A DEATH OF
DISTINCTION

A DEATH OF DISTINCTION

Marjorie Eccles

St. Martin's Press ✖ New York

A THOMAS DUNNE BOOK.
An imprint of St. Martin's Press.

A DEATH OF DISTINCTION. Copyright © 1995 by
Marjorie Eccles. All rights reserved. Printed in the
United States of America. No part of this book may
be used or reproduced in any manner whatsoever
without written permission except in the case of
brief quotations embodied in critical articles or
reviews. For information address St. Martin's
Press, 175 Fifth Avenue, New York, N.Y. 10010.

Eccles, Marjorie.
    A death of distinction / Marjorie Eccles—1st U.S.
ed.
    p.   cm.
    "A Thomas Dunne book."
    ISBN 0-312-18566-9
    1. Mayo, Gil (Fictitious character)—Fiction. 2.
Police—England—Fiction. 3. England—Fiction. I.
Title.
PR6055.C33D46 1998
823'.914–dc21   98-5568
                                                              CIP

First published in Great Britain by Collins Crime, an
imprint of HarperCollins*Publishers*

First U.S. Edition: May 1998

10 9 8 7 6 5 4 3 2 1

1

'. . . what could well be the end of civilization as we know it. We are not only systematically destroying our own planet, we're destroying our society. Drugs are endemic, rape and murder have become commonplace. But what is more unforgivable than the rest is the destruction of childhood innocence.'

Jack Lilburne paused briefly. With undisguised love and a total absence of irony, his eyes rested on his daughter, Flora, sitting next to him at the dinner table. Eighteen years old, her mass of tumbling, tawny-blonde hair falling to her shoulders, her painted lips pouting invitingly, full, creamy breasts threatening to spill from her dangerously cut neckline.

'Decadence is projected at our children every day from our television screens,' Jack continued, a handsome, vital figure with thick white hair, lively brown eyes and still-dark eyebrows. 'They are encouraged to believe that violence is the answer to every trivial disagreement, that even the most casual encounter between boy and girl must involve sex . . .'

Anthony Spurrier, uneasy in his hired dinner jacket and black tie, ran his finger round the inside of his collar, adjusted his spectacles and with an effort managed to drag his gaze away from Flora. Chasing crumbs of Bath Oliver and Stilton round his plate with a celery leaf, he looked covertly at his watch. Jack could be guaranteed for at least another ten minutes, though from one end of the long, shining expanse of mahogany to the other the guests were listening with every appearance of interested attention.

Well, they would be, wouldn't they? For one thing, nearly everyone present had a soft spot for old Jack. He could go on a bit sometimes, he was inclined to be somewhat overfond of the sound of his own Geordie-accented voice, but nobody doubted his sincerity, the passion of his involvement. And tonight, they

1

were prepared to be indulgent, goodwill had marked every phase of the evening; even the controversial subject of the new wing had been tacitly swept under the carpet.

Candles flickered against dark panelling and banked flowers, silver and napery gleamed, wine glowed in crystal glasses and wafts of the Mayoress's statement-making scent drifted down the table. It was all very civilized, a polite gathering of colleagues and civic dignitaries invited to dine here in the municipal splendour of the Town Hall. A semi-official function, hosted by one of the town's industrialists and given the blessing of the Mayor. A recognition of Jack's OBE award in the New Year Honours list, for services as Governor of the Conyhall Young Offenders' Institution, but recognition also because he was a respected figure in the local community, a friend and like-minded colleague. Nods of approval followed his words.

'However,' he continued, on a more optimistic note.

Anthony had heard it all before, but it was the lingering echo of the word 'sex' which drew his gaze, as if with invisible strings, back to Flora's cleavage, of which he had a full view, since she was sitting directly opposite him in her red, crushed velvet frock, tight and fashionably tarty. Sinking further down into his chair, as Jack showed no immediate signs of drawing to a close, he idly began to fantasize about removing the frock. He had reached the point where he was sliding down the zip when Flora's mother, sitting correctly upright on the chair next to him, picked up her water glass and took a small, delicate sip. Immediately, Anthony too sat upright, sharply reminded to sublimate such thoughts. Dorothea had an uncanny knack of being able to guess what was in your mind – or at any rate, her laser gaze made you feel she did.

Drawn the short straw again! Anthony had thought with a hint of unaccustomed temper, having hoped to sit next to Flora and finding instead that he'd been put next to her mother. OK, so it was an honour to be placed next to the governor's wife, but Dorothea was hard work. Her hair done in a smooth, beige French pleat, all well-bred politeness but rarely smiling, she would field a conversational ball pleasantly enough, but never bat one of her own, so that there were long, intimidating silences while you were left searching for another opening. Especially tonight, when your other neighbour was Councillor Ponting's ancient and very deaf wife, preoccupied with her food.

2

The one topic which could be guaranteed to evoke a response in Dorothea Lilburne was anything on the subject of gardens, but that was soon exhausted, since Anthony scarcely knew a daffodil from a dandelion, whereas Dorothea's gardening was in the RHS Committee Member class. The Mayor, on Dorothea's other side, holding forth on a scheme for a new municipal rose garden, had done rather better than Anthony, whose nearest approach had been that all-time conversational low, the weather, and its effects on Dorothea's herbaceous border. Dealt with in about five minutes, all permissible adjectives to describe the last appalling weeks having long since been used up.

It had been the sort of spring which broke all records: curtains of rain had swept for weeks across the sodden landscape. The lower parts of the town had been flooded several times to the extent where the canal and the river, running parallel for some miles, had almost joined. It had been bitterly cold, though Anthony and Flora had scarcely noticed. They'd drawn the curtains in his room, lit the lamps, listened to the rain lashing the windows and turned up the gas fire to make love on the rug in front of it.

Flora. She was like a magnet. He could no more stop looking at her, only a candle flame away across the table, than he could fly: her skin flushed and downy, she was ripe as one of the out-of-season peaches piled in the centre fruit bowl. In her red velvet she glowed like Rembrandt's Saskia against the mostly dowdy blacks of the other women; against her mother's discreetly tasteful navy lace, the one she'd worn to the Palace with a matching hat and a silk coat when Jack had collected his OBE from Her Majesty.

He was willing to bet Flora's frock had received a chilly reception. Dorothea waged a low-key but persistent war of attrition against her daughter's choice of clothes. Nothing so obvious as a clash of wills, because she would never descend to such – and anyway, Flora wouldn't join in – but a constant disapproval that was intended to wear her down, though she must have known it would never succeed. You didn't win with Flora.

Anthony was only too aware of this. He was up to the eyebrows in love with her, and though they'd been sleeping together on and off for three months, he still couldn't get her to say how she really felt about him, and could in truth see

3

nothing coming of it, especially if her parents had any say in the matter. They were from such utterly different backgrounds – Anthony from working-class Walsall, where his father was a foreman tool-maker and Flora . . . well, Jack Lilburne himself was proud of coming from Northumbrian mining stock, but he'd escaped before he was out of his teens, got himself a scholarship to Durham University, then married Dorothea and come into comparative wealth and social standing. In his more charitable moments, Anthony allowed himself to believe that Jack must have fallen in love with Dorothea's cool, patrician beauty, but Jack had a canny streak, and anyway, Anthony didn't see anyone marrying Dorothea for anything other than her money and her position as a daughter of one of the county families.

Flora, born latish in their lives, had never known anything but this privileged, nothing-ever-denied-to-her, lifestyle. Over which Anthony, on the lowest rung of his particular career ladder, quietly despaired. He'd come to the Prison Service after qualifying as a psychologist, and couldn't aspire to anything likely to be acceptable to Flora's parents in the foreseeable future.

Jack finished his speech to a round of applause, glasses were raised once more, and the main purpose of the evening being over, guests were free to disperse, though most of them found it pleasant to linger. Chairs were pushed back, legs stretched, seats exchanged for a word with friends. The Mayoress, accompanied by Dorothea, sailed away in a cloud of Obsession to the end of the room, in order to inspect more closely the various splendid presentation gifts which Jack had received during the course of the evening, while Flora went to sit next to Anthony, giving him the full benefit of her radiant smile.

'Poor love, you've been having a hard time with my mother.'

'Not really.' Anthony was embarrassed that his boredom had been so evident, but Flora only laughed.

'She's all right, you know. She just never knows what to say to people unless they know about gardens.'

Anthony felt a rush of love for her. Nobody, seeing Flora for the first time, would imagine how kind and good-natured, how *nice* she was. He ought to try, like her, to see the better side of people. But even so, his imagination stopped short, trying to envisage an endless future with a mother-in-law who talked of nothing but chrysanthemums and compost.

'D'you like my frock, Anthony?'

'I like you in it,' he replied diplomatically.

Flora glowed; then made a *moue*. 'My mother doesn't. She wanted me to go and change, but it was too late. They'd sent a car with a chauffeur for us and it was waiting.'

Clever Flora! But even Anthony had to admit the frock was a bit much, certainly for tonight – probably a recycled number from her own rather iffy little venture into business, called Mark Two. She and her partner, Charlotte Delamere, knew plenty of women who didn't bat an eyelid at spending on designer-label clothes what would be a month's wages for some people. To be worn only a few times and then sold, discreetly, to places like Mark Two, who advertised them as being for 'women with more fashion sense than money'. No shortage of women like that in Lavenstock, but few who were able to afford even the second-hand prices of the clothes in Flora's shop. Anthony was giving the enterprise another three months, with luck.

Jack sat back with relief now that he'd done his bit, but with an unaccustomed feeling of anti-climax. He'd reached what most would regard as the pinnacle of his career: was there no way ahead then, except downhill? Retirement had been spoken of several times that night. He was only three years off sixty, the time when most people began counting the days, but he was looking towards it without much enthusiasm. He came from a long-lived family, his father had died digging potatoes at ninety-four. At that rate, he'd more than half the years of his present life yet to live.

As yet he'd formulated no plans beyond a vague intention to write a book or two based on his professional experiences, or possibly to travel, preferably to remote parts of the world where Dorothea would not feel it incumbent upon herself to accompany him. A guilty thought made less guilty by telling himself that, enduring martyrdom away from her garden, she would indeed be a dreary companion. Secretly, he nourished a hope (not as secret as he thought) that sixty wouldn't, in fact, bring a total severance from his present occupation: that some niche, somewhere, would be found for him. Work suited him. He didn't want to be put out to grass, not yet. He still had a lot to offer: he was physically active and rich in experience, and second to none as an administrator; added to which, no one knew better than he how to handle the difficult youths who came under his care, having held the reins of Conyhall in his hands since a few years after its inception. His OBE had been an acknowledgement of the fact.

If the truth were told, he didn't want to relinquish those reins at all, though choice in the matter wasn't an option. A new governor would be appointed willy-nilly, and he was unlikely to be consulted. Someone with stiffer ideas about discipline, no doubt. It was quite possible that the person chosen to head the team of governors who ran Conyhall could be a woman. The next logical move for someone like Claudia Reynolds.

She was seated at three removes, on the same side of the table as he was, so that he couldn't see her without craning forward, but he was aware of her, as a strong personality and as an attractive woman. Pity about her . . . However – he comforted himself with the thought – Claudia was a matter of indifference to him, and her promotion would certainly mean relocation.

'Ten-thirty tomorrow morning, then, Jack?'

Denis Quattrell, his bank manager, had slipped into the Mayoress's vacant chair. He was a long, thin, desiccated man, who said little but, one had to assume, thought a lot. The type, in any case, to have as friend rather than foe. Jack had been careful to cultivate Quattrell. The decision on whether or not the new wing should be built couldn't in any way be his, but as Chairman of Conyhall's Board of Visitors, his support and recommendations on the need for more administrative space would go a long way. Also, as a member of Lavenstock Town Council, he could be invaluable in stemming the tide of local opposition. An unofficial, friendly meeting between himself and Quattrell could do no harm, Jack knew, to the fulfilment of his plans.

'Half past ten, Denis. I'll look forward to seeing you.'

Quattrell said carefully, 'Don't count chickens, but no doubt there's room for coming to some – mutual accommodation.'

Jack felt triumphant. He knew it! It had made sense, all along, in these difficult times, to add a new admin block to the present building, old as it was, rather than spend Government money on new premises. There was a vociferous element locally, who objected to the scheme on the grounds of what they saw as the gradual encroachment of the prison buildings towards them – disregarding the fact that the proposed new wing would be well within the Conyhall boundary, and on Prison Service land.

But such protest groups were listened to more and more, and Jack knew he couldn't afford to disregard them. He was sure, however, that some solution, other than direct confrontation, would be found. He felt himself riding on a crest of optimism at the moment, when everything was undoubtedly going his way. For a moment, remembering recent troubling events, he had a flicker of doubt, but once more he put it out of his mind.

2

Taking a short cut through the narrow lane at the back of the Town Hall had been a mistake: Marc was wedged in between a following car and a big truck being loaded with huge pots of flowering plants. Probably from the previous evening's function, he decided, and now being transported back to the Parks Department glasshouses. He waited impatiently, but it wasn't long before the driver gave him the thumbs up and he could get past. It hadn't really delayed him much, he made good time and his mother was still there when he arrived.

The resiny smell of new wood filled her small flat as he carried in the planks, shouldering with ease the six three-foot lengths of three-quarter-inch-by-nine. Good, sturdy shelves that he left leaning just inside the door while he ran back down the narrow stairs to fetch his saw, plane, drill and sander, the Rawlplugs and screws. He'd always been good at practical things, and he was eager to prove his carpentry skills, to get on and see the results. They'd be just the job when he'd finished them, three shelves in each of the alcoves either side of the small cast-iron fireplace that was only just big enough to house a barely adequate gas fire. Even so, she wouldn't have enough books to fill them, or even any small ornaments and such to make up the spaces. He wondered what had happened to them all, and whether she missed such things.

The tiny flat, once a bedroom floor, just this one room partitioned off to make provision for somewhere to cook and wash up, plus a minute bathroom and a shoebox-sized bedroom, was sparse and comfortless.

'I could get you a few pictures, some cushions,' he'd suggested. 'A cat?' Even a budgie. Something, at any rate, to love.

'No! No, thank you. I have everything I want.'

Her refusal was quiet, but uncompromising, as if through the need to convince him that she'd grown away from the necessity for luxuries. He thought of her Spartan bedroom, its walls bare except for the crucifix above the narrow bed, seeming to dominate the room. It made him uncomfortable, this reminder of the faith that, despite everything, was still the main principle of her life.

He'd left the door propped open while he went for the tools, and when she heard him return she called to him from the kitchen area.

'Please – don't call me that,' he said, leaning against the doorframe, watching her as she moved quietly from one task to another. 'You christened me Marc, and that's who I am.'

She was silent for a moment, her head bent as she folded the tea towel and placed it neatly over the rail, revealing neither pleasure nor displeasure as she lifted her head and looked at him. 'If that is what you prefer.' He saw the shadows in her eyes, shadows that he'd come to accept were permanent now. The thought both saddened and enraged him, it had all been so bloody pointless and unnecessary. Then a sudden rush of tenderness swamped his anger, and with it came an ever greater determination to look after and protect her, as though their positions were reversed, and she was the child, he the parent.

She looked too young to be anybody's mother, let alone the mother of a grown man, though he recognized his own bone structure and colouring in her narrow, dark face, and knew exultantly that his own blood and genes and chromosomes were hers, too. She was still a beautiful woman. Her hair, which she was growing again, was sleek and dark, without a hint of grey. She was slim – perhaps too slim, he thought, professionally critical – and made even her cheap, chain-store clothes look elegant. Even without hearing her faint accent, the slight pedantry of her speech that persisted despite all the years in England, anyone would guess by the way she looked that she was French, he thought – it must be that Parisian flair they spoke about.

He reminded her, very aware of the time, 'Shouldn't you be on your way? It's nearly ten.'

'Yes. I have left you some soup and rolls for your lunch.' She indicated a carefully prepared tray he could see sitting on the two-foot-square work surface next to the sink. 'And there is fruit in the fridge.'

9

'I'll wait and have it with you. I don't want to stop for lunch anyway.'

He meant to work painstakingly, taking his time. He was always careful and precise when he needed to be. He would do everything perfectly, no lopsided or unsafe shelves – but even if the job went quicker than he anticipated, he intended still to be here when she returned, he wanted to see her face when she saw the shelves. Maybe he could use any spare time for a kip . . . you never got enough sleep, working the emergency rota.

'Don't wait,' she said. 'You will be hungry before I get back. I don't finish until half past two.'

He hated the idea of her job: waitressing, fetching and carrying, having to wear an overall and a cute, silly hat on her head. It was demeaning, cleaning up the sordid debris of other people's lunches – even if Catesby's restaurant was in a classy department store and though she'd recently been promoted from clearing tables in the self-service to the waitress-service area.

'I don't mind waiting, I had a big breakfast,' he lied, as she slipped on her coat. He could always nip out for a pizza if he couldn't last out. 'And I'm not due back on duty today. Bye, Marie-Laure.'

She didn't like him to call her Mother, or Mum. Nor did she kiss him before she left, but she touched his shoulder, which was an improvement on previous farewells.

He listened to her quick, light footsteps on the stairs and heard the front door close before turning to start on the shelves.

The small room quickly became very stuffy and within ten minutes he'd worked up a sweat. He stuck it for a while longer then, looking at his watch, pushed up the sash window which overlooked the street where the betting shop, the Halal Meat Emporium, the Pizza Hut and a small branch of the Bank of Ireland jostled each other, and countless overflowing black plastic dustbin bags lolled together along the pavement edges. He let in a rush of knife-edged air, breathed in the smell of diesel fumes and fried onions, heard the noise of traffic and the dustbin lorry grinding away further up the road, the hiss of air brakes. The Town Hall clock sounded the quarter and, simultaneously, he heard the bang in the distance – or rather, the loud crump, the thud of an explosion. Minutes later, through the open window, he heard the wail of police and ambulance sirens.

3

Reverberations from the explosion were heard miles away. The sound was muffled in the crematorium chapel, not easily identifiable, but several policemen stirred uneasily.

The service was nearly over, the coffin with its simple white cross of flowers, borne in by four stalwart constables, would in a few minutes disappear through the curtains. The chapel was full, with family and friends and row upon row of police: uniformed and plain clothes, top brass and other ranks, as befitted the funeral of a detective superintendent. Even the Chief Constable was there, out of sympathy for the widow and family, and to pay his last respects to a well-liked colleague.

Forty-seven. Christ, that was too young to die, thought Mayo, still numb with shock. To die of a heart attack or anything else . . . especially a man like Howard Cherry, careful of himself in every way – a non-smoker, a moderate drinker, a man who'd watched his health as carefully as he'd watched every step of his career moves, each one mapped out from the day he entered the Force.

'Man that is born of woman hath but a short time to live, and is full of misery . . .'

The last, at least, not true of Cherry, a man content with the career he'd chosen, and one who'd enjoyed a joke as much as any Yorkshireman allowed himself to. Mayo had known him all his working life. They'd started out in the same West Riding Force, become separated, and then found themselves by coincidence once again working together, here in the Midlands, in Lavenstock – Cherry as superintendent, CID, Mayo as chief inspector. There'd been none better to work for than his old friend. Not perfect, a bit of a bastard on occasions, truth to tell, over order and discipline. But fair. He'd earned the respect, if not the unreserved liking, of every man and woman on the station.

His marriage – to Anne, now facing a bleak future – had been happy enough, among the tide of police marital disasters, to cause comment and even envy. He'd left a youngish family: sixteen-year-old Melanie, now in tears enough to start the next Flood, poor lass. The twins, Adrian and Michael, hefty seventeen-year-olds, already tall like their father, pale with the effort of trying not to break down. Mayo, a big man with crisp dark hair, a square chin and a tough reputation, looked down at his feet, finding himself more than a little choked, too. A private funeral, with a memorial service later, wouldn't that have been less harrowing? Although there was something to be said for having it over and done with.

For some inexplicable but possibly private reason, 'Angel Voices Ever Singing' had been chosen to be sung as the coffin slid through the curtains and Howard Cherry went to his last rest, and when the final cheerful notes died away, Mayo followed the procession of mourners out of the chapel into the bright, scimitar-sharp morning.

Waiting for a word with Anne, he tried not to make it too obvious that his eyes were all for Alex, Sergeant Jones, standing some yards from him across the sea of wasted blossoms, the funeral tributes, spread out on the forecourt. She wore her uniform well, managing to make its mannish outlines look elegant, an emphasis to the creamy skin, dark blue eyes and sleek, short dark hair, precision cut under the uniform hat. She hadn't, through protocol, been sitting with him in the crematorium chapel and had evidently decided it would be circumspect to keep up the formality in the circumstances. Though there couldn't be many now who didn't know of their relationship. Their eyes met, and she smiled, and his heart, as usual, turned over.

Anne came across immediately she saw him. He kissed her, pressing her hand and murmuring words of sympathy. The usual platitudes were not enough, never could be, of course, but they were sincerely meant, and what else was there to say?

'Thank you,' she answered, dry-eyed and outwardly calm, as if they'd really helped. And they did. He knew that from his own experience when, years ago, his wife, Lynne, had died. They spoke a little more, then, as he was turning away, she added quietly, 'Take it, Gil, the promotion. It's what he would have wanted.'

Someone had been indiscreet. Cherry himself? Few others could have known how long he'd been dithering, uncharacteristically, over whether to go for it or not. It didn't matter now.

He'd made his decision some time since, gone through the rituals and the necessary procedures, even anticipated relocation and all the problems *that* would bring. But Cherry's death meant that a detective superintendent was now immediately necessary to keep the CID department functioning and here he was, in the right place at the right time. His meeting late yesterday with the DCC had set the seal on his new role as Superintendent, CID, Lavenstock Division. He'd never have chosen to achieve higher status this way, it felt too much like stepping into a dead friend's shoes. But he'd found out long ago that you couldn't pick and choose, rewards were dished out with one hand and taken away with the other.

A flurry of activity had broken out by the parked cars. One of his sergeants, Martin Kite, came running up to him and spoke hurriedly. Other men were already rushing to their cars, the Chief Constable was turning to see what was wrong. Radios squawked as vehicles sped through the spruce, well-barbered crematorium grounds. Mayo turned apologetically to Anne Cherry.

'I'm sorry, there's been an incident . . . I'm sorry, Anne.'

She watched them go. It seemed, somehow, an appropriate postscript to the funeral.

Conyhall Young Offenders' Institution had started out as a gentleman's residence – a stately Gothic pile built a hundred years ago to replace an earlier, Elizabethan manor house, considered by its Victorian owners to be unfashionable. The family had been of some standing, consequently the house was large, almost a mansion. It had previously stood in many gracious acres, on Lavenstock's outskirts, but as the town grew in size, so Conyhall's grounds became reduced, sold off piecemeal for the semi-rural housing estates which now almost surrounded it. Twenty-five years ago, the house and most of its contents had followed, put on the market to pay off death duties and to allow the incumbent heir to continue to live the jet-set life he felt was his due. The sale completed, he had departed smartly to make a large hole in the proceeds, leaving behind only a few marble nymphs and some urns in various niches and interstices of the building, plus several time-obscured and unremarkable oil paintings in the hall to add gravitas to what was then to be a local detention centre. What had now come to be the Conyhall Young Offenders' Institution.

Several acres of land still remained behind the main house, with a small lake providing a home for a few ducks, and within the perimeter fence, separated from the housing estates by a belt of trees, was an area of kitchen garden to help support the prison, plus soccer and basketball pitches. The original house was now the administration section, and alongside was a motley collection of purpose-built accommodation blocks, kitchens, workshops, etc. Lying beyond the wire was the Elizabethan Home Farm, which had escaped the restoration of the big house and was now the governor's private home.

Before the others were down to breakfast, on the morning after the celebrations at the Town Hall, Dorothea Lilburne was out in her garden, on her knees in the beech coppice, dividing snowdrops.

The swelling buds of the ash trees were black against the light, pearly sky, early daffodils danced, crocuses spreading purple, gold and white across the grass. It was a perfect morning, though still bitterly cold for mid-March, and she was glad of her padded body warmer. Snowdrops, she thought, lifting the bulbs tenderly, were probably her favourite flower. Fair Maids of February . . . She had twelve different kinds, double, single, some pink-flushed, scented, or tipped with yellow. So pretty they'd looked, a few weeks before, carpeting the ground beneath the trees with the meek, drooping white chalices hiding their delicate green stamens, but they were in danger of becoming overcrowded. There wasn't much nourishment between the gnarled, twisted, surface roots of the beeches, and they were vying for what there was of it with the naturalized daffodils and fritillarias.

'Wouldn't move 'em if I was you, missis.'

Tom Barnett stood sardonically regarding her efforts. With his shambling figure, his spade over his shoulder, ill-shaven, with a knitted cap pulled down over his ears and mud-caked gumboots, he looked like some oversized and disagreeable old Nibelung. 'Snowdrops is like you and me – older we get, less change we like.'

'Oh, rubbish!' Dorothea answered coldly. 'If you catch them

after they've flowered, before the leaves or bulbs have the chance to dry off, they'll transplant well enough.'

'Oh ar. Have to see, then, won't we?' Parting his lips in a knowing grin, he clomped off to dig the vegetable plot, which was the only sort of gardening he thought worthwhile, and the only reason he was employed – for that, and to trim the hedges and cut the lawns. And even there, a conflict of interest arose between her own preference for gently curving borders and his conviction that they should be ruler-straight.

Dorothea rammed her handfork into the hard earth. Tom Barnett was a miserable old grump who didn't know the first thing about flower gardening. Which didn't stop him having a lot to say about it. She hadn't yet forgiven him for digging up what he swore had been a moribund shrub which nothing could save, when she'd been away once, and planting a row of onions in its place. She still mourned the little Judas tree, grown from seed, not dead, merely a reluctant specimen she'd coaxed along for years.

And how dare he put her in the same age bracket as he was?

You get back to your cabbages and leave me to my flowers, she thought huffily, nettled because he might well prove to be right: beautiful as they were, snowdrops were temperamental creatures, often sulking if they were disturbed. She'd planned to put them where they could colonize the empty space left by the crinum lilies, which hadn't survived a hard winter followed by this terrible wet spring, and she wasn't going to let the likes of Tom Barnett put her off. Firmly dealt with, they would thrive. She rose rather stiffly from her knees to cart down there the now-full trug. As she did so, the telephone rang, and went unanswered. Jack must have finished his breakfast and was probably in the shower, and Flora, who, after the late night last night, had announced she wasn't going into her shop that morning, would be fathoms deep in sleep. Reluctantly, Dorothea turned to go and answer it.

The dogs, in whom the telephone always, for some mysterious reason, engendered frenzied excitement, materialized from some far corner of the garden as she hurried towards the house. Nearly knocking her over, they rushed in as she opened the door, barking, scattering the rugs in the wide, stone-flagged hall, which had a door at each end, front and back. Delightful in summer, when one could leave the garden door open and see the long matching borders with the swathe of grass between, but cruel in winter, when the draughts whistled like a whetted knife between the doors.

'Quiet, Sam! And you, Kip!' She leaned on the door to shut it against the wind, paused to slip off her muddy gardening shoes, and the wretched telephone stopped. Dorothea, who was not the swearing kind, clicked her tongue in annoyance. The old spaniels, disappointed, floundered up on to the cushioned window seat above the radiator, one eye on her because they knew this was forbidden. They were Flora's dogs, and very spoilt.

'Who was that on the telephone?'

Jack, now showered, shaved and dressed in his best suit, ready to drive round to his office via the main road for his meeting with Quattrell – Jack who was as fit as a flea but never walked when he could drive – came into the hall as she was shooing the animals off the window seat. She explained what had happened but he was barely listening.

'Enjoy it last night, did you then, hinnie?' he asked, smiling at her, throwing an arm around her shoulders, using the northern endearment she would only allow in private. Not that she was *ashamed* of his origins – but there was no need to flaunt them quite so deliberately. She'd once overheard him described as a professional Geordie, and was afraid this could be true.

'It was very pleasant, Jack,' she answered, lying for his sake, because it had been an evening very special to him, although such occasions were torture to her. She'd no small talk, and was afraid of making a fool of herself by speaking on topics of which she knew nothing. She knew she was thought dull when she failed immediately to laugh at a joke, or see the point of something, but she didn't catch on quickly, and repartee was beyond her. So she'd gradually learned to take refuge in polite smiles and anodyne remarks, like the Queen, and though she knew her reserve was often mistaken for coldness, she didn't know how to remedy it. Strange that Jack, who always seemed to be able so easily to recognize inadequacy in the youths in his care, had never seen that.

He failed to appreciate her lack of response now. 'Aye, it went very well. Our lassie looked lovely, didn't she?'

'Flora always looks lovely.'

But oh, that frock! Dorothea sighed deeply, though truly it was the least of the things on her mind about Flora. Not to approach Jack with, however, who could see no wrong in his daughter, and certainly not at this time, when he was evidently feeling optimistic, brimming with goodwill for all the world.

'I hope your meeting goes well,' she contented herself with saying as he picked up his briefcase.

'Oh, it will, I'm sure of that.   uattrell as good as gave me the nod last night.'

He sounded so confident that she didn't voice her own doubts about the strident local element who were vociferously opposed to his scheme. The new block, if and when completed, would come within fifty yards of a children's playground. That it would merely consist of additional offices, and be staffed by civilians, made little difference to the objectors, who were out to make trouble.

In a rare gesture of spontaneous affection, she kissed him. He looked surprised, but pleased, and patted her cheek. 'Be back about twelve. I'll dodge the mess today. Sandwich for lunch, eh? After last night, I'd better be on short commons for a bit.' He drew in his flat stomach, well aware that he weighed no more than he had when she'd married him, twenty-one years ago.

Smiling, rattling his keys, he made for the front door, pausing, as she knew he would, to filch the newspaper and read the front page before flinging it on to the back seat of his car and driving off with it.

He was halted by the appearance of Flora flying down the stairs clad only in flip-flop mules and a short nightshirt with a naughty slogan across the bosom, calling out, 'Da! Wait for me – I want to ask you something.' Dorothea tut-tutted as she went out to the car arm in arm with her father, just as she was, barely decent. The front door opened and the garden door, insecurely caught on the latch, burst open as was its wont. Dorothea forgot them both.

From where she knelt, pulling on her garden clogs, she could see the left-hand border, twin to the right, in summertime effulgent with colour, heady with scent, and was reminded of what she'd meant to do this week. During this last long spell of wet weather, when it had been too damp even for her to contemplate working outdoors, she'd spent the time in her dark little room under the eaves rearranging, on squared paper, some

17

of the plants and shrubs in the borders, seeking for better plant associations, and she now had all sorts of exciting projects in view.

It was there that Flora had found her the other day, with her head bent over her plan, occasionally looking up from it to consider the sodden garden below, and getting a whiff of fragrance from the sprig of *Daphne odora* in a vase on her desk.

'Blimey, it's gloomy in here! Don't you want a lamp on, Mother?'

'No, thank you.' Dorothea spoke absently, surveying her handiwork. 'I'm just wondering whether the colours are too pale towards the middle – here?' Had she followed received gardening wisdom too slavishly, or did the pale froth of pastels need something more daring, a touch of thunder-purple, or perhaps crimson? She had it – a *Cosmos atrosanguineus*, its delicate feathery plumes and purple-black flowers would make a perfect foil for the strong heads of the pale pink phlox and that creamy scabious . . .

'Moth-*er*! The garden's perfect as it is. Why d'you want to make more work for yourself?'

'More work? Good gracious, the work in a garden's never finished – and if it were, I wouldn't want it. Don't you see?'

'Heavens, no!' Flora threw herself into the sagging old armchair next to the bookshelves, crammed with Dorothea's gardening books. 'I'll *never* understand how anybody can enjoy breaking their back and their fingernails gardening! I suppose I'm far too lazy, not like either you or Da.' She always called Jack Da, the name he'd called his own father. 'There are better ways of enjoying yourself.'

Oh, Flora, Flora! thought Dorothea now, preferring not to imagine the ways Flora had meant, pushing aside these troubling thoughts with the decision to drive down after lunch and order the *Cosmos* from the specialist nursery she used. Only first, she must finish the snowdrops or she might not get round to it again today.

She went outside and took the trug of snowdrops to their new home, and it was then that the deafening explosion occurred.

The sky went dark, the very ground rocked beneath her feet. Dorothea never afterwards knew whether she'd imagined the silence between the explosion and the terrible sound of falling debris and broken glass, or whether it was merely her own heart which had stopped beating. But after that, there certainly was a silence, when even the birds stopped singing. Into it came a distant, smaller crash, which later she was told was one of the stone nymphs, slowly toppling from its alcove above the front door of the main building. Followed by the noise of the ducks on the little lake, filling the air with panic-stricken squawks and beating wings.

By the time the real pandemonium broke out, the ducks had settled to paddling around in aimless circles, to an occasional indignant quacking, upending themselves into the mud, wondering what all the fuss was about.

4

There wasn't much left of Jack Lilburne's Nissan, and still less of Jack Lilburne.

If anybody could have been naive enough to believe it might have been an accident, the team of experts from the army bomb disposal unit quickly removed the idea. A bomb it was, though what type they weren't saying, not yet, until they'd more to go on. Shouldn't be long, the major from the Royal Engineers said. They'd already begun to poke about among the wreckage, now that the pair of well-trained sniffer dogs had made sure there were no more devices likely to go off. But Christ, one had been enough!

Mayo stood outside the cordoned-off area, surveying the disaster with something approaching disbelief. A pall of yellowish, choking dust, redolent of old plaster, still hung like a miasma. A car wheel, intact, lay in the gravel drive, and shreds of blue fabric seat-covering had caught on a piece of dangling spouting. Broken glass splintered sunlight on to the yellow, stripped blossom from a huge forsythia, lying scattered like confetti in front of the house. Miraculously, the only apparent damage to the old house itself was that all the front windows had shattered and the ceiling of a downstairs room had come down.

It was the heap of wreckage under the half-demolished barn which was the focus of the horror. Of Elizabethan vintage, the same age as the house, what was left of it suggesting it had possibly been decrepit even before the bomb had blown half of it away, the brick and timber building had stretched at right angles to the house, with a gravelled forecourt lying between them. Half the roof now leaned crazily to one side, its corner still shakily supported by a single upright beam of stout weathered oak. From beneath the heap of bricks and roof tiles poked an obscene mass of buckled steel and tangled wires. Some of the man who'd been in the car might still be there, too. Parts of him were already in black plastic bags awaiting the attentions of the pathologist.

Mayo turned aside from the milling crowd of uniformed and plain-clothes men and women, the army personnel in their camouflage fatigues, the scenes-of-crime team. He felt cold to the bone, nothing to do with the biting wind, an inner cold that thick boots and a serviceable padded anorak taken from the boot of his car and donned over his sober funeral garments did nothing to alleviate. Alive one moment, then – oblivion. Howard Cherry, Jack Lilburne . . . Well, it happened, but thank God, not often like this . . . a heart attack, yes, but bombs, until now, hadn't been part of the Lavenstock police scene.

'When did he last use his car?' he asked abruptly of his assistant, Inspector Abigail Moon.

'About half-four yesterday. Parked it where he always did, parallel with the barn.' Her face was pinched and pale under her cap of bronze hair, but resolute, determinedly professional, she'd already sussed out the necessary. He'd have been disappointed in her if she hadn't.

'Which is why the barn took the brunt of the damage. Lucky he didn't leave it nearer the house.'

'You'll want to see Mrs Lilburne later, I suppose. She was out in the garden at the other side when it happened, but – '

'I'll want to talk to anybody who was around when it happened, yes, but Mrs Lilburne can wait. She's enough worries at the moment, poor woman. Plenty others we can see first.'

'That's what I thought. I've arranged for us to see Miss Reynolds, the deputy governor, over at the prison, in about twenty minutes.'

The prison, the YOI, the Young Offenders' Unit. It was very near. Apparently not near enough for the house to be included in its security system, being outside the perimeter fence, but close enough for the bomb to have caused some panic over there, no doubt.

' – and there's a Mr Spurrier who's asked for a word – Anthony Spurrier, one of the governor-team.'

'Oh? What does he want?'

'He hasn't said, but he was out with the Lilburnes last night, at some sort of celebration at the Town Hall – for the governor's OBE, I gather. A chauffeur-driven limo arrived at about seven to pick up Lilburne and his wife and daughter, and then brought them home at eleven.'

'So the bomb could've been planted on the Nissan any time between seven and when it went off – by virtually anybody. Wonderful!' Mayo looked at his watch. 'If I'm not due to see Miss Reynolds for another twenty minutes, we've time to see Spurrier first.'

'No point in driving round to the main building, there's a short cut through the garden.' Her tone was resolutely neutral.

'And you'd like to get a look at it.' Mayo smiled. 'All right, all right, I suppose one way's as good as another.'

The scene behind was grim, Abigail was still shaken, but she recognized a generous offer when she saw one, a chance to get herself together. It was especially generous, coming from a man who'd never been known to pick up a spade – at least willingly. Career-orientated and single-minded about it, she'd discovered a keen gardening streak in herself since she'd become the owner of a derelict cottage with an even more derelict garden. He could still surprise her. Something was making Mayo more benign these days, and she'd put money on it being the settling down of his relationship with Alex Jones. Good for them, she thought, but unenvious, her own love life, her association with Ben Appleyard, editor of the local *Advertiser*, being quite satisfactory at the moment, thank you.

She could feel the colour coming back into her cheeks. 'You never know, you might pick up a few tips yourself.' A bit cheeky, that, but she knew him well enough now to know when to risk it. He didn't seem to mind. Might be different from now on, though, with more rank between them. His new status could put their partnership at risk. Pity, really, when they'd just got into stride, as you might say.

'I'll have you know I appreciate a nice garden as well as the next man . . . under the strict proviso that I don't have to look after it,' he replied equably, unlatching the gate which opened on to extensive lawns that sloped down to a beautifully land-scaped garden. Its immediate area was still thick with policemen of all sorts, some of them engaged in picking up scattered debris, and worse, for the explosion had been big enough to blast some of it as far as a shallow lake, about a hundred yards from the house. This wasn't deep enough for frogmen, and several un-happy police officers were wading through the mud and the water lily pads with dragnets, further disturbing the affronted ducks.

Leaving the main centre of activity behind, they followed the serpentine curves of a shredded bark path, alongside tranquil beds and borders where the graceful shapes of bare-branched trees, evergreen shrubs and spreading conifers gave form and substance to a landscape bursting forth from its winter sleep. Abigail, still subdued by the succession of events – the funeral, followed by the explosion – felt her spirits lifted by the sight of rare shrubs beginning to burst into flower, underplanted with bright blue scillas and narcissi and what looked like acres of crocuses – purple, white – and gold, too, she noticed jealously. Why were these left alone, and not hers? In her own little garden, hooligan sparrows had descended in marauding gangs to decapitate all the yellow ones – the yellow ones only – that she'd so painstakingly planted in the autumn.

As the path turned, they came across an old man forking over a patch of ground near to where the garden ended and the perimeter fence began. He glanced up, without stopping what he was doing, as they drew level, and the smell of damp, newly turned earth came to them.

Mayo paused beside him and introduced himself. 'And this is my colleague, Inspector Moon. You must be the Mr Barnett who was working in the kitchen garden behind the house when the bomb went off?'

Pausing to crumble a ball of soil in one horny hand, the old man nodded, apparently unaffected by the shock of what had just happened, though you could never tell, shock took people all ways, and perhaps for him getting on with the job was its own kind of therapy.

'Tell me what happened.'

'Dunno, rightly. Just parked me bike in the barn and got me barrer out not five minutes afore I heard this hell of a bang. How is her, then, the missis?'

'Bearing up,' Abigail said. 'The chaplain's with her now.'

'Oh ar.' The two laconic Lavenstock syllables that could express anything: agreement, disbelief, approval, scorn . . . His boot on the fork, he drove the tines into the earth again.

'Spare us a minute of your time, if you will.'

Barnett removed his foot, even went so far as to lean on his fork and look at Mayo, but he was a surly old devil, not inclined

23

to be forthcoming. Mayo nodded to Abigail and then watched in silence while she questioned the gardener. His answers were as short as he could make them and didn't tell them much: he came twice a week, yesterday being one of his days, and he'd worked as usual, leaving at about quarter to five, having checked that all the tools and garden machinery were in place in the barn where they were kept, before locking up. Noticed nothing out of the ordinary, but he'd been anxious to get off. He lived with his daughter and she went on at him summat rotten if he wasn't home on time. 'Don't want me to think her's hoping I've fallen off of me bike so her can collect on me insurance,' he remarked sardonically. The barn had still been locked when he arrived this morning at nine-thirty, and hadn't been disturbed as far as he could see. He'd noticed nothing at all unusual, and he'd be glad, his attitude implied, if they'd let him get on with his digging.

'Nothing and nobody at all?'

'Not unless you count that there chap with the camera last week.'

'Oh? What chap was this?' Mayo put in, holding on to his patience.

'Up by the house. Taking pictures for one of them posh magazines, I reckoned. Wouldn't be the first time – though the missis said nowt to me about it, and he nivver come into the garden – it was just the house he was snapping. But he soon took his hook when he saw me watching him.'

'Didn't you think to mention it to anybody?'

'Why should I? There's a footpath from the lane into them woods over yonder. He coulda been one of them hikers, couldn't he?'

Just possible. The house was picturesque enough to have provided that excuse, anyway, had the photographer been challenged. It wouldn't have disgraced a calendar, above a month in spring or summer. But this had been early March and the recent weather conditions for photography had been appalling. And to disappear so promptly when he was aware of being watched?

'Describe this man to me if you can.'

'Youngish.' Which, in Barnett's book, meant anywhere between eighteen and forty-five, Mayo discovered. Wearing one of the padded jackets they all wore nowadays, green or blue, maybe, he couldn't remember. It had to be Thursday or Friday

24

when he'd seen him because those were the days he worked here. Beyond that, he couldn't go. Whether the man was tall or short, fat or thin, dark or fair, it was too much to hope that he'd remember, and he didn't.

Mayo thanked him, said it might be useful to talk to him again, and prepared to follow the path which skirted the perimeter fence to the front entrance of the prison, leaving the old man to get on with his work. But once stopped, Barnett seemed to have lost the will to continue. Looking vacantly across the garden, his shoulders sagged, as if the stuffing had gone out of him.

He said slowly, scraping his hand across his chin stubble, 'Reckon that was it, then? He was the one as put the bomb in the car?'

'I'd say there's a good chance.'

'Bloody hell.'

Mayo briskly disposed of any feelings of remorse. 'If he is, you couldn't have known.' Briefly, he laid a hand on the old man's shoulder. 'Go home, Mr Barnett. You've had a shock. There's plenty of cars up at the house. Somebody'll drive you home.'

'Mebbe. When I've finished what I'm at,' the old man countered stubbornly. And when Mayo looked back at the gate, he saw that he'd started his digging again.

'It wasn't the governor's practice to check under his car before getting into it, then?' Mayo asked when they'd been through the rituals of admittance, and Anthony Spurrier was finally ready to talk to them in his office. This after several minutes' delay while he made a distracted and abortive search among his chaotic papers for a file which had apparently gone missing, the sort of activity the mind fastens on when events are too shocking to contemplate.

'What? Oh, it wouldn't have entered his head,' Spurrier replied, his eyes still wandering in search of the elusive file. 'Such things happened to other people. Jack always thought he had a charmed life. Maybe he should've checked – but that's a counsel of perfection. One tends to get relaxed about these things. He wouldn't have thought anybody could've had it in for him.'

Abigail said, 'Somebody did. The bomb couldn't have got there by accident.'

'But who, for God's sake?'

25

'You must have some pretty dangerous guys banged up in here.'

'Some. And banged up's the word! If they could've got as far as the house, you wouldn't have seen them for dust – wouldn't have been stopping to plant bombs, I can tell you – even if they'd had the means.'

Dangerous, Abigail had meant, in that they had friends outside, who might conceivably have done the job for them – for reasons which hadn't yet offered themselves.

Spurrier had the stunned look of someone in deep shock. His hands were restless. Long, thin fingers fiddled with a treasury tag, folded and refolded a scrap of paper, rearranged a collection of biros, pencils and odds and ends in a mug with a crude, fat-lady seaside joke on it.

'You wanted to see us, Mr Spurrier?' Mayo prompted, with difficulty refraining from looking at his watch. He was anxious to get going. Kite, his high-energy sergeant, had already set the wheels of the inquiry rolling, and plodding old Atkins would be setting up the incident room, but this wasn't going to be any straight-down-the-line inquiry. There'd been no claim so far from any disaffected or subversive organizations. There was still time for that, but no point in waiting for it: a bomb as a means of settling a personal score was unusual, but not unheard of – and that meant starting here where grudges were more than likely to have originated. 'We'll need to interview everyone,' he'd told Abigail on the way over, 'prison officers, inmates, civilian staff – everybody.' He was anxious to brief his team, establish firm lines of inquiry. And there was Miss Reynolds, the deputy governor, still to see.

And here was Spurrier, still skating around the edges of what he had to say. 'They pushed the boat out for him last night at the Town Hall. Because of his OBE. The Mayor and Mayoress, speeches, champagne, the works. I was there as a friend of Flora . . .' He added quietly, in absolute misery, 'Oh, God.'

Ah yes, Flora, the governor's daughter. Mayo watched the restless fingers unfold the piece of paper once more, begin refolding it even more tightly, as he added, 'He was well liked, the governor. Respected and well liked. Better than most I can think of.'

Mayo nodded, resigned to accepting that this wasn't going to be quick. 'Sure. I liked him myself.'

'I didn't realize you knew him.'

'Met him occasionally in the course of business. We had a drink together once or twice.'

It was true that Mayo had liked Lilburne – within their limited acquaintance. He'd sent him a congratulatory note on reading the announcement of his OBE award, believing the distinction conferred on him was, in this case, well deserved. A hail-fellow-well-met type, Jack Lilburne, yet patently dedicated to his job. On the face of it, the last person to provoke enough personal animosity in anyone to make them put a *bomb* under him, to want to blow him out of existence. Maybe it *had* been a gesture of another sort . . . an anarchical gesture, a declaration of subversion.

Spurrier had pushed his chair back and walked to the window, standing with his back to them, looking out. The room was old fashioned, had seen better days. Cream paint was chipped and darkened to the colour of old yellow teeth. Thumb-tacked posters, visual-aid boards, were screwed on to one wall, contemptuous of what had once been fine panelling. A hole in the plaster indicated where the doorknob had crashed into it too many times. Files and books spilled on to the floor, a jacket was slung over a peg, with a bump poking out just under its collar. What would Spurrier, a psychologist, have made of the room, what construction would he have put on its owner's character, had its occupant been someone else? That he was a bit of a slob, for sure – and he'd have been dead right, Mayo thought. Spurrier's shoes were unpolished. (To Mayo, who had to be reminded to get his hair cut, and wore his own suits until they were only just this side of respectable, this was the ultimate sin.) More, Spurrier's shirt was open necked and looked rough dried, his cords were baggy at the knees, as well as elsewhere, the lenses of his glasses smeary. About thirty, with worry lines on his forehead, and a slightly defeated droop to his shoulders. But his reactions were quicker than his procrastinating manner indicated and his eyes, behind the dim lenses, shrewd. Almost certainly, underneath the haphazard exterior, was a depth of understanding and compassion.

He swung round and slouched back into his chair. 'Look,' he said eventually, 'most lads in this establishment are between eighteen and twenty-one . . .'

'But quite capable of carrying out threats against the governor?' Mayo supplied when he failed to finish the sentence. And giving him a further push, 'Is that what you wanted to see us about?'

Spurrier adjusted his slipping spectacles with a forefinger, hunched his shoulders, still unwilling to get to the point. 'You know as well as I do the sort we get in here. Most of them are defiant and resentful when they come in, and we have to accept that a lot are still resentful when they go out. We aim to change attitudes, to prepare them for release in every possible way – and some of them do respond positively. We're proud of our success rate, of the high percentage – relatively speaking – who go straight after they leave us. But some we haven't a hope with, we know for a fact that eighty per cent will be back. You have to understand, they've already been conditioned by their past experiences, their background . . .'

Perhaps he was used to glazed looks from his listeners (though to do him justice, his conversation was relatively free from jargon), perhaps he saw a certain scepticism creeping in. At any rate, he checked himself and continued on a different note. 'But yes, of course, threats are made, all the time, against all of us – '

'By anyone specially?' Mayo asked.

'Oh, I can give you names, dozens, but mostly threats are all it amounts to. Empty threats, sounding off, trying to appear big. Not *seriously* meant. He wasn't like that, the governor, not the sort of sadistic – well, he maintained there was hope for everybody.'

'*Never* any serious threats?'

Spurrier said reluctantly, 'Well, maybe . . .'

'You've someone specific in mind?'

'He's out now, he's done his time, no point in hounding him . . .' Mayo waited. At last Spurrier said, 'All right, his name's Davis, Derek Davis, better known as Dex. I hesitate to point the finger, but he's consistently made threats – and he's capable of carrying them out – though I wouldn't have thought this was his style.'

'What was he in for?'

Spurrier said with an unexpected touch of humour, 'The first time, he was the getaway driver, what else, in a wages snatch. You wouldn't believe how many of them we have in here,

28

nearly as many as those who've been stitched up by the police! They're never the ones who've done the job, who've done the smacking. The second time he smashed a night watchman at a clothing factory on the head with a hammer. Lucky for him it wasn't murder.' He sighed. 'Always a difficult lad – poor home background, a history of anti-social behaviour as a child – bunking off, exclusion from school, and then the usual story when he left – no chance of a job, started getting into real trouble, nicking cars, thieving . . . He became a right tearaay, no holding him down, a hell-raiser – '

Breaking off suddenly, he jumped up, and dived into what appeared to be a pile of wastepaper on the floor, emerging triumphantly with the missing file. Having retrieved it, looked at it as though he didn't know what it was, he then dropped it on to the paper-strewn desk, where there seemed every chance of it disappearing as completely as it had before. He seemed to have lost the thread.

'How long is it since Davis was released?' Abigail prompted.

'What? Oh, four months. Mid November.'

That was exact enough to tell Mayo that Spurrier, despite his initial reluctance to name Davis, had been sure enough of his suspicions to have checked the records and to have had the dates at his fingertips. 'What did you mean about this not being his style?'

Spurrier thought for a moment. 'I suppose I meant it wouldn't have been enough for the governor to go out, bang, just like that. Dex would've had to see to it personally. He'd have chosen some other way, preferably sadistic, where he could see Jack's reaction when he realized it was Davis, taking his revenge.'

The telephone rang at that moment and Spurrier sprang towards it. His hand fumbled, lifting the receiver, but he caught it before the second ring. 'Yes? Thank God. She hasn't? I see. Yes, I will. Thank you, Mrs Lilburne.' He put down the receiver and sat looking blankly at it for a minute. When he looked up, his glasses were misted. 'They've examined Flora and found nothing wrong with her except for cuts and bruises – and shock, of course. She's been heavily sedated and hasn't come round yet. That was her *mother*, would you believe? – Flora's mother, ringing from the hospital to let me know.'

He sounded almost as shocked by that as by the news that

Flora herself had escaped death by a hair's breadth. Mayo speculated, as they left him, on how the governor and his wife had regarded what had all the indications of a heavy relationship between Spurrier and their daughter. And what Spurrier might feel if their reactions weren't favourable.

5

The chaplain had driven Dorothea to the hospital with every intention of staying with her until Flora came round. But Flora was still sedated, and though he disliked the thought of leaving Dorothea on her own, he gave in when she insisted.

'You've been so kind, Dick, so kind, but I mustn't stop you from going about your business any longer.'

'My dear, who else but you *is* my business at this moment?'

But perhaps she really wanted to be alone, he thought, even needed it, now that she'd talked herself silent. Although they'd always got on well together, in a quiet way, and his wife Meg was the nearest Dorothea had to a close friend, during the last couple of hours she'd talked to him more than in the whole seventeen years of their acquaintance, as if she needed to spill out things she might now be regretful of saying.

Why? Why Jack Lilburne? And who? Who could have contemplated doing such a thing to Jack? *Jack*? Everyone was asking the same questions. Everyone except Dorothea and the Reverend Dick Felden.

As a prison chaplain, he was a man tolerant of behaviour in all its forms, non-judgemental, hopeful of goodness and repentance, but nevertheless with an unshakeable belief in the very real existence of evil and its occasional manifestation in the human soul. It was not at all beyond his capacity to believe that one of the youths who had at one time been under his pastoral care had planted the bomb.

And Dorothea was too shocked as yet to be looking for blame, indeed, too shocked for real grief. He found it in himself to wish she hadn't taken so calmly what was by any standards nothing short of disaster. A storm of cleansing tears would have been better, would have started the healing process. Even anger would have helped. This too-calm acceptance that Jack was dead, that Flora, but for a split-second miracle, might very easily have been dead, too . . . It was all wrong.

'Don't worry about me, it'll be harder for her, my poor child, they were always so close,' she'd said at one point, almost to herself, as if she'd forgotten he was there, gazing out of the window of the little annexe to Flora's room, at the end of the corridor. Staring, unseeing, at a view of the hospital's old-fashioned boiler house, whose minimal interest had long since waned.

They'd always left her behind, those two, Jack and Flora, Flora and her da. She wasn't agile-minded enough for them, too slow to catch their jokes, to share their laughter. There was nothing new for Dorothea in that situation. She'd been the youngest of a boisterous family of three boys and two girls, and it had been the constant cry of her childhood, as she ran on her short legs after the others, 'Wait for me, wait for me!'

It had taught her to be good at waiting. To find consolation in her beloved garden, in something she alone excelled at. To bide her time until things worked themselves out, as they almost always did, in the end, if you were patient enough and prepared to accept what you couldn't change. Even though you were hurt to the point where it threatened to tear you apart.

'Jack always said,' she observed now in a detached voice, 'that it's important you don't rock the boat, though I'm afraid he didn't always follow his own advice. "Just wait until something tells you what you can do about a situation," he used to say, "and then have the courage to go ahead and carry it through, no matter what the consequences."'

'My dear,' Dick Felden repeated, giving her a worried look and receiving in return only an absent smile. Finally, he, who'd helped countless numbers of people through the agony of bereavement, was forced to leave, with a wretched feeling that he'd been no help to her whatever.

After the talk with Spurrier, Mayo and Abigail were escorted by a member of staff from the administration offices, where an air of tense and feverish excitement pervaded the atmosphere, into the main body of the prison, where Miss Reynolds was presently occupied. Their guide was a woman prison officer whose badge gave her name as PO Corsham. 'Make it Sylvia,' she smiled, a young woman with a mop of dark hair, buxom arms beneath the short sleeves of her white uniform shirt and a cheerful line in chat. Although evidently agog with curiosity, she quickly took the hint when Mayo parried her questions about the bomb.

The old house was separated from the newer sections – the sprawl of buildings that had gradually grown up to form the various wings and functions – by a long zigzag walkway with high windows either side and a succession of doors, each one opened with the big key hanging from the prison officer's belt and relocked behind them.

The crisp, blowy morning, glimpsed through the corridor windows, appeared cold and fresh in the bright sunshine. Mayo had a sudden urge for the joy of stretching his legs across miles and miles of open moors, a favourite addiction he'd certainly have to forgo until this investigation was over, but one he could look forward to. The key turned in another lock and the thought was abruptly killed. Behind these locked doors nearly four hundred healthy, aggressive, anti-social young males were shut up from the outside world, a perplexed and guilty society's only answer to dealing with the crimes, from petty to horrendous, they'd committed. But it wouldn't do to think too much about freedom, about the tensions and ugliness of prison life, its confused, recalcitrant and sometimes despairing inmates. It was counterproductive, as well as depressing.

Food trolleys and an institutional smell of stew indicated that lunch was in the offing. Some of the inmates were receiving their portions to take back to eat in their cells, but several of them were hanging around in the vicinity of a small office in one of the wings. 'Any of the lads have problems, they can see Miss Reynolds,' Sylvia had told them. 'Home leave, parole boards, anything really. She's pretty good at getting them sorted.'

How many of them had legitimate calls on the deputy governor's time, Mayo wondered, how many of the requests were fabricated? There was, after all, plenty of time to think up ways of relieving the tedium.

And Claudia Reynolds was nobody's idea of a prison officer. A small, cool, elegant blonde, she was wearing a smart rust-coloured suit that showed her figure to excellent advantage, hair pulled tightly back into a knot from a classically featured face, big pearl and gold studs in her ears. Noting the expensive-looking cream leather shoes that did a lot for her legs, Mayo added another reason to the list of why the inmates might try to wangle time to see her.

'How can I help you?' she asked, having briskly dealt with the preliminaries, without wasting too much time on expressions of shock or horror – or sympathy, either, he noticed. 'Have you any ideas about the bomb, so far?'

He didn't want to speculate at this stage, mainly, he reflected gloomily, because there wasn't much to speculate *on*. 'The usual suspicions when a bomb goes off – terrorists, subversives, idealistically motivated groups, someone with a personal grudge . . .'

'Such as one of our disaffected ex-inmates?'

'Possibly. Or someone connected with one of them.'

'We've nobody here with extremist connections, not that I'm aware of . . . though we've a fair sprinkling of ethnic minorities, a lot of them with axes of some sort to grind. A good percentage of Irish, come to that, although I suppose that shouldn't be a consideration since the ceasefire.'

'Did the governor have strong political views that might have been the cause of him receiving any threats recently?'

'If he had, he didn't tell me. Or make them public in any way. I should think it extremely unlikely.'

'Then we can't rule out revenge, the need to settle a personal score. At any rate, it's something we may need to follow up. In which case, we shall need access to records, of course. As well as interviews with inmates – and staff.'

She gave him a sharp glance, but said, 'Sure. May I ask if you've anyone particular in mind?'

'Mr Spurrier's suggested we look at a Derek Davis, released about four months ago, for one.'

'He'd be top of my list, too,' she said crisply. 'Along with a couple of dozen others.' Mayo raised an eyebrow. 'Oh, don't let their age fool you. We've some really evil types in here. In for far worse crimes than nicking cars – and Dex Davis was one of them. The governor put a lot of effort into his rehabilitation programme during his last few months – without much success, needless to say. Not the sort to respond to the softly-softly approach, our Dex.'

Meaning what? Mayo asked himself. That this kind of approach was one she didn't approve of – and therefore, by association, hadn't been a member of the Lilburne fan club either? He might not have thought of this if it hadn't been for Spurrier's surprising last words: 'Don't attach too much importance to what Miss Reynolds says about the governor,' he'd said, as they were leaving him. 'They didn't get on too well, never mind what she might say.' And when Mayo had asked him to clarify this, he'd answered cryptically, 'About a lot of things – but the new wing was the touchy subject of the moment.'

'Why did Davis make these threats? Did he have a special grievance?' Abigail was asking.

'They all think they've a grievance,' she answered drily. 'But he was an incorrigible troublemaker, and a bully. He was segregated more times than you've had hot dinners. He's always had a general intolerance of any kind of authority, a total non-acceptance of his need for punishment. Another who thought he was being discriminated against.'

The profile seemed to fit. An anarchic personality, a bomb. 'Is Davis capable of holding on to a grudge?'

She laughed shortly. 'Oh yes, more than most. Vindictive – and deep. He'd wait for his chance, all right.'

It was the sort of vengefulness most people connected with the law encountered. Mayo had come across it himself, more than once. 'I'll get you for this, one day,' was a threat he'd heard more times than he could count, down the years. Maybe he was just lucky that so far it hadn't materialized.

'Hm. Tell me about this proposed new wing, if you will. I gather there are objections to it from outside.'

She took the change of direction in her stride, though he sensed she was less comfortable with it. 'Not only outside! I wasn't for it, myself, because as I see it, it's only a cosmetic answer to the problem. It would help, but not much. Frankly, the whole place needs a bomb under it, and rebuilding.'

It was, in the circumstances, an unfortunate turn of phrase, and she made a rueful face. But if there was compassion – and he wasn't necessarily questioning that – it was well hidden. He said merely, 'Is that likely? Rebuilding, I mean.'

'Unfortunately, no, at the moment, and as long as we contrive to make do with this sort of piecemeal solution, it never will be. Funds won't be made available for anything better. Mr Lilburne didn't agree with that, however. He was more inclined to go for what I see as the short-term advantage.'

'Half a loaf?' Mayo suggested.

'And look where that sort of thinking in the past has got us. A hotch-potch of buildings – ' She broke off, spreading her hands. 'Well, you've only to look.'

She said what she thought, Ms Reynolds. She was a cracker to look at, she had a clear skin and large blue eyes, she smiled often, but he was not charmed. The concept of her attractiveness as a spur to wangling a few minutes in her company was fast losing ground, as far as he was concerned. In contrast to the cheerful young woman who'd guided them here, it was gradually being borne in on him that beneath the softly rounded bosom in the rust-coloured suit could beat the heart of a female Gauleiter.

She looked covertly at her watch, a gesture not lost on Mayo. He chose not to see it. 'What about the local residents who're objecting to this scheme?' he asked.

After a pause, she said, 'They *are* objecting strongly – and groundlessly, of course – but I can't see them going to the extent of putting a bomb under his car to put their point across.'

'Possibly not.' This wasn't something worth arguing about at the moment. 'How did Mr Lilburne get on with his staff? Was he easy to work with?'

'I never found any difficulty.'

That wasn't an answer to the question. She was beginning to show signs of an underlying obstructiveness, though he'd have put money on it that Claudia Reynolds was normally the type to make it in her way to get on with anyone if it suited her, on the surface.

'What about personal involvements – enmities?'

A tumbler of water from which she'd been drinking stood on the table, and she reached out a hand to take another sip, perhaps to give herself time. Unfortunately, she wasn't looking as she did so and her sleeve brushed against the glass, knocking it on to the hard composition floor, where it broke with a crash, the glittering fragments scattering in a wide arc. She gave a little cry and immediately sprang from her chair to clear it up.

'Watch you don't cut yourself,' Abigail warned, but she was too late. Claudia Reynolds was looking with horror at a cut on her index finger and had turned as white as paper, though it was little more than a scratch, so slight, in fact, that the blood was having difficulty in oozing out. A few tiny red drops on the white skin of her manicured hand was all that could be seen, but, looking at them, she gave a soft little moan and fainted dead away.

'Was it something I said?' Mayo wondered aloud, sitting beside Abigail as she drove him back to the station with the competence that characterized everything she did – and which was why she was sometimes resented by those of her male colleagues who couldn't measure up to her standards, most of whom she'd skimmed past, barely touching ground on her way up to the coveted position of detective inspector. 'Or did it just prove she was human after all? Cut her, and she bleeds . . .'

'Rather clumsy diversionary tactics – knocking the glass over, I mean.' Abigail drew smoothly up to a set of traffic lights. 'The faint was real enough though, wasn't it? She's obviously one of those people who can't stand the sight of blood. Blood phobia must be a bit of a hazard in her line. But knocking the glass over . . . I think there was something she just wanted to avoid at that moment.'

'Personal relationships? That's what we were talking about just then. Was there something going on between her and Lilburne?'

'Nothing amorous if there was,' Abigail said drily.

That had been obvious, but the conversation with Claudia Reynolds had been unsatisfactory all ways, Mayo reflected. She was prickly, to say the least – a woman in what was very much a man's world, who hadn't yet learned how to cope with it gracefully, though he was damn sure she wouldn't have thanked him for thinking that. Perhaps that was the reason she'd drawn in her horns about Lilburne. He felt she could have said a lot more, had she been so inclined, and whether it was relevant or not, he'd have been better pleased to have heard it – to know what it was she'd kept silent about, and why.

6

Flora woke with a dull, throbbing pain in her head. Her eyelids felt weighted, it was a tremendous effort to open them. When she did, she saw a white coverlet on a high narrow bed, pulled taut across her feet, flowery curtains and shiny, cream-painted walls, a sink in the corner and an open door into a corridor, from whence she heard the squeak of rubber tyres on plastic tiles. There was a smell like none other, compounded of fish and antiseptics and polish, which immediately told her where she was, but not why. Slowly, she turned her glance sideways and saw her mother sitting by the bedside, her head bent; she shut her eyes again, terrified of remembering something unspeakable and as yet unrecalled on the edge of her consciousness. The room swam around her, and presently, she slept once more.

Mayo still hadn't become used to his flat being so spruce, though anywhere where Alex Jones lived was destined to be tidy. It had been perhaps the tiniest thing on the debit side of her coming to live with him — the fact that he'd have to put his clothes away, and his shirts and socks out for washing on a regular basis, not just when he'd come to the last clean ones. But on the credit side, he could see the difference — a home, as opposed to a bachelor pad. There was something to be said for having it dusted and polished and cared for, and not to have to face a sinkful of washing up every time he came home. It wasn't perhaps as pristine as Alex would have kept it, left to herself. Mayo was gradually educating her otherwise. She now occasionally left a cushion rumpled.

It had been a day and a half, and wasn't finished yet.

Moses, the old grey cat who belonged to his landlady, but thought he ought to belong to Mayo, was waiting outside his door as usual when Mayo arrived home, in the ever-optimistic but never-to-be-fulfilled hope that one day he might be allowed inside. 'Hard luck, mate,' Mayo said, closing the door on his jealous miaow as Bert the parrot squawked out his usual low-class greeting from inside.

He knew Alex was off duty and was looking forward to a welcome from her, to the hopeful prospect of savoury odours coming from a meal simmering to perfection point in the oven while he sipped a single malt. Some music, perhaps, the latest acquisition, with his feet up for half an hour on the old sofa whose ancient springs had learned to accommodate themselves to his shape.

The whisky was there, but Alex was not, and the flat smelled only of the spicy bowl of potpourri on the coffee table. He read the note she'd left, informing him she'd be home shortly, there was cold food left ready for their meal in the fridge. Shrugging philosophically, he poured himself a judicious slug of Glen-finnan and crossed to the sofa, which was also not there.

He stood contemplating its replacement. Lois, he thought.

When Alex had finally agreed to live with him, they'd de-cided on his flat rather than hers because it was bigger, and had agreed to pool resources and so keep the best of both worlds. Mayo, not caring one way or another, had left the choice of redecorating it to Alex, with professional help from her sister Lois, who was an interior decorator. He, Mayo, was merely the one who slapped the paint on. Now that they'd finished decor-ating it and Lois's desire to go the whole hog with 'amusing' furniture and dramatic lighting effects had been tempered by Alex's insistence on a comfortable mix of old and new, it looked unbelievably smart and coordinated, with even the parrot matching the colour scheme (though he fancied he'd seen Lois casting a speculative eye on him more than once). He had to admit it was an improvement on the all-over magnolia job he'd walloped on when he moved in because he couldn't think of anything else.

He was becoming accustomed to seeing familiar pieces of furniture disappear and to stumbling over others he'd never seen before, but he was so bemused with joy that Alex was actually here at last, in his flat and sharing his bed, that he'd made not a murmur. The only thing he'd drawn the line at was interference with his collection of old clocks, which were sacrosanct.

And the sofa.

Though to be fair he hadn't actually stipulated this last item. He'd have thought Alex would have *known*. He'd had it since before he was married, and it was second-hand then, but it was deeply comfortable and it had been the first piece of furniture he'd ever bought. There was a lot of history in that sofa.

This one was as stylish as the rest of the decor, pretending to be a Victorian chaise longue, with a curved, buttoned end and a carved wooden back. It was stuffed as tight and unyielding as a Christmas turkey. It was velvet. It was *rose pink*, for God's sake.

And it was undoubtedly Lois's choice. Sometimes he wondered which sister was supposed to have moved in with him.

There had been an improvement in relations between him and the spiky Lois since she'd been involved in the Fleming case, a particularly nasty murder he'd had to investigate two or three years ago, but he couldn't yet feel she approved of him entirely. He still felt it was her influence which was partly responsible for Alex refusing to marry him, never mind all this bollocks about wanting to keep her independence. There was also a question hanging over Alex's professional future. Did she want to stay in the police service or would she – the latest proposal – yield to Lois's continuing pressure to join her in her interior-decorating business?

He went to set the new dining table with the new table mats and the new cutlery and then, as a gesture to his own independence, swept them away and set out the old stainless-steel knives and forks on the kitchen table.

'I don't know what you're making such a fuss about,' Alex said when she came in five minutes later. 'It's only gone to be re-covered, and resprung. It'll be back in a week.'

'Oh.' Mayo wasn't so sure about the respringing. 'It won't be too hard?'

'Feather and down cushions.'

'Not rose pink?'

Alex burst out laughing. 'You surely didn't think this – *boudoir* piece – was permanent? Would I do that to you, Gil? It's on loan from Lois, until the other's ready.'

He felt a fool. He could just hear Lois, in that brittle, particularly infuriating manner of hers: 'Well, really, Giles!'

But Alex was saying, 'Well, we've more to talk about than that old sofa. What a day it's been for you – Superintendent!' She gave the impish grin that had first made Mayo see distinct possibilities for letting herself go behind the cool exterior she presented to the world.

'Hey, just because you live with me doesn't give you the right to get uppity, Sergeant Jones.' He grinned. 'And the day's not finished yet, not by a long chalk. I've only come home for a couple of hours – to get out of this gear, have a shower and something to eat, then I'm off again.'

Alex also being in the police, he could announce these sort of intentions without fear of sulks or recriminations. Just as he could talk about his current cases without the risk of being either indiscreet or boring. She was as interested as he was in the present one.

'How is she – Flora, the daughter?' she asked when they were sitting down to carefully sliced cold chicken and a beautifully prepared but boring salad, with a jacket potato done in the microwave by way of a bonus. Alex might be his dear love but her best attributes didn't lie in inspired cooking – that was left to his daughter, Julie. Mayo lived in hopes that, one day, she might turn up from Australia or Outer Mongolia, or wherever her next letter said she was living at present, and give Alex some lessons, but meanwhile good plain cooking was the most he ever got. He put more dressing on to his salad and kept mum, like Alex when she'd seen the table set in the kitchen. Perhaps they were both learning.

'Flora Lilburne?' he repeated. 'She's OK – but incredibly lucky – concussion and minor cuts and bruises, that's all. Shock, of course. She must've walked away from the car seconds before it blew up.'

'The worst's probably still to come, for her.' Alex spoke from experience. She knew what it was to be the victim of violence. It had taken her weeks to recover physically after being injured when tackling a thief who turned out to be armed in a petrol-station heist, a long convalescence which she could see, how-ever, in retrospect, as a respite, an opportunity to take stock of her life, just then at a crossroads, professionally as well as privately. Whether she'd chosen to take the right direction in returning to her job or not remained to be seen; what she was increasingly certain of was the rightness of her decision to make a real commitment in her private life, to have moved in here with Gil Mayo. Since she wasn't a person who undertook such commitments lightly, it had taken her a long time to make her mind up. She knew he thought she was fighting shy of marriage due to a conflict between that and her career. If it were only that!

And also, she'd known his wife, Lynne, very well. Despite the fact that it hadn't been a marriage of unalloyed bliss, mostly due to the exigencies of his job, Alex was by no means sure that he'd totally recovered from Lynne – that he still didn't have hang-ups, reminding him of the mistakes he'd made. She didn't want that kind of a marriage, with a man always looking over his shoulder. She needed to show him that theirs would be different.

'Still nobody claiming responsibility for the bomb?' she asked as she poured his second cup of excellent coffee. Coffee she *was* good at.

He shook his head as he accepted the cup from her. 'And I've a nasty feeling there won't be.' He half hoped his intuition would be proved wrong, that some subversive organization would call and say they'd planted the bomb, then the investigation would be in other, specialist hands; if not, it was likely to remain his responsibility . . .

'We've never begun an investigation with less to go on. No clues, no suspects, not even a body. No real leads at all, except maybe a so-called photographer who might, on the off chance that we can find him, turn out to be genuine. Oh, and a slim chance on one of the ex-inmates at Conyhall.' He wasn't, he realized, pinning many hopes on Dex Davis. Despite his record at the YOI, despite Spurrier's reluctant conclusions, and Claudia Reynolds's convictions.

'Not even a jealous husband?' Alex asked.

'A what?'

'Well, Jack Lilburne was quite a dish, wasn't he? Very attractive.'

Mayo was taken aback. 'If you say so. Must confess, he never turned me on!' But this added a dimension he hadn't so far envisaged. 'Is that right? The sort to play away from home?'

Alex shrugged. 'Maybe. The sort who couldn't help giving a woman the eye, at any rate.'

'Well, well.' All the clocks in the flat reached the hour and joined together in a joyful noise, while Mayo thoughtfully finished his coffee and Alex waited patiently until they could speak again.

'We may have more to go on when I've seen Mrs Lilburne tomorrow. And one or two of my lot should have reported in by the time I get back . . .'

It was going to be mostly legwork at this stage: all that interviewing at Conyhall . . . Farrar detailed to trace Dex Davis . . . Jenny Platt with her ear glued to the telephone in an attempt to trace the photographer . . . None of them fighting for the privilege of questioning Lavenstock's small but occasionally troublesome and always volatile Irish community. Although so far any local political affiliations with the Provisional IRA were unknown, they had to check whether any mistaken vestiges of sympathy remained, whether the violence had been channelled against the governor as a legitimate target. The task had fallen to the unenthusiastic Sergeant Carmody and DC Deeley whose names, it had been agreed by popular vote, would give them a head start. Deeley only got a big laugh when he protested that his ancestors had come from darkest Devon, and Carmody hadn't had a leg to stand on from the outset. He was Liverpool-Irish right down to his toenails.

Marc Daventry unhooked the clipboard from the iron footrail of the bed and read the notes carefully. Replacing it, he smiled at the patient. 'Won't be long before you'll be home, I should think.'

Flora said nothing, just turned her head and stared out of the window. Marc looked at the pale, lovely profile and, despite himself, felt a stirring of pity for her. She'd been told what had happened, her memory of it had come back and she was taking it badly, though everyone kept repeating that it was a miracle she should be thankful for, that she'd escaped with barely a scratch and was still alive. Marc understood and sympathized. He knew from intimate experience how bad she must be feeling: he could recognize the numbness and the unwillingness to believe what had happened – only for him the shock had been twofold, and a long-drawn-out agony, because, unlike her father, they hadn't died immediately, the two people he had until then loved as much as he'd loved anybody. An icy road, a

43

drunken motorist taking a corner too wide, too fast, with the result that they'd ended up in hospital, he in a coma, and she still conscious but attached to a blood drip.

A malign fate had decreed that Marc had been on duty, working overtime, when they'd been brought into Accident and Emergency at the hospital where he was working. Of course, he wasn't allowed, when it was discovered who they were, to continue working in the theatre, and he understood and accepted that. They told him sympathetically to go home, another ODP would take his place in the support team, they'd let him know when there was any news. But he waited at the hospital, his nerves twitching – this time an anxious, waiting relative on the other side of the fence, drinking endless cups of coffee from the dispensing machine. They couldn't keep him, later, from their bedsides.

He hadn't, until then, known their blood groups; there'd been no reason why he should. June, he read on her chart, was A negative – and Frank, he later saw with a shock that still sent tingles down his spine, was also A negative. While he himself, their son, was B positive.

It wasn't possible. Two A-negative parents with a B-positive child. He'd done his haematology stint during his training, and knew it couldn't be. Something was seriously wrong.

Frank died the next day, and it was to June that Marc spoke, even though she was so ill. *Because* she was so ill. He was all too aware how little time there was left, and he had to know the truth. He'd felt no compunction at pressing her, since any explanation must be so cruel to himself that he felt he was absolved from any necessity to spare her. All the love and kindness between them was forfeit after what those two had done. One of them was not his true parent. Or perhaps neither.

'Tell me the truth,' he demanded, 'that's all I want. Am I adopted, or what?'

She was sensible enough to give him a painfully whispered answer, to beg his forgiveness. 'We should've told you . . . we always meant to . . . but it wasn't a story for a young child . . . then somehow . . .'

Through stiff lips, he asked, 'What do you mean, not a story for a young child? Why not? Who am I?'

But she'd passed beyond him, spent, and though she lingered for several days, she was never able to speak coherently again.

Marc went to their double funeral, a quiet ceremony attended only by himself and a few shocked friends. There were no relatives, and for the first time his total lack of any aunts, cousins or grandparents struck him as peculiar. He'd always been told that both June and Frank were orphans, and accepted it, but now he wondered if that were false, too. He endured the ceremony with stoic indifference, which his parents' friends remarked on as courage. It was anything but. Those two people, whom he'd loved and trusted, had suddenly become nothing to him. They'd lived out a lie, and had forced him, unwittingly, to live one, too. They'd robbed him of his birthright.

Who am I?

The question had hammered and throbbed in his brain until he'd thought he was going mad. Why had they kept the facts from him? He'd always thought they were truthful, sensible people, who would surely have recognized the well-publicized dangers of not telling a child he was adopted. Remembering June's last words, he could only conclude bitterly that there had been something too shameful or disgraceful about his birth to discuss.

He looked now at the patient on the bed, at Flora. She looked so pale and pure, like a nun, with the coif-like bandage around her forehead, and he felt another stab of pity for her, and an impulse to touch and comfort her, an innocent, accidental victim, through no fault of her own. Then a different, painfully pleasurable but unwelcome emotion took him by surprise as he found her looking at him with wide, hazel eyes.

With long working hours and all his spare time occupied with what had come to be an obsessive search for his true identity, Marc had found little time for women – or to develop personal relationships at all, for that matter. He had rather a lot of acquaintances, but almost no real friends. His intensity was inclined to put people off from getting too close, and if they had, he wouldn't have reciprocated. He'd had brief encounters with women but nothing more. The deep stirring of sexual desire he felt now as he looked at the innocent, virginal figure in the bed, the urge to touch and fondle her, filled him with self-disgust. He drew back. Emotional complications he could do without. He had enough on his plate at the moment. She had to remain what she was, a stranger to him.

45

'Are you a doctor?' she asked suddenly, aware of his intense scrutiny.

'Not exactly,' Marc said.

Far from it, really, though he would like to have been, if the long years of training before he would be qualified hadn't deterred him. He'd been working as a hospital porter when he'd heard about Operating Department Practitioners, or ODPs, as they were known, who worked in the operating theatres and assisted the surgeon and the anaesthetist. The idea appealed to him immediately, and it turned out to be almost as good as being a doctor: he'd studied subjects allied to surgery and anaesthetics during his two-year training, which wasn't too long, though it was rigorous and needed a lot of study and application. But because this was something he really wanted to do, he'd passed both practical and theoretical exams with flying colours and would soon be on the second grade, a senior ODP, and could, theoretically, rise to Assistant Chief, or even Chief, though he wasn't sure he wanted that. It involved too much administrative work for his taste, whereas he enjoyed the practical side – setting up the technical equipment, checking that the ventilators were working, even monitoring the patient, occasionally, when the anaesthetist was called away. He liked the responsibility and power it gave him, particularly the feeling of having control over life and death: if he were to make a mistake, or failed to anticipate the anaesthetist's needs, if he allowed his attention to wander, no doubt about it, the patient could very easily die.

7

Josie Davis, small and very slim, with short, bleached, neatly cut hair, wearing tight jeans and a sleeveless T-shirt, was whipping round the weekend chores with her usual brisk efficiency.

Every Saturday morning the small house was blitzed from top to bottom, windows cleaned, floors vacuumed, furniture dusted and polished, while the week's washing was whirling around in her new combined washer and tumble dryer. Nobody was going to get the chance to say she didn't keep her home nice, though it was bloody hard work, keeping it spotless and looking after the children, besides working full time in the mail-order office. But if she hadn't had the job, never mind that it bored her out of her mind, there wouldn't *be* a house, not to mention the little luxuries she felt they were all entitled to. They'd taken on a bitch of a mortgage, dependent on their combined wages, hers and Barry's, to buy it. The house was brilliant, a new one on a small estate, better than the last grotty old shack – or anything she'd ever lived in before.

She was hoping to get the ironing done before getting the bus into town to shop for some clothes – you couldn't go on wearing the same things day after day in the office, the other girls would look down their noses – and to buy some ready-prepared meals from Marks. Dear, but you had to pay for convenience: when the twins let themselves in from school all they had to do was to microwave boeuf bourguignon or chicken tikka masala to eat while they watched *Neighbours*.

She rubbed the windows even more vigorously, cheered by the idea that she might buy herself something smart this afternoon that she could wear that night. Being Saturday, they'd a sitter coming in so that she could go down the club with Barry.

Busy, busy, busy, every weekend the same.

So she wasn't exactly delighted to see two men walking

purposefully up the path beside the handkerchief-sized lawn. Especially when she recognized them immediately for what they were.

She told them grudgingly that they'd better come in, evidently on tenterhooks that the neighbours might see and hear. It was a fear Martin Kite often played on to his own advantage – getting the door banged in your face earned you no medals. He smiled seraphically in the face of her scowl and allowed her to lead them indoors.

Two neat little girls of around ten, as like as two peas, slightly darker editions of their mother and dressed almost identically to her in jeans and T-shirts, with knowing little faces and gold sleepers – smaller versions of their mother's earrings – in their ears, were doing what looked like homework on the table in the dining end of the living room.

'Go out and play,' their mother ordered, 'this won't take long. Don't forget your coats.' They exchanged sulky looks, but after a silent debate, did as they were told, and presently could be seen, clad in shell-suit jackets in vivid fluorescent colours, rather desultorily bouncing a ball about on the front lawn. Smart wench, this, approved Kite, knew how to keep her kids in line, at any rate – he should be so lucky with his own lads. DC Farrar was thinking he wouldn't have argued, either. Sharp-faced madam, Josie Davis, with a tongue to match.

'Dex? You mean *Derek*, I suppose? Well, I don't know why you've come here!' she bridled, taking a cigarette from a half-empty pack of Rothman's King Size and snapping a lighter to it. 'Think I'd have him back, after what he's done?'

'Any idea where he is?'

'Should I have?' she countered, dragging on the cigarette with hard, angry little puffs.

'If *you* don't, I don't know who would.'

'Why don't you try his mother?'

The two detectives exchanged glances, immediately realizing the mistake that had been made. 'We should've known you're too young to be his mother, love,' Farrar said, favouring her with one of his knock-'em-in-the-aisles smiles.

She gave him the once-over. Didn't half fancy himself, this one. Though come to that, she might have fancied him, too, in other circumstances. She laughed. 'What gave you that idea? If that nasty little sod had been mine, I'd have done something about him before he ended up where he did. I'm only his stepmother, thank God.'

'This was the address he gave his probation officer when he was released – where he said he was living.'

'What of it? He doesn't have to report no more.'

Kite was looking hard at Josie. He wasn't as baby-faced as she'd thought, even if he did look like he couldn't hardly knock the skin off a rice pudding. Sergeant then, was he? After a moment, she shrugged.

'Well, he did come here, then. It was his dad let him, not me. Stopped for a bit, and that was enough for all of us, even Barry. He didn't like the discipline and we didn't like him, know what I mean?'

Kite nodded. The picture was clear enough. 'Where's your husband – Barry, is it?'

'What d'you want him for? He can't tell you no more than me.'

'He's Dex's dad, isn't he? He might've told him where he was going.'

'Pigs might fly! And I don't want you bothering Barry, specially at work. They don't like coppers snooping around down the garage . . . Why can't you leave us alone? What d'you want to come bothering us for, just when we've got our lives sorted!'

Taking in the puffy, beflowered three-piece suite, the state-of-the-art music centre, the twenty-seven-inch telly, the frilly Austrian blinds, Farrar said, 'Down the garage? Which one?'

'If I told you, you'd know, wouldn't you?'

'Come on, sweetheart, give us a break.'

'Don't you sweetheart me!' She stubbed out her cigarette. 'Tell you what, though. I can give you her address – his mother's – yeah, you go and pester her. Not that he'll have gone to that cow if he'd any sense.'

When they'd gone, she picked up and dialled. 'Barry? Guess who I've just had here. Yeah, they're on to him – what have you two been up to, the pair of you? What? No, I bloody didn't, but I will if they come here again. I'm not letting that little bleeder mess things up for us again, so you'd better be telling me the truth.'

'Well,' said the major from the army bomb disposal unit, 'there you are, can't have it clearer than that. All the Provo IRA trademarks, though now we're all friends . . .' He shrugged eloquently. 'Doesn't rule out other subversive organizations, mind, animal liberation weirdos, or even some maverick IRA bugger – somebody who knows what it's all about from the good old days. They knew how to pack a bomb – though clueless, you wouldn't believe it, sometimes, I tell you. If I were you, I'd be looking for somebody with access to several pounds of Super Ajax, Swiss-made detonators and a helluva grudge. And the ability to put it all together in a plastic lunchbox with weedkiller and sugar.'

'Commercial explosive, hm? And Continental detonators? Not something you buy over the counter.' Mayo looked across the desk at the young man. 'We're not talking amateurs, then?'

'Doesn't follow. The stuff's easy enough to get if you've the right sort of friends. And most of the components you can buy anyway from any electrical store. But take it from me, this was no Mickey Mouse box of tricks.'

'And the know-how?'

'Elementary chemistry. Plus a lot of care – unless you want to spread yourself all over the ceiling.' He laughed, this clean young man whose everyday business was dealing with death and destruction, who came within a hair's breadth of his own death every time he defused a bomb.

'So it wasn't simply a warning – ?'

'It was meant to kill, all right. Fixed to the underside of the vehicle, wired up to go off immediately the car was vibrated in any way.' He described the mercury tilt switch which had been used, sensitive to any movement of the car, to the rocking of the suspension when anyone lowered themselves into the driving seat, which would have activated the chain reaction which exploded the bomb.

'All this from the debris,' Abigail said. 'Rather you than me.'

'Piece of cake, this one. You should see some of 'em.'

He was tall and fair and ruddy, his cropped hair as short as his clipped speech. His smile was bright as a toothpaste ad, as white as his certainties. He adjusted his black beret to the correct straight line above his eyebrows and left them without any room for doubt.

Nearly everyone was already there in the incident room – the team assigned to the inquiry, around thirty men and women –

constables, three sergeants and two inspectors. The hum of conversation died, computer screens were abandoned as Mayo took up his position facing them, the window behind him thrown open in a vain effort to clear the air of the cigarette smoke that rose to the ceiling and hung in a carcinogenous pall. The gesture failed to make any impression on the serious smokers. Mayo called the room to order.

'Right, let's see what we've got, then.'

Six-thirty in the evening of day two of the investigation. Not a lot achieved as yet, but the initial turmoil settling down into ordered chaos. Not a lot of hope that much *would* be achieved quickly on this one. Plenty of enthusiasm, though. Nobody liked the idea of a murder, especially a cold-blooded bombing that could rip apart flesh and tissue, wipe somebody off the face of the earth in a split second, and they were all out to get the bastard who'd done it.

'That feminist animal liberation group in Hurstfield we had trouble with some time since,' Mayo said, after repeating what the major had told him. 'Ted? You were looking into that, weren't you?'

'Disbanded, after we nabbed the ringleaders.' This was Carmody, long face lugubrious, plodding and patient as ever. 'And not started up again, as far as I can find out.'

'Let's hope so. But by the very nature of the crime we can't overlook terrorist involvement, local or otherwise. In the absence of any sort of claim, it's beginning to look remote. But we need a result on this one, quick, always bearing in mind it could be the start of a series of attacks directed against specific targets. There's been a lot of call lately for stiffer sentencing for young offenders, for instance, we all know that, and this might have been some loony sort of opposition to it. So regarding Conyhall, how're we doing on the interviewing there, Inspector Moon?'

'Still going on. Every inmate's being questioned, all the prison officers, and the civilian staff. Any recent releases will be seen, plus any earlier ones, if any look like being worth checking on. Especially Derek Davis, when we find him, known to have made specific, personal threats against the governor.'

'Davis. Yes, but he's a long way from being the only one who felt he'd a score to settle.'

51

Though it had to be said, that of all those so far interviewed, nobody had evinced a particular hatred of Jack Lilburne. Not that there hadn't been a few who had the obvious if unexpressed wish to see off *all* persons of authority – the filth, judges, magistrates, screws in general. But shock, genuine or otherwise, had been expressed at the attack on the governor.

'The general consensus of opinion among the Young Offenders' Institution population,' Mayo said drily, 'seems to be that he was "all right". Which I suppose means he was probably held in fairly high esteem. We can't take it for granted, though. And this brings me to the next thing – that from now on, we concentrate on Lilburne himself . . .'

'Sir,' Jenny Platt put in diffidently, her face pink under her curly brown hair. Mayo always expected her to put her hand up before speaking out at these meetings, which was odd, because she was neither shy nor incompetent; on the contrary, though young, she was one of his best officers. 'What about that scrap of paper, sir? The one we found in Lilburne's breast pocket?'

'Glad you mentioned that, Jenny. I was coming to it later, but we can just as well talk about it now.'

Scattered among the macabre bits of Lilburne's person had been shreds of clothing, and at the bottom of what had once been the breast pocket of his suit had been found a scrap of crumpled paper, folded and creased, as though it had been pushed down by his wallet. It could have been there some time and was probably of no importance now, though presumably it had meant something to Jack Lilburne when he put it there in the first place. All the same, it had been subjected to the usual tests. It comprised the last few lines of a page of typing – typed, not produced on a daisy wheel, dot-matrix, bubble-jet or laser printer, which was of itself significant. In this age of computers, typewriters were fast becoming as obsolete as LPs and treadle sewing machines. It wasn't even typed on an electric typewriter.

'Anything else, Dave?'

Dexter, the Scenes-of-Crime sergeant, never overoptimistic, said economically, 'It was a very old portable, manual Olympia 66. Flaw in the alignment, and the shift lock doesn't depress properly so that the caps are above the line. Several worn or damaged keys – distinctive, if we find the original to compare it with. The paper was good quality typing paper, eighty-gramme bond.'

The typing had read:

> . . .*what you said. You might at least see me. I'll be in the coffee shop at the Hurstfield Post House at eleven on November the 20th, if you can bring yourself to admit that I'm right, though I don't expect . . .*

The page ended at that point, and a question mark had been pencilled in the margin, on the bottom line. 'For Lilburne to check his business diary, to see whether he was free?' Mayo asked.

'At eleven o'clock on November the twentieth, according to his secretary, Lilburne was with his area manager,' answered Kite, on the ball, as usual. 'Had lunch with him and was with him until half past two. But we don't know how long that paper had been in Lilburne's pocket, of course. Might have been November the twentieth the previous year.'

Mayo acknowledged this was possible. 'It was obviously a personal rather than a business letter, and it's not much, but there's an aggrieved tone about it that does indicate perhaps everything in the garden wasn't smelling of roses – which brings me to what I was going to say: that from now on, we concentrate on Lilburne's personal life. I want everything we can get on him – and I mean everything. Right from where he was born to how often he changed his socks. Talk to people, see what they thought of him. Go through his past with a tooth comb. See what he did before he came to Conyhall. Dig up the dirt, if any. Everything so far indicates that Jack Lilburne was a well-respected and well-liked man, with an apparently blameless life, but nobody's that perfect. There must have been something.'

Bridie O'Sullivan woke when the alarm went off in the next bedroom. It was still dark, and she pulled the bedclothes up round her ears and turned over to sleep again. But the noise as he clumped about, getting dressed, stomping down the stairs in his Doc Martens, prevented her. She reached out to switch the light on and look at the clock. Half past five. Jesus, the middle of the night! His car, parked in the road outside, revved up, the roar split the silence. What in the name of God was he doing, going out at that time? Most mornings, she couldn't get him out of bed till noon.

But Bridie had long since learned to put disrupting thoughts about Dex to the back of her mind. She'd done everything she could for him since he entered his teenage years, tried pleading with him, threatening, reasoning, belting him round the ear . . . she'd spent hours of her life in police stations and magistrates' courts with him . . . and it'd got neither of them anywhere, except to exhaust and make an old hag of her. Dex was grown up now and she couldn't be responsible for him any more. He came and he went, more secretive than he'd ever been, he was tight lipped about his affairs, but she knew he mixed with a right lot of villains. Money came from time to time and Bridie no longer asked where from.

The other four kids were grown up as well and though Tara and her boyfriend were still with her, occupying the back room, and Tara already pregnant with her first, Bridie had her own life that she was determined to lead. Now that *he*'d upped and left her for that Josie and her two kids – and much good would that do any of them! – there was still time to try and recapture some of the youth that had passed her by since leaving County Kerry to look for better things . . . she was only forty-three, for God's sake, and though she sometimes felt nearer sixty, she knew she didn't look it. Sure, she'd put on a bit of weight, but her troubles hadn't yet robbed her of her abundant black hair and white skin and her blue, black-lashed eyes. There was still time to be Bridie O'Sullivan again, the name she'd been baptized, Bridget Philomena Mary O'Sullivan, devil take Mrs Barry Davis.

She stretched her legs blissfully to the cool corners of the bed that was hers alone, luxuriating in hitherto undreamed of freedom. No more cooking him the tripe and onions that made her stomach heave – nor having to tart herself up to go down to the club or the pub with him, whether she felt like it or no. No watching him becoming roaring drunk, either, and getting beaten nearly senseless when they got home. Best of all was this stretching herself out in a bed she didn't have to share, unless she wanted to, knowing that her body was all her own. Without lying awake afterwards, sleepless, sinfully praying there wouldn't be yet another pregnancy.

She reached out for her first cigarette of the day, propped herself up on the pillows, looking forward to a free weekend from the school where she worked as a dinner lady. Little knowing it was to be her last day of peace for a long time.

54

Marc had come across the papers in Frank's desk when he was sorting things out after the funeral, a neat collection of newspaper cuttings and some old letters clipped together. Avidly, he read every word, his excitement mounting, and when he'd finished, he'd known at last who he really was: the child of two people called Marie-Laure and Charles Daventry. Now he'd learned their story, there was no longer any need to wonder why he'd never been told of his origins.

He tried out his new name – Marc Daventry – and liked it infinitely better than the bland, nothing sort of name he'd had for twenty years. He repeated it like a mantra, and gradually things which had previously puzzled him began to make sense: half-forgotten things which could have had no connection with June and Frank came back to him. The way, for instance, he'd amazed his teachers at his senior school by picking up French so quickly, almost as if he'd learned it before. He remembered – or thought he remembered – from the dim distances of childhood, someone telling him he was going to live somewhere else and have a new mummy. And he knew now the source of the recurrent nightmare he'd had until his teens, the dream in which he'd been a small boy again, being pulled screaming from some woman's arms. The letters explained the other disturbing memories that had flashed, unexplained, across his mind for as long as he could recall.

When his so-called parents had been brought into the hospital and he'd made that devastating discovery, he'd felt as though the centre of his life had fallen apart, as though he'd lost his identity and become nobody, a nothing without a past. He'd hated them then, June and Frank, but now he felt only indifference towards them. Well, he'd always been undemonstrative, unable to show his emotions, and though he'd taken it for granted that because they were his parents, he must love them, he'd never been conscious of feeling any particular closeness with either of them, and no wonder: there'd never been any blood tie.

Finding the papers had re-energized him, he was born again, with another, real identity waiting to be reassumed. He discovered in himself a strength he hadn't known he possessed, a determination amounting to a fixation, to find his true, biological mother and put things right. It dominated his thinking, even after all inquiries fetched him up against a brick wall, all his requests met with refusals. Of his father, Charles Daventry, he didn't think at all.

He'd imagined it wouldn't be hard to find her, but he soon discovered that if a person doesn't want to be traced, they needn't be. He tried all the usual channels when the obvious one, to his rage, failed him, but without luck, and at one time he became so desperate he'd even contemplated the ultimate step of going to the police – though not for long. As if they'd be interested! Useless bastards, he thought scornfully, they didn't want to know unless they were forced into it, unless the missing person was underage, or there were mysterious circumstances. Nothing, in fact, had come of anything.

Months went by – a year – it was Christmas again, and he was no nearer finding her.

After the funeral, he'd continued at the hospital in Birmingham until he'd acquired his qualifications, then come to work here at the County Hospital. He'd drifted, out of sheer lack of interest, into living in drab accommodation in the Branxmore area, a 'garden flat' – actually a back-of-the-house, one-room pad with a scullery attached, nasty, second-hand furniture and a landlord too tightfisted to do anything about the rotten window-frames or the mould growing in the corner of the room, despite the exorbitant rent he charged. Marc had spent as much of Christmas as he could working, and in return he'd been invited to a New Year party by the man whose Christmas Day shift he'd taken over. Returning to his own depressing surroundings from the snug, happy little home which Peter Mansell and his wife had created, it suddenly occurred to him that it was sheer masochism to live like this, when he didn't have to. It wasn't what he'd been brought up to. June, whatever her faults, had always kept an attractive home, which he'd taken for granted and grown accustomed to.

The sale of 14, Rumbold Avenue, even though it had been beautifully maintained, hadn't fetched much – because of declining property values, he was told. But it had left him with a useful amount of money, which at first he'd sworn never to touch, a gesture he now saw as futile, benefiting no one. Why shouldn't he make use of it? It was what they'd intended when they'd willed it to him, hadn't they? It was what they *owed* him. He was earning a decent salary, so it shouldn't be beyond his means to take out a mortgage and buy and furnish some attractive flat, or even a small house, where he could live independently, and – this was what clinched it – where he could bring his mother and take care of her, make up to her for everything, he swore, his determination feeding on his sense of injustice. Just as soon as he found her, which he would, one day, of that he was utterly convinced.

That day, however, seemed a long time in coming. He'd read somewhere that the Salvation Army was very helpful in tracing missing persons, and he was on the point of approaching them when he stumbled on something which was to lead him to where she was, quite by accident. By one of these amazing coincidences which no one admits to believing in, but which are happening to someone, somewhere, every day . . .

8

Dorothea Lilburne, accompanied by a pair of noisy spaniels with ear-splitting barks, came directly from the garden to speak to Mayo and Abigail Moon when they'd made their appointed way to the governor's house the next morning. There was earth beneath her fingernails, and her hair was escaping from its pins but she was regally calm. Apologizing in a well-bred way for not being ready for them, she explained that she had to see Flora at the hospital later and she'd thought to get an hour in the garden before their arrival. 'I'm afraid I lost track of time.'

Abigail nodded understandingly, as if she found nothing at all strange in grubbing about in the earth, outdoors on a freezing morning, while your life was literally in ruins about you. No accounting for tastes. There was no hope for her, Mayo saw, she was hooked, already a card-carrying member of the universal brotherhood of gardeners. Abigail Moon and the governor's lady were sisters under the skin.

'I need to change my clothes.' A rueful glance at the workmanlike garments – Viyella shirt under an olive sweater, green padded body warmer and cotton trousers, black at the knees . . . 'Would you like me to make you some coffee while you're waiting?'

'Show me where the kitchen is and I'll make it,' Abigail offered.

'Oh, would you really? How kind.'

The two women disappeared and Mayo, left to himself, wandered round the pleasant, comfortably shabby room at the back of the house. Although it was so cold outside, bright sunshine poured into the room, on to the delicate pink flowers of a huge cyclamen on a round table by the window, bringing forth the heavy scent of blue and white hyacinths. A large photo in a silver frame stood next to the hyacinths . . . Jack Lilburne in morning dress and grey topper, outside Buckingham Palace on the occasion of his investiture, flanked by his wife and daughter – his wife in navy blue and a becoming, wide-brimmed hat; Flora, a laughing girl in an eye-catching yellow outfit. A charming family group.

The room was low ceilinged and with an open hearth where the ashes of a dying fire glowed red, and stored warmth still pulsed from the bricks. He reached out and threw on another log . . . it was beyond him to let what was obviously a permanently lit fire go out through fear of taking a liberty. He sat himself in a big, roomy chair, listening to the flames catching hold. In a few minutes he was joined by the smelly old spaniels, one of whom jumped up to occupy the chair opposite, while the other, with a soulful gaze challenging Mayo to boot him away, sat on his feet. Much too close to the fire for a dog with a problem like his, but he let the poor brute stay, fondling his ears.

'And where were you two, when somebody was creeping around on the gravel with bombs – the dogs who didn't bark in the night?' he asked, and sat back, dangerously at ease in the warmth of the fire . . .

He'd stayed late at the station the previous evening with Abigail, working out strategies, sent her home and then spent several more hours upstairs, alone in his new office, getting used to not having the hurly burly of the CID room next door, accustoming himself to sitting in Howard Cherry's chair and to his new role as His Nibs, arranging the disposition of his forces and assessing the reactions of the men and women downstairs to his appointment.

Goodwill, for the most part. But wariness, as well. Relief in some quarters, no doubt, that he'd been kicked upstairs. But if you value your jobs, my friends, he'd thought sardonically, don't count on it making that much difference. He'd no intention of taking his finger off the pulse, not for a minute. Nor did he mean to regard the position as merely administrative. The previous incumbent, Cherry, had done the job in his own particular, if pedantic, way, and done it well. And he'd carry on, doing it in his own style.

Much later, he'd walked home through the sleeping town and up the moonlit hill, eager now to get home rather than indulge in one of his famed night prowls through the shadowy reaches of the silent town. And with him had walked the shadow of the one now permanently occupying his thoughts, the guilty one, the one who'd so violently taken a life, who might even now be awake, sweating – or gloating – contemplating his crime. Or might be sleeping like a baby. All were equally possible.

Arriving home, not wanting to waken Alex, he'd decided to spend the rest of the night on the sofa, before remembering it wasn't there. She was awake anyway, and called out sleepily to him. He slid in beside her, into the soft, warm embrace of her arms, and he was instantly fathoms deep in sleep . . .

Abigail and Mrs Lilburne met at the foot of the stairs and he sat up with a start as they entered the big drawing room together. The dogs were immediately shooed out of the room and Mrs Lilburne took up her position in a straight, tall-backed chair. Quietly impressive, if not intimidating, in a classic outfit of camel skirt, beige and cream sweater, with a matching scarf tucked into the neck, pearls in her ears and her hair in an immaculate French pleat, she was very composed. Perhaps she'd done with weeping, perhaps it was still to come.

It's Flora who'll feel it, they'd said. Real Daddy's girl, the apple of his eye. The wife was a bit of a dragon, a snooty piece, one of the old county families. Perhaps because of this, Mayo couldn't feel at ease with her yet, unable to rid himself of the idea that a degree of forelock-tugging was expected. Abigail, on the other hand, settling herself to take unobtrusive notes as Mayo began to find out what Mrs Lilburne could tell them that they weren't already aware of, seemed quite at home with her.

'We're going to have to ask you some personal questions, Mrs Lilburne. If they seem intrusive, please remember that it helps us to know as much background as we can,' he began, though nobody knew better than he that in the search for who had perpetrated the outrage against Jack Lilburne, they were going to have to take his affairs apart. Intrusive questions would be the least of it.

The faint nod Mrs Lilburne gave could have been appreciation of the tact which had prompted the statement, but she gave no other sign, listening politely and answering decisively as he went through the routine of establishing whether Lilburne had had any strong political affiliations – he had not – any antipathies against particular organizations – no. Had there been threats, had he had any recent quarrels, upsets, any enemies – ?

'A man in his position can hardly fail to have attracted a few enemies during his career, Mr Mayo,' she answered firmly. 'In which case, shouldn't you be looking in the direction of his professional life?'

'We should and we are – but we can't overlook the possibility of any more personal connection.'

'Then I can't help you there. Jack wasn't the sort to go out of his way to upset people – as you must know,' she said stiffly, reminding him that he'd been acquainted with her husband.

'You'd no family problems?'

'None whatever,' she answered, with more conviction than most people could have done, faced with the same question. And if he were to bring up what Alex had suggested, the possibility of other women in her husband's life – which as yet he saw no reason to do – he was sure it would have been met with the same firm denial. 'We were a very united family, he was the easiest of men to live with.'

This last was very likely true, from what Mayo remembered of Lilburne. She was right, though, he *must* have had his enemies, he was in a position to attract them, as all prominent men were, more than most, in fact – especially enemies who'd take revenge in so extreme a fashion.

'Let's talk about the new wing he wanted to build. There's been some local opposition, I gather – how did he feel about that?'

'He was inclined to dismiss it. I personally felt he under-estimated the force of the objections – but since the protestors appear to be still going ahead – I hear there's a meeting sched-uled for this week – they couldn't have seen him as posing enough of a threat to do anything so – so utterly evil.'

As the stiff, guarded speech faltered to a close, for the first time she appeared to lose some of her composure. Mayo saw fit to give her an encouraging smile. His highly selective smile, bestowed only on favoured recipients – or those he meant to disarm. Abigail was interested to notice that its effect on Mrs Lilburne was the same as on most people: they began to wonder why they'd found him intimidating, something that almost certainly hadn't occurred to him. She was pulling herself to-gether visibly, even summoning up a faint answering smile of her own, as he went on, 'I'm inclined to agree with the principle of what you say, but we can't take it for granted.' He added soberly, 'Unfortunately, there are plenty of people fanatical enough.'

When it came to discussing the actual events of the last two days, rather than abstract opinions, Dorothea Lilburne became surprisingly less sure of herself.

'I've been over it all in my mind so often, it's becoming a blur – I hardly know what did and what didn't happen.'

'That's understandable – just tell us what you can remember.'

What facts she was able to tell them threw no new light on the situation. The two days had followed their normal pattern, apart from the celebration dinner at the Town Hall, and the fact that Lilburne had left for work later than usual the next morning, for a scheduled meeting with Denis Quattrell, whose name Mayo was familiar with as manager of a local bank. He was interested to learn that Quattrell was also on the council planning committee, suggesting that Lilburne had maybe not been above using a little persuasion to achieve his aims.

'You've an interesting house here. Lovely garden. Very photogenic,' he remarked, just when Abigail thought he'd forgotten, when he'd already indicated that they were about to leave. 'I understand it's appeared in magazines?'

'Not recently. It was featured in the county magazine, and in *House & Garden*, but that was last year.'

'Another one planned?'

'No, why do you ask?'

'Oh, I wouldn't want to miss it, if there was.' He thought it better that she shouldn't know the reasons for asking, not yet. He was sure, anyway, that it was going to come to nothing, that the man who'd been doing the snapping might well have been just another walker with a camera, as Barnett had suggested, and not someone using it as a screen for making a close inspection of the premises.

Mayo was silent, deep in thought, for a long time on the way back.

'Mark that lady down,' he remarked as they drew into the station yard. 'We haven't finished with her, not by a long chalk.'

Abigail paused in the act of unstrapping her seat belt. 'You're not suggesting she was the one who put the bomb under her husband's car?'

'Hardly. But I wouldn't fall over with surprise if she didn't have ideas about who did.'

He didn't choose to enlighten her further, and Abigail knew better than to press him. He'd tell her if, and when, he was good and ready.

In fact, his instincts were telling him, strongly, that there had been another one who hadn't been entirely open with them. That something crucial, something vital it was necessary for them to know, had been withheld. It had been a negative sort of interview, in every sense, an image in which the reversal of tones might have given quite the wrong impression. Guilt there certainly was, but whether it was merely the guilt felt by nearly everyone when someone close to them dies – what might have been, sins of omission and commission – or guilt of a very different nature, it was difficult to say. What was certain was that they had merely skimmed the surface. There were interesting, and possibly even murky, depths to Dorothea Lilburne they hadn't plumbed.

Well, he was experienced at being very patient indeed when necessary. What he needed he would get from her in due time. He was just as certain of that as he was sure that Mrs Lilburne was a woman who would only give if she could do it of her own accord.

Afterwards Marc Daventry was to wonder what had made him choose that particular house agent from all the ones advertising in the local paper when he'd finally decided to buy a house. He thought perhaps it was the name – Search and Sell, which sounded both optimistic and approachable, though he couldn't decide whether it was some sort of pun or not.

There were scores of properties advertised in the windows, all with attractive-looking photographs. The prices gave him a jolt but he went in, refusing to be put off. It was warm and welcoming inside, with a blandly soothing decor in shades of coffee, cream and caramel, a lot of potted plants around and comfortable chairs to sit in – though not so luxurious that customers might start grumbling about the commission they were being charged.

He was asked to fill in details of his requirements at this initial stage, and to write down his name and address and his occupation in block capitals. When he handed the form back and the woman behind the desk had read it through, she looked up, repeating his name. 'Marc Daventry. Marc with a "c"? That's French isn't it?'

It gave him a strange, proud feeling to be able to say: 'My mother is French.'

He'd been aware of the woman's fixed stare all the time he'd been filling the form in, and now she studied his face as if she were about to say more. She was a plain, overweight woman in her late thirties, or perhaps older than that, with pale-lashed eyes and sandy hair scraped back from her face with two tortoiseshell slides, wearing a short-sleeved blouse in a bright shade of coral which was the uniform of the assistants, and added a touch of colour to the decorations, but didn't suit her complexion at all. Her name, he was informed by the plastic tag pinned to her chest, was Avril Kitchin.

She was so long in replying that he asked, 'What's the matter? Anything wrong with my name?'

'No, no! Just checking I'd got it right. It's unusual, that's all.' She shuffled papers together clumsily, put details of all the properties she had available into a folder, slid it across to him and suggested making appointments to view several of them immediately.

'I'll study them first,' he told her.

'Well, don't leave it too long. Anything that's worth having goes immediately,' she warned him, which he found rather hard to believe, considering how long it had taken to dispose of the house in Rumbold Avenue. He put it down to sales patter, though she wasn't exactly the dynamic sales type – a stodgy sort of woman, without much get up and go. Unsmiling, not the sort you warmed to. He felt her gaze following him as he went out of the shop.

When he'd gone through the contents of the folder, thought about them and read between the lines, he sat back, dismayed by the miserable sort of properties being offered within his stipulated price range, and began to feel it would be pointless to waste time in making an appointment to view any of them. If this was all he was going to be able to afford, he thought he'd better forget the idea. Peter Mansell told him it was worth going to have a look at almost anything – you wouldn't have believed what a slum their house was before they'd bought it and done it up. But Marc didn't fancy spending all his spare time searching for property that he would have to spend further time on renovating. He would have to think of some other way of talking to Avril Kitchin again.

By now, he knew he had to do this. The encounter with her had unaccountably stayed with him, and due to his heightened awareness of anything to do with his name, he felt that although she'd denied it, it had meant something to her, even that she'd perhaps known, or still knew, a woman called Marie-Laure Daventry who had once had a son called Marc. The bizarre notion actually passed through his mind, though he quickly dismissed it, that Avril Kitchin might *be* Marie-Laure Daventry, who had changed her name.

After two or three days, he'd been able to bear it no longer, and he'd decided to go and talk to her again. It was lucky that, because of working night shifts and standby rotas, he sometimes had free time during the day.

Opposite Search and Sell was a small open space where a row of picturesque, but near-derelict, almshouses had once stood. After years of argument with the local preservation society, the town council had finally won their battle to have them demolished, and in their place had planted a low-maintenance but ugly shrubbery of evergreen viburnums and berberis and spotted laurels, into which all manner of rubbish blew, and stayed, and which the local yobs added to with their discarded fish-and-chip papers and Coke cans. Because of this, it was not the pleasant place the council had originally envisaged, and the seats placed round the periphery were not much used, except of necessity by the elderly or infirm, pregnant mums or those with a long wait for the next bus at the stop further along.

Marc took up a seat there with a car-maintenance magazine as a pretext at about twelve, and settled himself to wait until Avril Kitchin came out for lunch. If she didn't, he was prepared to return just before the agency closed, and wait for her then, though he hoped he wouldn't have to. Mid January, even with your warmest clothes on, wasn't the best time to sit about on park benches. He'd be getting some funny looks if he sat there too long. But at half past twelve, one of the other women who worked in the agency returned and two or three minutes later, Avril Kitchin emerged.

She was wearing moon boots and red woolly gloves and a quilted anorak in dark blue over her coffee-coloured uniform skirt, with a patterned scarf over her head, and she was carrying a shopping bag. Marc thought she looked like a Russian peasant going to queue for food, and indeed, she was heading purposefully in a flat-footed way towards Sainsbury's. He crossed the road and followed her, but it seemed she was going to have her lunch before doing her shopping. When she reached the small coffee shop next door, she went in.

Marc stood two behind her in the self-service queue, bought himself an orange juice and then took it to the table where she sat with a Danish pastry and coffee in front of her. 'Is this anyone's seat?'

She shook her head, barely glancing at him. 'Please – ' She gestured to the free chair, pulled off her scarf and bent down to reach a paperback from her bag before starting on the pastry and beginning to read.

'Miss Kitchin,' Marc said.

She looked up, surprised at hearing her name. Perhaps if she'd been prepared, she might have been able to conceal the consternation on her pudding face and in her pale, round eyes when she realized who he was. As it was, she looked almost panic-stricken, and it was this that told Marc he'd been right, he was on to something. He felt a surge of elation so sharp that it hurt.

'Miss Kitchin,' he began again, excitement almost choking his voice.

'Mrs,' she corrected automatically. Well, there were women who refused to wear wedding rings, and he could believe she might well be that sort.

'I'm sorry to bother you over your lunch, but I couldn't think how else to get hold of you in private. I think you can help me.'

'You should've come to the agency – or telephoned, if there's somewhere you want to view.' The annoyance in her voice didn't hide the fact that she was deliberately misunderstanding him, of that he was sure.

'It's not about a property. It's about my mother. Her name is Marie-Laure Daventry. I think you know hr, don't you?'

He thought she looked frightened. The dull colour rose in her cheeks, but she tried to cover up by pretending further annoyance. 'Well, you've got a nerve, I must say, following me around and badgering me like this while I'm having my lunch!'

She pushed aside the apple Danish as if he'd quite made her lose her appetite.

It was insufferably hot in the café. He could smell tea and hamburger, and felt the sweat inside his collar. A woman at the next table was watching and listening to their conversation quite openly. Other people were beginning to stare. Marc lowered his voice.

'I'm sorry, I'd no intention of bothering you. I wouldn't have approached you at all, only I've tried every other way I can think of to find my mother. You *do* know her, don't you?'

She eyed the food she'd pushed away as if regretting the action, and then rather defiantly pulled the plate towards her again. No point in wasting it, her attitude said. Marc could see her thinking what she ought to say as she munched her way stolidly through the pastry, and he deliberately held himself back from saying anything else until she'd finished. 'What if I do?' she said at last, wiping her mouth on the paper napkin.

'You can tell me where I can find her.'

'What makes you think I know? Why should I tell you, anyway, even if I did? What makes you think she *wants* to be found? You've no right to invade her privacy.'

She spoke rapidly, in a low voice, her face flushing even more unbecomingly as she realized the admissions she was making. 'It wouldn't be like that,' Marc said. 'I just want to see her and talk to her. If she doesn't want to keep in touch after that, I'll leave her alone, I swear it. It's up to her.'

He sensed there was some sort of inner struggle going on, but he felt this was all to the good. At least she wasn't dismissing his proposal out of hand. 'Tell me just one thing – is she living near here?'

Her expression told him that he'd guessed correctly, but she was scrabbling in her bag for her scarf, not looking at him, suddenly in a hurry, regretting having allowed herself to be pushed as far as she had been. 'Look, I've only an hour for my lunch.' She scraped her chair back. 'I'm sorry, but I've some shopping I must do.'

'Will you see me again, then?'

'No! No, that would be a mistake. It isn't that easy – '

'Why not?'

'I can't! You've no idea what you're asking!' She was plainly panicking now.

He looked steadily at her, with that intense compelling look which he'd long since discovered usually made people do what he wanted. 'I shall find her, you know, even if you won't help.' He would stick closer to Avril Kitchin than a postage stamp, follow her until finally, in one way or another, she led him to his mother.

Suddenly, she gave in. In a panic-stricken way, she said, 'I can't promise anything, but, well – all right, tomorrow. Tomorrow's my half-day. I'll meet you here tomorrow, the same time.'

Of course, she was playing for time, she perhaps wanted to speak to Marie-Laure before seeing him again, to prepare her for what was bound to be a shock. He didn't mind that. It would give him time, too, to get used to the idea that at last, he'd found her, he was going to meet her . . .

After the two police officers had gone, Dorothea began stacking the used coffee cups in the dishwasher. Halfway through, she stopped to write a note to Sue, the young woman who came in three times a week to do the cleaning, to remind her to do the larder shelves, then remembered it wasn't her day . . .

She had to collect some things of Flora's to take to the hospital, but she'd forgotten what . . .

Toilet things, surely? And a nightdress, perhaps that new white silk one of her own she hadn't worn yet, more suitable than those silly things Flora usually wore . . .

And there was something else she should remember, though she couldn't think what that was, either . . .

She stared across the gleaming surfaces of the kitchen Jack had recently had newly fitted for her, without seeing it. Was it always going to be like this? This lack of concentration? This hard knot in her chest, making her want to cry out loud in her need for Jack? With the source of tears that might have washed it away, dried up?

And that other person inside her head, whispering, whispering . . .

The clock in the hall struck ten and she began to move automatically. She was due to meet Anthony Spurrier at half past.

Twenty minutes later, she was taking the garden path across to the institution, carrying the small bag with Flora's things in it.

Her car, as well as Flora's Polo, both of which had been garaged in the old barn, had been damaged in the blast, hers a total write-off, Flora's probably reparable. She was going to have to do something about finding another car, summon up energy to decide on something in which she'd little interest. She must ring the garage and tell them to send her the nearest replacement to her old one they could find. She couldn't go on being dependent on other people to ferry her around.

It was impossible in any situation, however fraught, for Dorothea to pass through the garden without casting a critical eye around, as she did now. Walking quickly, but observantly, she tried to assess what damage all those policemen, tramping over every square inch of the garden yesterday, had caused; paused briefly to see whether the paeony buds were yet pushing prematurely through, while there was still danger of frost. They were not, but her gaze fell on a stray escape of ground elder, against which she waged implacable war. She pounced, her fingers burrowing deep to pull it out by the roots, otherwise it would send out fat white rhizomes under the soil, to surface where you least wished it to be – right in the crown of another delicate plant, most likely, threatening to choke it. She tugged the weed out at last and for several moments stood staring down impassively at it lying in the palm of her hand, as if reading her life in it, the delicate, trefoil leaves pretty and inoffensive, the roots unbelievably tenacious and invasive. Then she let it drop on to the path, later to be put on the bonfire. Burn it, destroy it, the only way to get rid of any infestation, completely and permanently.

Brief as it was, the incident had delayed her; she must hurry, or Anthony Spurrier, who was taking her down to the hospital, where he would see Flora for the first time since her accident, would be waiting. Dorothea, who was always punctual, except when she lost track of time in the garden, couldn't allow him to think she was letting down her own standards.

He was, she reflected, a rather naive young man, despite his impressive qualifications and the nature of his work, which she felt should have taught him more of the subtleties of human nature. She'd evidently astonished him by knowing about his relationship with Flora. He'd been overwhelmed that she'd bothered to set his mind at rest about her injuries and to keep him informed of her progress. Dorothea was wryly amused at this. How little they all knew her! She understood and cared more about Flora than anyone dreamed of.

All the same, the depth of Anthony's anxiety had demonstrated to her that perhaps it might not be so bad – Flora and Anthony Spurrier. He might be the one to make her happy, after all. It wasn't in the least what she'd envisaged for her daughter – no big wedding, no alliance with a son of one of the best families. Anthony was never likely to be rich, though that scarcely mattered now – Jack had left Flora well provided for; he was several years older than she was, and that might even be an advantage. Flora needed a firm hand, a father figure . . . the knot in Dorothea's chest tightened again and she walked more quickly, images she would rather not see blurring before her eyes.

She'd almost reached the group of slender birches near the gate where the crinums had flourished until lately, before she remembered the snowdrops.

She was upset, out of all proportion, at this evidence of further confusion in her mind. How could she have forgotten her precious bulbs? So completely? When it had been the last thing she'd been doing before her world had shattered? Was it too late to save them, when they'd been lying out there in the cold, drying winds ever since, with their roots exposed to the sun?

When she reached the place where she'd left the trugful of bulbs there was, however, no sign of them – and the space which she'd designated for them was now filled. Planted in a neat square, in regimented rows like soldiers on parade, were the snowdrops, some of the leaves still a little limp and drooping, others already picked up. But planted, saved from withering away.

Tom Barnett! Whoever would have believed it?

She stood looking down at the rigidly disposed plants, aware of the soft smell of newly turned earth, of new life stirring all around her, of a blackbird singing on a flowering currant.

uite suddenly, the tears welled up unstoppably. She leaned against the corky bark of a nearby beech, sobbing until at last she could cry no more, the hard knot in her chest slowly dissolving.

Finally, she blew her nose, smoothed back her hair and hurried on towards the admin block, anxious to find the women's cloakroom before meeting Anthony. Her hands were filthy from grubbing out the ground elder. She'd never in her life faced anyone with her eyes red, her face blotchy, and she wasn't going to start now.

9

The long, depressing street of villa-type brick houses was clotted with on-street parking, but Farrar found a space only four doors away from the house where Dex Davis's mother lived.

Dingy curtains and battered paintwork, a neglected plot of grass in front, roughly the dimensions of a grave – there could hardly have been a greater contrast to the house they'd previously visited, the house of the woman who'd supplanted her.

They knocked on the front door. Twice. As Kite lifted his hand for the third time, a voice from inside called, 'Round the back!' Kite jerked his head at Farrar, signalling him to go down the passage between the houses, waiting while Farrar, always fastidious in the extreme, was picking his way along a broken and oil-stained concrete pathway, through a garden where only grass and dandelions survived, past a line of doubtful washing, a motorbike propped up on bricks, minus its front wheel, an overflowing dustbin and a week's supply of empty milk bottles.

Presently, Kite heard him shouting through the front-door letter box. 'Have to go round the back, Sarge. Can't open this.'

The front door hadn't been opened for years. Couldn't be, the way it was blocked from behind with a log jam of discarded and broken objects, old shoes, and a coatrail so overburdened it had lost half its grip on reality and sunk lopsidedly towards the floor, making access to the upstairs something of an assault course.

'Mrs Davis?' Kite inquired, when he, too, had negotiated the hazards of the back entry and was in the kitchen.

'No. Bridie O'Sullivan. I've reverted to me maiden name,' replied the big, handsome woman with the cloud of dark hair and the rich Irish brogue grandly, making him wonder if there wasn't something more than tea in the mug she was swigging from.

He wouldn't have blamed her. Something had to compensate

for her wretched surroundings, and by all accounts her wretched life, though she hadn't lost the sparkle in her blue eyes and
her smile was as wide and generous as her hips. Breakfast was
not yet over – a jar of Silver Shred with a knife sticking out of it
stood on the cloth, next to a hacked-off white loaf and a plastic
tub of marge, scored with the bread-knife serrations. Automatically, she reached for two more mugs and poured a black,
evil-looking brew from the teapot, sugaring both with a heavy
hand and pushing them across. Kite's look defied Farrar to
refuse.

'We're looking for your son, Dex, Mrs – '

'Bridie,' she plugged the hesitation. 'What's he done this
time?'

'Nothing so far as we know, yet. Is he living here?'

'Only because he's nowhere better to go.'

'Short of money, is he?'

She laughed.

'Who's he associating with these days?'

'It's no use asking me these sort of questions. I don't have any
answers.' Her eyes were suddenly empty as a rain-washed Irish
sky. 'What do you want him for?'

'Just a word in connection with that bomb that went off at
the Conyhall Young Offenders' Institution.'

'The bomb that killed the governor?' She was jerked into
mobility, drawing herself upright on the kitchen chair. 'No! He's
a terrible little toerag, so he is, but he wouldn't do a thing like
that, not Dex!' But he read fear and uncertainty in her voice.

'We only want to talk to him, m'duck.'

'Then you've struck lucky, haven't you? For that's his car just
pulled up outside. Oh, Jesus. What have I ever done to deserve
this?'

Bridie sank her head in her hands, banging her elbows on the
table in frustration, but all it did was to make her keen with pain
as she struck her funny-bone and the nerve sent excruciating
tingles down her arm and hand.

'What's up with you?' demanded the youth who shambled
through the door.

The pain in her arm had receded, leaving only numbness, but
the other pain, the one clutching her heart, was still there. She
sat where she was, looked sorrowfully at the son who'd caused
her nothing but trouble for the last six or seven years, and

decided she'd had enough of what life decided to throw at her. Sure, she'd go on fighting. She hadn't been born Irish for nothing. But this time she was going to fight for herself.

'You've got visitors,' she said.

If Dex Davis resembled either parent, it wasn't his mother, except that he was big. Muscular. Dangerous. A close-cropped head, a hard face devoid of expression, empty grey eyes, jaws moving rhythmically on a piece of gum. Leather jacket. Ironmongery in his ears. Washed-out black T-shirt, the mandatory skin-tight jeans and Doc Martens. A hard man in his own opinion.

He didn't frighten either policeman.

He looked older than his years, old with more knowledge of the seamy side of life than his age warranted. Nobody with sense would have trusted him with a bag of boiled sweets, let alone bought a used car from him. Life had already stamped on him what he was to become, a hopeless case, destined to spend the best part of his life under lock and key, the rest of it in the dubious activity that was to put him there.

'Derek Davis?'

'What of it?'

'Detective Sergeant Kite, and this is Detective Constable Farrar. We'd like a word.'

'What about? I've done nothing.'

'Glad to hear it, Derek. But for starters, how long have you had the motor?' Farrar indicated the car drawn into the kerb. It wasn't new – a red, H-reg Orion – but if Dex could afford to buy and run that, legit, then Farrar was looking to him for a bit of advice.

Dex shrugged. 'Week or two.'

'Must've cost you.'

'Got it cheap, off of one of me mates, didn't I?'

'Yeah, we know mates like yours, sunshine,' Kite said. 'Get you anything you want, can't they? Dodgy, is it? Nicked?'

'No, it bloody isn't. Paying for it on the knock, if you must know.'

'And you on the dole? Come again.'

'Dunno what you're on about,' Dex answered, taking refuge in playing stupid.

'We're on about that bomb that went off at Conyhall. And what you know about it.'

His expression didn't change. His jaws masticated. But Kite was interested to see that a light sweat broke out on his forehead. 'Hey, man. You can't pin that on me.'

'Don't hold your breath.'

'I don't know nothing about it.' Dex made a show of indifference and turned as if to go upstairs.

'Don't go, Derek.'

He slouched into a chair. 'Told you, I'd nothing to do with it.'

'Then you won't mind coming down to the station, nice and quiet, like a good lad, and telling that to our inspector.'

'Hey, hey!'

'Get your coat on. Come on, don't hang about.'

'I tell you, I dunno – ' Farrar took hold of his arm. He wasn't such a ponce as you'd think. Dex began to look hunted. 'Ma?'

'Don't look at me, you daft little bugger, you're only getting what you asked for. I've done with you, so I have!' And Bridie, who'd seen off more policemen, probation officers and social workers in her time than she could count, sat immovable in her chair, while Farrar collared her son out to the waiting police car.

Halfway to the door, Kite turned back. 'Thanks for the tea, Bridie, and good luck to you. Here,' he added, seeing the tears now spilling from her eyes and rolling down her cheeks, 'don't let him get you down, m'duck, he's not worth it.'

'And who the hell are you to say he's not worth it?' she rounded on him, swiping at the tears, blue eyes flashing, Irish temper up. 'I'll thank you not to talk about my son as if he was rubbish – and you harm a hair of his head and I'll have your guts for garters, so I will – and don't think I'm not capable of it.' She picked up the smeary bread knife from the table and brandished it. 'You get out of my house!'

Kite got. That she was capable of *anything*, he didn't doubt for a minute, and there were other parts of his anatomy that he valued, even more immediately accessible than his guts.

The side ward where Flora had been was now occupied by an old lady with a broken hip, but although she was physically not there, Marc couldn't get her out of his mind.

She haunted his dreams and, when he least expected it, his waking hours. In the operating theatre, checking the technical equipment, he would see the sweet pale face, with its tremulous smile; the rich hair tumbling over her shoulders after the bandages had been removed, shining like gold when the sunlight caught it, making him shiver when he thought what it would be like to run his fingers through it and feel its silky softness. His brain and his hands worked on autopilot: when his arms were round a patient, lifting them on to a trolley, it was Flora's soft body he felt; when he prepared anyone for surgery, squeezing their arm for the needle, he was squeezing the plump creamy flesh of her bare arms and seeing the swell of her breasts under the white silk nightdress. He was disgusted with himself at the gross impulses he felt, yet excited.

This was all so totally unexpected. The last thing he wanted was to become involved with *anybody* at the moment yet, one way or another, he had to see her. She'd be glad for them to meet again, he was sure of that. While she was still at the hospital, he'd made it in his way to pop into her room for a few minutes several times a day, though he'd no valid reason to be there, other than to see her, and she'd thanked him gravely and told him his little visits made the time pass less slowly. He felt there was an instinctive understanding between them. He could talk to her as he'd never talked to anyone else: when he'd told her about the accident to June and Frank – though he hadn't spoken of his shattering discovery that they hadn't been his real parents – her eyes had filled with sympathetic tears.

She'd looked so lost, so in need of being cared for. She made him feel manly and protective. The question of how best to get in touch with her and help her was quickly becoming an obsession with him, the way things did, the way it had become an over-riding need with him to find his mother . . .

Waiting for Avril Kitchin outside the coffee shop, the day after he'd spoken to her in there, seeing her approach from a distance, he had thought again how dreary and peasant-like she appeared, with the same shopping bag dangling from her arm, the same look of frowning doggedness on the face under the headscarf.

And again, he couldn't help noticing the heaviness of her features, how grudging her greeting was, how guarded. She still wasn't sure of him, what his motives really were, how far to trust him, and he knew he was going to have to tread softly.

'I thought we'd go somewhere else, it's not very private in there,' he said, indicating the steamy café behind him with its beige Formica-topped tables set too close together. He felt rather sick with apprehension at what this coming meeting was to reveal, his stomach was tied in knots, and he didn't think he could face the smell of hamburger.

'All right.' She seemed indifferent as to where they went. 'Where would you like to go?'

'I thought the pub over there. It seems quiet.'

He realized immediately they entered the Crown and Anchor that it was quiet because it was a pub of the spit-and-sawdust variety, not having much to offer at this time of day, either in the way of comfort or even a decent selection of bar food. He could see it might have a kind of welcome for some in the evening, when all the lamps were lit and the juke box going and people were talking and playing darts and noisily enjoying themselves, but at midday it was deserted, stale with the aftermath of cigarette smoke and beer. Christmas decorations, though it was now the middle of January, still hung in festoons from the ceiling, a pair of dispirited cardboard Santas stood pointlessly at either end of the bar, dubiously regarding the few uninteresting sandwiches of debatable age which were displayed there. Marc and Avril agreed on cheese, and Marc ordered a lager for himself, though Avril asked for coffee. The barman raised his eyebrows and said he'd see what he could do, much as if he'd been asked for champagne cocktails, or a bottle of Château Lafitte.

They carried their food across to a corner where two slippery vinyl-covered banquette seats met, with an indifferently wiped table between them. 'You needn't finish them if you don't want,' Marc said, pushing his sandwiches away after a few bites. 'Though I don't know what else I could get you, except maybe a bag of crisps.'

'They're all right. I've eaten worse,' she replied ungraciously, working her way through stale-tasting cheese between doughy slabs of bread with the same concentration she'd given to the Danish pastry in the coffee shop. The consumption of food was evidently a matter of serious intent to Avril Kitchin. He sat back and waited with mounting impatience, guessing he wouldn't get anything out of her until she'd finished eating.

As soon as she'd demolished the last crumb, he asked, 'Well, what happened, what did she say?'

Avril looked round for her coffee, which was not yet forthcoming, before answering. 'I'm not sure.'

'What d'you mean – not sure? You *did* speak to her?'

He leaned across and took hold of her plump wrist, not realizing he might be hurting her until she angrily pulled her hand away. 'Yes, I did. But I meant I'm still not sure whether it's a good idea or not. She's beginning to make a life for herself, she's learning – '

'Where does she live?' he interrupted roughly.

'She's staying with me. I've a flat in Branxmore.'

'Branxmore!' He stared at her, feeling the blood rush to his head.

Avril Kitchin looked offended. 'It's not a very select area, I know, but it's not that bad! I can think of worse places than Coltmore Road.'

'It's not that, it's just that I live in Branxmore myself,' Marc said, forcing himself to be calm. He could hardly take it in. She'd been living in Branxmore, all the time! Three or four streets away from where he himself lived, only just around the corner, you might say. He could actually have passed her in the street, they might even have stood next to each other at the supermarket checkout, or in the launderette. Though he felt, somehow, he would instinctively have known her if they'd met, even though she must have changed considerably, and the only photo he had to fix her image in his mind was the blurred and grainy newspaper cutting.

The coffee came, a predictably grey, watery-looking substance, some of which had slopped into the saucer. At least it appeared to be hot, judging by the steam rising from the cup. The landlord took away their plates, unsurprised by Marc's unconsumed sandwiches.

Avril sipped the scalding liquid and then she said slowly, reluctantly, as if she'd rather not be saying it, 'She wants you to come round, on Wednesday night if you can manage, for coffee, and something to eat. It won't be much, just a snack.' She watched his face, the beginnings of his smile, and her own expression hardened. She said roughly, 'I have to tell you, it wasn't my idea.'

He didn't care. It didn't matter to him what this woman thought or said. It was his mother who'd invited him – his *mother*! She had *asked* to see him! He was going to see her at last, face to face, he hadn't had to plead, something he'd been very afraid of having to do. He said, doing his best to conceal his fierce elation, forcing himself to use a more humble tone than he wanted to, 'Won't you tell me something about her first, how she came to be living with you?'

'No. If she wants to tell you, she'll tell you herself. But I warn you, go easy on her. She's been through a lot.'

'I know.'

'No, you don't,' she contradicted flatly. 'Nobody does, who hasn't experienced it.' He knew, without her saying it, that it had been an experience Avril Kitchin had shared.

They left the pub, and most of the coffee even Avril hadn't been able to drink. Dizzy with euphoria, Marc had watched her clump sturdily away into the January afternoon in her moon boots, her shopping bag over her arm.

10

When Dex Davis saw that the inspector sitting on the edge of the table in the interview room and waiting to question him was only a woman, a near-redhead with a tasty figure and long legs, he visibly perked up. He knew how to treat women like her, you just had to give them the eye, it was going to be a doddle. Wasn't a tart yet he hadn't been able to twist round his little finger. His sisters had always stuck up for him, sworn black was white, lied like the clappers to get him out of trouble if he'd sweet-talked them. And up to now he'd only ever had to smile at his mother and say he was sorry and he'd been all right.

Twenty minutes later, he was sweating. A right cow, this one. Nearly as bad as that butch screw, Reynolds, at Conyhall. Even worse than that Kite, who was sitting with her.

After two hours, eyes narrowed, he knew he wasn't going to get away with it, and was rapidly calculating what his chances were, while automatically repeating that he'd had nothing to do with the bombing.

Abigail sighed. 'Don't mess me about, Derek. You swear you're going to get your own back on the governor – and then as soon as you're outside, he cops it! And you expect us to believe you'd nothing to do with it?'

It gave Dex a big charge, satisfied his need for revenge, the idea that Jack Lilburne had been blown to smithereens, but over the years he'd learned not to show his feelings.

'You'll not walk away from this, you know. It won't be a couple of years this time, it'll be life. And it won't include any safari trips, I promise you.'

He was known as a hard man, proud of it, his street cred depended on it. But *life*! Christ. He knew they weren't bluffing, not this time. 'There's no way I'm going down for that bomb,' he said, 'no *way*!'

'Now we're talking, my friend.' And half an hour later, she said, 'OK, this mate of yours, the one you say you met in the pub – '

'He's no mate of mine. Just some guy that was around, I tell you. He asked me if I could get him the stuff and I said no problem. If he used it to do for Lilburne, that's down to him.'

'Why you?' Kite said. 'If he'd never met you before, how did he know you'd do that for him? Shooting your mouth off, were you?'

'Just talking to the others, that's all.' He saw their scepticism. 'I might've said, "Somebody should put a bomb under that bastard."'

'Might have? And added that you knew how it could be done?'

'Well, I'd had a jar or two, you know how it is. This guy must've heard what I said. When I went to the gents, he followed me and told me he could make it worth me while, like. But I didn't do the bomb.'

'Just got the stuff for him.'

'No, I never! I just told him I knew somebody who could.'

'Names?'

'I don't grass on me mates.'

Not if he'd any sense, he wouldn't. If he'd any choice. Which Abigail could tell Dex was beginning to see he hadn't. Even though the criminal fraternity had never been renowned for their long-term forward thinking. She changed tack. 'How much did he pay you?'

'Half a grand.'

'Five hundred pounds! Pull the other one.'

'And a couple of grand for the stuff – '

'Ah, at last. The bomb materials. Where did they come from?'

Dex looked shifty and refused to say. On and on it went, turn and turn about – how much were you *really* paid? What did he look like, this man you met in the pub, are you sure you don't know him, where did you get the explosives, how did you know who to go to . . .?

They were presently joined by the big man, the super, who sat himself down and said nothing, just listened and watched, which unnerved Dex more than the woman and the sergeant's endless questions . . . 'We want names, Derek,' Abigail said. 'A lot more information, and names.'

'If I tell you – '

'I'm not dealing with you, Derek. You're not in a prime position for that.'

In the end, he came up with a name – Clarke, he said, gazing into space, John Clarke. And then the admission that the bomb equipment had been left in the unlocked boot of a car parked in a deserted demolition lot down by the river . . . sticks of explosives, leads, detonators in a biscuit tin. To be replaced with the required money in used tenners, no problem. But he wouldn't yet say who'd agreed to supply the materials.

'All right, Dex,' Abigail said at last, standing up and taking her jacket from the back of her chair, ready to follow the superintendent out, who'd left the room as quietly as he came in.

'You mean I can go?'

She and Kite exchanged smiles. 'Not on your life! We're keeping you in here till you tell us who provided those explosives. And there's still the matter of that dodgy Orion of yours.'

Barry Davis, Dex's father and erstwhile husband of Bridie, had not at first been cooperative in the matter of the Orion, which his son had eventually admitted he'd bought from the backstreet garage where his father worked. Possibly because Davis Senior had been interrupted in the consumption of a vast plate of chips, under which lurked black pudding, bacon and fried eggs, with maybe a fried tomato or two as yet undisclosed. Accompanied by thick slabs of bread and butter. All adding another dimension of strain to an already complaining waistband, tight over a check workshirt, open to reveal a white T-shirt.

He was an older version of Dex, even less bright. Trying hard to retain his youth, and keep up with his new young wife, with tight jeans and his hair short on top and tied at the back, a gold identity bracelet and a gold earring – it seemed to be a family adornment – in one ear.

Bright enough to know, however, that he was in it up to the eyebrows, as far as the car was concerned, he and the man he was working with. The Orion, to nobody's surprise, had been nicked, resprayed, given new number plates before being sold to Dex at a giveaway price.

The greasy spoon where these revelations took place was

located just around the corner from the garage where Barry Davis worked and were continued in the garage itself. Dex's father was a slippery customer, whose own record was none too clean, though up to now he'd been going straight for some time. After twenty minutes, both he and his partner were apprehended. Further inquiries, in an interview room not far removed from the cell where his son was presently languishing, brought forth no information on the provenance of the bomb materials. After half an hour, Kite was certain in his own mind that Barry Davis was telling the truth when he said he didn't know anything about them.

Throwing her jacket over the back of a chair, Abigail reached for the cup of tea she'd been just in time to claim as she walked into the incident room next morning, just before Mayo's morning briefing. 'We can forget the Conyhall Residents for Freedom from Rapists and Murderers,' she announced as she grabbed herself an unoccupied chair.

'That's what they're calling themselves?' Mayo murmured absently, perched on the edge of a desk, deeply immersed in a file, falling for it before realizing he'd been caught napping. He looked up, grinning sheepishly . . . 'OK, OK, OK!' . . . then looked again, wondering why his inspector appeared so radiant this morning. Bronze hair, recently regrown after a brief flirtation with shorter haircuts, now a shining, curved bob hanging below her ears, hazel eyes glowing, bursting with energy – she made him feel a hundred, sometimes. 'Why can we forget them?'

'They're a harmless lot, mostly young mums, only anxious for their kids' safety. Mistaken, maybe, but bombers they're not. Just happy to know there'll be no more danger from the desperate crooks and villains behind the wire than there ever was, even if the new extension goes ahead, which now seems unlikely. Claudia Reynolds made them see that.'

'Claudia Reynolds?' Mayo was surprised enough to show it.

Abigail smiled. 'She addressed the residents' meeting last night. Explained what it was all about, and why. Used her elfin charm to convince them that they'd actually benefit, since the new block would really form a bigger barrier between their children and the inmates.'

'How do you know all this?'

'I was there with Ben Appleyard.'

As editor of the *Advertiser*, he'd planned to send one of his juniors along to cover the protest meeting but when the bomb had occurred he'd written the meeting off, assuming it would certainly be cancelled. By the time he'd learned it was still on, he was short of someone to send, although even without it there was plenty of mileage still to be squeezed from the incident. Ready for the next edition was the gardener's photo, to be displayed under the caption, 'Pensioner escapes death bomb by minutes': more than that, one of the youngsters on the staff knew Flora Lilburne and was hoping for another front page human interest story from her, though so far he'd been foiled in his attempts to contact Flora, either by the hospital staff or by Flora's formidable mother. But then it had occurred to Ben that Abigail – purely from a professional point of view, of course – might be interested in the meeting, and might, incidentally, be persuaded into snatching a quick supper afterwards, and after that . . . He'd been lucky on all counts; they'd both left her cottage this morning in their respective cars feeling very chipper.

It wasn't always that easy, straddling the gap between press and police territory, Abigail had thought, inching her way through the one-way system, but since she and Ben were both aware of the danger areas and had been scrupulous in avoiding them, whatever they had going between them had so far worked very well. How far it would continue to do so when the heat was really on, they hadn't actually faced. They were both ambitious, dead keen. So far theirs was an undemanding and uncommitted relationship, suiting them very well; neither had admitted yet to the growing strength of the bond between them.

She sipped her tea and wished she'd stopped for more breakfast. On cloud nine, food wasn't a priority, but back in the real world she was aware that a cup of coffee and half a bowl of muesli wasn't going to sustain her long. But it was almost eight-thirty, the briefing was about to begin, with no time to nip out for even a Mars Bar, and Mayo, twirling his pen, thinking about what she'd just said, was observing, 'If it was so easy, why didn't Jack Lilburne do the same thing, call a meeting and avoid trouble in the first place?'

Abigail had no answer to that, either.

*   *   *

The investigation wasn't proceeding quickly enough for Mayo, nor for the Chief Constable, whose breath Mayo was beginning to feel on the back of his neck. Tossing ideas around was no substitute for action, but at the moment, ideas were pretty much all they had, as long as Dex Davis persisted in keeping silent.

'What about his father?' Mayo asked.

'I think he's clean,' Kite said, 'as far as the bomb goes, anyway. The car's another matter, and he's been charged, him and his partner. As far as Dex goes, he's more frightened of what'll happen to him if he splits than what'll happen if he doesn't.'

'We can't keep him in much longer,' Mayo warned.

'I'm reliably informed that he hangs out at the Black Bull in Holden Hill, him and his mates,' volunteered DC Tiplady. 'And we all know what their clientele's like.'

'Right.' Mayo observed his new DC. Jim Tiplady was a short-ish, stocky, slightly balding man who rarely smiled, newly re-cruited from the uniformed branch, known universally as Tip, he struck him as a forthright and sensible sort of chap, the sort needed to form the backbone of CID. 'Get up there and see what you can find, then.'

'We could try the quarry, sir,' said Farrar. 'That's in Holden Hill, too.'

'First place we made inquiries, remember?' Kite said, giving him a look. 'No dice.'

'I know, but wouldn't it be worth trying again?' He meant to imply that if *he*'d done the asking . . .

Mayo knew quite well what Farrar meant. 'You can go up to the Black Bull with Tip as well, Keith. Discreet inquiries, both of you, as to whether any of the customers have connections up at the quarry.'

'Oh, right, sir.' Farrar's smart response was more enthusiastic than his desire to waste an evening at the Black Bull, among the great unwashed of Holden Hill, but he was becoming wise enough not to let it show. Served him right, he should've kept his mouth shut.

On that cold January night, that first time he'd met his mother, clutching his bunch of exotic hothouse lilies, Marc had approached the house in Coltmore Road feeling more nervous than he'd ever felt in his life. He'd bought flowers, rather than chocolates or anything else, for no other reason than that June had always taken them when visiting someone socially, and though he'd never bought flowers for anyone before, he wasn't embarrassed, as some men would have been. Once having decided to do something, Marc went through with it without bothering what other people thought.

'I'll take all those,' he'd told the florist, making his decision immediately, pointing to a container of the biggest, most flamboyant flowers he could see.

'The Longhi lilies? Well, there's eight there — and they're three-fifteen a stem.'

'That's all right.' He hadn't batted an eyelid, not letting on that he'd no idea what flowers cost, and if he'd given the matter any forethought, he might have expected to pay something more like three pounds fifteen for the bunch, rather than over twenty-five pounds.

The assistant tenderly wrapped the flowers in daisy-dotted cellophane, fastening the wrapping with a huge pink satin bow. 'There you go! They cost a lot, but they *are* lovely, aren't they? I'm sure she'll like them.' She smiled, evidently thinking he was splashing out for a favoured girlfriend. He didn't tell her they were for his mother.

It wasn't the first time he'd been down the road since Avril had told him the address. It had been two whole days since they'd met in the Crown and Anchor and, unable to wait until the appointed time, he'd driven down the previous evening and sat in his car on the opposite side of the road, watching the house, hoping for a glimpse of Marie-Laure in the upstairs flat. But all he'd seen were shadowy figures behind the curtain, a chink of light down the middle where they were imperfectly drawn. The light had gone out about ten. They were obviously not night owls. This evening, he must beware of outstaying his welcome.

He didn't have to hang around this time. It was so near to where he lived it hadn't been worth bringing his car, and he walked down to Coltmore Road, the huge bunch of lilies like a banner before him. He rang the bell under the name of Kitchin and waited, his heart beating painfully. What should he do if it was Marie-Laure, his mother, who answered the door? Would she recognize him? Would she burst into tears? Would she expect him to kiss her?

He needn't have worried, it was Avril who came to the door, in ill-chosen trousers and an unexpected, lacily knitted pink top. Her hair, though still parted in the middle and scraped back with the tortoiseshell slides, was seen to be quite a pretty auburn shade under the hall light. There was no welcoming smile on her doughy face.

'Come in.' She must have thought the flowers were a gift for both of them because she held out her hand, but Marc guarded the bouquet jealously, not wanting to relinquish the first present he'd ever bought for his mother. Avril made no comment but led him upstairs and through a door which opened straight off the landing at the top.

He'd been right, he thought later, when they were sitting down to supper, he would have known her anywhere. Thin and dark, also wearing trousers, she was much younger looking than he'd expected. With her hair worn boyishly short, seeming at first to be another edition of himself, he could see now why Avril had so easily recognized him. Then he saw that although she was so extremely slim, the trousers revealed a shapely figure, and when she smiled, her femininity was in no doubt. She wore no make-up and no jewellery except for a small ivory crucifix on a gold chain around her neck, which she fingered constantly.

There'd been no question of her wanting to kiss him, then or in the weeks which followed.

It wasn't easy, that evening, though he could see that someone had gone to a lot of trouble, by having everything scrupulously clean and tidy and polishing what there was to polish, to make the tiny room look welcoming, a room of such small dimensions as to make his own poky bedsitter seem spacious. They had to eat off plates balanced on their knees because there was no space for a dining table. The narrow divan which nevertheless took up so much room was, he learned later, where Marie-Laure slept, while the curtain across the alcove contained Avril's bed.

Avril had put the liles in a hideous moulded glass vase, where they looked graceless because there were too many for such a narrow container, and there was nothing to soften their stiffness, but she said it was the only vase they had. She had to put it on the floor by the fireplace, where the heat from the gas fire brought out the heavy scent of the flowers.

They ate rice with coronation chicken, bought from the super-market, they told him, because neither of them were much interested in cooking and it was easy to eat with a fork only. This was followed by trifle, which delighted him – he was sure that his mother must have remembered that it had always been his favourite sweet.

The food was brought out immediately, which was a good idea because it served to bridge the first awkward moments. But the conversation remained stilted, on general subjects, about his work at the hospital, Avril's at the house agency. She told him that the name of the owner really *was* Search, but Sell had been added as a sales gimmick. He learned that his mother worked as a waitress in Catesby's restaurant.

Marie-Laure sneezed several times during the meal, and her eyes watered as if she were coming down with a cold. Marc saw Avril raise her eyebrows and his mother shake her head imper-ceptibly. He noticed jealously how often the two women ex-changed these sort of glances, how they seemed to know what the other was going to say, before they spoke, the sort of wordless communication that comes when two people understand each other perfectly. It made him slightly uneasy, without knowing why.

Before they reached the coffee stage, Marie-Laure's cold had become worse, until in the end she could scarcely control her sneezes. 'I'm sorry, I'm sorry,' she gasped between bouts.

Without saying anything, Avril picked the flowers up and squeezed past Marc where he sat uncomfortably perched on the edge of the divan, and presently Marie-Laure's sneezes grew less. 'I'm sorry, your lovely lilies, I'm allergic to flowers of any kind. I thought I would be able . . .'

Marc tried to hide his chagrin. Not because he'd spent a fortune on the lilies which would obviously have to be thrown out, but because he couldn't help wondering why Avril, knowing his mother's allergy, hadn't left them in the kitchen sink, with some tactful remark about arranging them later. Or why she'd put them by the fire, where their scent was bound to be stronger.

He felt depressingly that the incident only emphasized the huge yawning gap which lay between himself and his mother, how little he knew of her, how much there was for both of them still to learn. How much he needed to know, not to mention what he had to conceal from her.

He desperately wanted to mention the idea he'd had of buying a place where they could live together, but though this was very obviously a one-person flat and even two people living there made it unacceptably overcrowded, he sensed it was much too early to broach the subject, that his mother would need time before being willing even to consider such a suggestion.

She was, he saw suddenly, as nervous as he was. Her hands continually strayed to the crucifix round her neck, as though to seek reassurance or comfort from it, and she seemed to find difficulty in speaking naturally and without constraint, though this was understandable. He wasn't an easy conversationalist, himself, and Avril didn't help. After supper, she picked up some knitting, seemingly to disassociate herself, but though her fingers flew as if with a rhythm of their own, her eyes silently watched the two of them. The uncomfortable evening wore on and he was still no nearer knowing what had made Marie-Laure take that last, inexplicable step.

It wasn't until they were drinking their second cups of coffee that she had suddenly said, 'Well, where shall we begin?'

It was easier for both of them after that, after she'd made the first move. They talked, gradually becoming easier with each other, and the more he listened, the more he became buoyed up and encouraged with the knowledge that whatever he might do for her, it would not be too much.

He also knew that she hadn't told him the most important thing that he wanted to hear, swallowing hard on the fact that perhaps she never would. The last secluded years had added to her natural reticence; perhaps she felt that if she revealed every last thing, she would truly have nothing of her own left. He could hardly blame her. After all, there were certain things he'd also kept to himself.

It was very late by the time they finished. And all the time they were talking, Avril knitted, and listened, and hardly spoke a word.

11

Nothing much disturbed WDC Platt's good humour, and as usual she'd given as good as she got from the rest of the team about her present assignment. Having said her piece, she then grinned and got on with it, this allegedly cushy number she'd landed, working here in Lilburne's private study at his home, a room which overlooked the sweep of the gardens. It was a task which was in fact turning out to be mind-bendingly dull. Her brief was to go through Lilburne's personal papers, with no particular guidance on what to look for, except to pick up anything unusual. So far the files in his desk – those left after Inspector Moon had lifted his bank statements and so on – hadn't yielded anything except routine stuff . . . receipted bills, copies of guarantees and agreements, insurances and the like. She was very nearly finished with them, then it would be on to the letters of congratulation which he'd received on the announcement of his OBE award in the press. Crikey, there were hundreds of them, or so it appeared, all saying much the same thing in different ways, as far as Jenny could gather from an initial flip through.

'You'll see he'd marked the ones he'd answered, which I think was most of them by now. He was working through them steadily, answering as many as he could manage each day,' his wife had told her. 'I don't know what you're likely to glean from them, but you're welcome to try. They weren't all complimentary, by any means – you know how some people feel about the Honours List – but I think he had the good sense to throw those away.'

Mrs Lilburne had accepted the invasion of her privacy without question and seen to it that Jenny was comfortable, had switched on the electric fire which supplemented the small radiator and sent in coffee and biscuits – best china, chocolate digestives. While appreciating all this, Jenny was, however, in danger of nodding off, reflecting that even Deeley and Carmody, in the thankless pursuit of all persons Irish or terroristically inclined, might be having the last laugh after all – at least they weren't cooped up indoors. She went to turn the fire off and open a window to let in some fresh air, and with her hand on the window latch, noticed a girl with a couple of old spaniels at her heels, walking aimlessly across the lawn towards the house, dragging her feet. She was wearing black leggings and heavy, lace-up shoes and a big, loose, dark-grey sweater that covered her from chin to thigh. Her hair blew about her face and she was very pale.

Had it not been for the dressing on her forehead, Jenny would have had difficulty in recognizing her as the sexy Flora Lilburne who waltzed around her upmarket second-hand clothes shop, a bright, bouncy young woman with a sunny smile and an easy, friendly manner. Jenny had been tempted into Mark Two once or twice, but had always come out empty-handed, the prices being way beyond her careful budget and most of the clothes, when it came down to it, too extravagant for her lifestyle.

As Flora came listlessly towards the house and then disappeared, Jenny notched the window open and returned to the papers. Half an hour passed, with no more success than she'd had before, and she was nearly ready to start on the pile of letters when there was a knock and Flora came in, asking if she'd finished with the tray.

She had seemed entirely absorbed in her own unhappiness, but as she came forward, she looked curiously at Jenny. 'Haven't I seen you somewhere before?' she asked, her brow wrinkled. 'I know, you're a customer of ours – Mark Two, the dress shop in Fetter Hill? I'm Flora Lilburne.'

'Jenny Platt. Not a customer, I'm afraid, only a browser, so far. Out of my price range.'

'We're always open to negotiation.'

'Even so.' Jenny smiled, pushing back her chair to get the coffee tray.

'No, leave it, I'll get it.' Flora wandered across to the small table where Jenny had left the coffee things, but she didn't pick up the tray immediately, nor did she leave. Sinking into an armchair as if the effort of walking across the room had exhausted her, she sat pale and dejected, absently nibbling one of the remaining chocolate biscuits, watching Jenny as she resumed her work.

'What made you decide on such a boring job as the police?' she asked after a minute or two, as Jenny closed the last file.

'It's a job.' Jenny shrugged, then feeling that this was somehow letting the side down, she added firmly, 'And it's not boring – well, not always, quite the opposite, sometimes. I'm just doing what I'm told. At the moment.'

'One of the ambitious ones,' Flora said.

'Sort of.' And what was wrong with that, Jenny asked silently. And not half as much, anyway, as some she could name – Abigail Moon, for instance.

'I've never wanted to do anything that badly. Well, I used to think I'd like to be a nanny, once.'

'Why didn't you?'

'Oh, I don't know. My mother nearly had kittens at the idea. And anyway, you need to be a saint to look after other folks' kids . . . and I'm not brainy enough for anything more interesting.' Her voice trailed off and she shrugged. Then, as Jenny drew the basket of letters towards her, her interest sharpened. 'Don't tell me you have to go through all those?'

'Afraid so.'

'Why? You don't suppose the person who murdered him wrote to him and announced his intentions first, do you?' she said disbelievingly. 'Anyway, he threw all the hate mail away.'

'Hate mail?' Jenny inquired, ignoring the first part of what Flora had said. 'Did he get much?'

'Some – one or two. Well, no, not really *hate*. Letters from people who didn't approve of the honours system, or thought he should refuse on principle. Some who thought it was just a pat on the head from the Establishment – well, you know, the sort who can't bear anybody to have *anything* . . . What are you expecting to find?'

'A lot of our work consists of looking for things we don't know we're looking for until we find them.'

Flora had come to the desk and was beginning to leaf through the letters. 'Well, I can't see any of the nasties. He must have thrown them all away, as I said. These seem to be all the nice ones.' She lifted a clutch, picking out phrases at random. ' ". . . recognition of your sterling services . . ." ". . . no one deserves it better . . ." ". . . crowning your

92

career . . ."' Her lips twisted. 'And I'll bet half of them hardly knew him.'

'I think you underestimate people's sincerity,' Jenny replied, in a prissy tone she hardly recognized as coming from herself.

The doorbell rang, the drone of a vacuum cleaner somewhere in the house was switched off. The dogs barked, then stopped. The silence sounded very loud. 'Oh God, you're right, that was a hateful thing to say. I'm a bitch . . . people *were* pleased for him, really.' Flora had drawn her hands up inside the sleeves of the sweater, and crossed her arms, hugging herself as if she were cold. 'Which isn't surprising. Everyone liked Da who knew him.'

Her mouth trembled. A tear spilled, and rolled down her face. She dived into a pocket and pulled out a screwed-up wad of tissues and began to scrub her face. Jenny said awkwardly, 'Cheer up, it can't last for ever, you know.'

'I don't see why not.'

She was only eighteen, and she'd had a double shock, Jenny reminded herself, narrowly missing death and suddenly losing a beloved father, in a particularly horrible way. She obviously had a capacity for self-dramatization, but Jenny thought perhaps she was a girl who'd bounce back, that she was basically a nice girl, too, a lot nicer than in her own estimation.

A knock on the door was followed by a young woman clad in a short pink nylon overall cut like a tabard and worn over black trousers and T-shirt, her face barely visible behind a huge sheaf of cellophane-wrapped flowers which she held out to Flora. 'Who's a lucky girl, then?' she asked archly. 'Look what somebody's sent you!'

'For me, Sue?'

Flora, still sniffing, appeared mystified as she took the bouquet and searched for a card which she finally found tucked in among the elaborate loops and twirls of pink paper ribbon which decorated the cellophane. 'Oh.'

The prospect of having to arrange in a vase the unlikely combination of out-of-season magenta chrysanthemums, irises, pink hothouse roses and huge, Day-Glo, Magic Roundabout daisies was quite daunting enough, in Jenny's opinion, to account for the expression of surprise and dismay on Flora's face. Anyone who put together such a combination didn't deserve the name of florist. But it seemed to be the card rather than the flowers which was at fault. Having read it, Flora thrust it into her pocket with an abrupt gesture. From where she sat, Jenny hadn't been able to read the message, but the name at the bottom, written in the same round, schoolgirlish hand, probably the florist's, was clear enough, though it meant nothing to her. Mark, it said.

When they'd gone, bearing away the coffee tray and the flowers, Jenny sat thinking.

Ninety-nine per cent of the congratulatory letters she'd read were warm and sincere, glad to see such a distinction going to someone who really deserved it, rather than given as a gesture. Only a tiny minority could have written to him for reasons of self-interest, self-promotion, because it was the done thing.

But there was one which didn't fall into either category, and which in no way could be classed as hate mail.

One which she'd noticed on first flipping through the pile, and which Flora hadn't found, if that had been her purpose in shuffling through the other letters, because Jenny had already slid it under the basket.

For the second time in a week, Abigail snagged her tights on the doorjamb of the CID room, and swore in a fashion decidedly not ladylike.

'Doesn't anybody ever take notice of complaints around here? I've asked for this door to be reported twice. Do I have to bring sandpaper in and do it myself?'

One or two male shoulders were shrugged, but since it was a rhetorical question, demanded of the noisy CID room in general, few heard and nobody bothered to answer. It wasn't a problem they shared. Jenny Platt wasn't there and who else cared about snagged tights, one pound twenty a go, and this time no spare pair in her drawer? Abigail thought of the files piled up on her desk, looked at the clock and the serious ladder running right down the front of her leg and decided that for decency's sake, buying a new pair had to win. Catesby's, Lavenstock's answer to Harrods, was anyway only five minutes' walk round the corner. She leaned across Deeley's desk. 'Pete.'

'Ma'am?' the DC responded absently.

'Put a squib behind maintenance and get this damned door-jamb seen to, pronto. You, personally. I'll be back in about half an hour.'

Deeley sat up. 'Ma'am.'

For a provincial town, Catesby's wasn't bad. It still clung to many of its old-fashioned ways, but you could buy most things there, given you didn't expect London choices. Abigail rushed through Perfumery into the department selling underwear, gloves, hats and tights, decided to go for broke and grabbed a dozen packs of the most appropriate pair, not intending to be caught out again in the foreseeable future.

'Tell me how you do it,' said a cool voice across the Lycra support tights and pop sox. 'I've been here ten minutes and still haven't found the right shade.'

Claudia Reynolds, casually smart in cinnamon and black, big gold earrings swinging, blonde hair loose round her shoulders. Abigail envied the panache that could contrive elegance out of a zipped wool tunic over a polo-necked sweater, ski pants . . .

'Oh, hello. Case of needs must . . . Theoretically, I keep a spare pair at the office. It's remembering to replace the spare that does it.' She looked at the other woman, mentally re-arranged her schedule and said, 'Have you time for a quick coffee? I'd like to talk to you for a few minutes.'

Claudia looked at her speculatively, then smiled. 'Sure, why not? I've got the whole day free.'

'I hope it won't take that long.'

Catesby's coffee shop, leading off Ladies' Fashions, was never overcrowded midweek, though always well patronized, as it was today: young mothers meeting for coffee after seeing the children off to school, retired couples, dropping in on their way home from Tesco's, grandmothers remembering more gracious days when one wore hats to meet one's friends in Catesby's, for tea and scones and walnut cake, with a string trio playing in the background . . . ah, those were the days! Nowadays, it was espresso coffee and Coke, slices of quiche and pizza and micro-waved baked potatoes, and the string trio gone for ever.

'I saw you at the meeting the other night,' Claudia said as they found a place in front of a wide window that gave a panoramic view of the town.

Abigail hadn't expected to remain unnoticed, though she and Ben had sat at the back of the hall and slipped out as soon as it was clear as to which conclusion the meeting was leading.

'Sorry I couldn't stay . . . I admired the way you tackled it,' she said.

Claudia Reynolds acknowledged the compliment with a quick smile, then said with characteristic directness, though with a certain resignation, 'It's about my late-lamented boss you want to talk to me, I take it?'

'I confess I'm interested to know what you really thought of him.'

'Professional opinion, or a private one?'

'Both.'

'Ah.' Claudia, outside the confines of her job, leisurely shopping, prepared to enjoy coffee and a chat, was a different person, more likeable, more loosened up. Besides, she'd had time to think what to say, there'd be no accidental knocking over of glasses today, Abigail was certain.

'I'd nothing against him at all, professionally. He was brilliant, dedicated, absolutely the right person to deal with the sort of young men we get sent to us. I didn't always agree with what he did – but that's just because my style's different. No, he totally deserved that O B E . . . probably should've been a knighthood. But you can admire someone professionally without liking them very much. You're bound to hear, if you haven't already, that he and I didn't get on.'

She took cigarettes from her bag, recollected they were sitting in the no-smoking section and put them back with a shrug. 'I'm ambitious, and a lot of people equate that with bitchiness in a woman – you must know that – but that wasn't why we didn't hit it off. It was certain aspects of his private persona I found hard to take.'

'Like disagreeing with you over the new wing?'

'Oh, that! That was just a blip, we'd have sorted it out eventually. He was ultimately quite reasonable and sensible over things like that. That's not what I meant.'

She hesitated, staring out over the view across the car park and the municipal gardens and the Gothic splendour of the Town Hall, to where the town sloped gently upwards towards the tree-crowned hills, high on the skyline.

Overcoming her hesitation, she said eventually, 'Oh, well, here goes. He was a very attractive man, you know. Attractive to women. And vice versa. Not to me, though, he wasn't my type. Trouble was, he tended to think he was irresistible.' She smiled wryly. 'I came to Conyhall because I needed to widen my experience, but not in that way. I started out working with your outfit, before I decided this was what I wanted to do.'

Abigail didn't feel it necessary to say she was already aware of this, that it had been their business to find out about everyone at Conyhall, including the prison officers.

'I've worked now in nearly every kind of prison establishment,' Claudia went on, 'but what I really want to do is work with women, which I hope will be my next move. A bit of how's-your-father with Jack Lilburne to help me get there was definitely not in the scenario.'

Some tough lady, Claudia Reynolds, no question.

An elderly waitress came to clear the next table, wearing the green and white striped uniform and peaked hat Catesby's had chosen as a concession to modernity. She was slow and careful, but Claudia waited until she'd loaded the heavy tray and moved away with it before continuing.

'Anyway, that was one reason why he didn't like me particularly. Couldn't take the thought of any female saying no to Jolly Jack Lilburne.'

'Do you think his wife knew – about his affairs?'

A moment or two passed before she answered, rather quickly. 'It's hard to tell with Dorothea. She may have done. In fairness, I don't think they meant all that much to him. They were usually pretty brief. At least . . .'

'At least what?'

'There may have been one that was more serious. I did a previous stint of working at Conyhall some years ago, but of course I was much more junior then, not so in touch with the governor . . .'

'But you knew about the affair.'

'I put two and two together, from things I'd picked up, and what I saw. I'd a small cottage at the time, a few miles from Conyhall – I've always preferred to provide my own accommodation whenever I could. All that summer, I saw his car parked down a small lane which you could see from my bedroom window. It was there for hours at a time, and I assumed he was meeting someone. And then, suddenly, it stopped.'

Claudia stared down into her half-drunk coffee, which must have been quite cold by now. 'Something was evidently very wrong with the governor just about then. Whether it was because of that, I don't know, but he was unapproachable, which wasn't like him, and looking rotten . . . everyone noticed. Eventually, he put it about that his doctor had told him he was overworking and had advised him to take a long holiday. He went alone, walking in the Dolomites. When he came back, it was just as if nothing had happened.'

The Elgar cello concerto moaned softly through the room.

Mayo had taken it into his head to structure his listening – saturate himself in one composer so that he understood him more, and this tape was a new acquisition that he'd bought off a market stall. It had come to something, he reflected, when that was virtually the only place you could buy tapes now . . . he'd have to succumb to the blackmail in the end, get himself a CD player.

After hearing the piece through, he decided he could have saved himself the money and left it on the market stall. Disappointing. A slow piece, which the conductor took even slower, it wasn't Elgar at his confident best. Downbeat, uninspiring, despite the occasional beauty of the solo cello, with none of the sweep and vigour and majesty of the Variations.

Alex sat on the floor, leaning against his legs, writing a letter to her mother, the pad propped on her knees, finishing off a Bounty bar. She had a very sweet tooth, which he didn't share. He *hoped* the letter was to her mother, squinting at the rapid, decisive handwriting, and not to her former lover, the execrable Liam, who had given her a bad time but still had a nasty habit of popping up when least wanted or expected. Ashamed of the aberrant thought – Alex wasn't like that, promises and decisions once made were kept – he got up and went to make a pot of tea. They'd had a lean and virtuous meal of steamed plaice for supper, with new potatoes and peas. He hated plaice, a tasteless fish, even with parsley sauce, which they hadn't had. Alex was still absorbed in her letter when he came back and took her teacup from him, with a quick smile but not so much as a glance at the three-decker corned beef and tomato sandwich he'd made himself, dripping with pickle, mayonnaise, calories and cholesterol.

He felt more at one with the world after he'd eaten it.

Because the sofa, his favourite seat, was still missing, he sat in a chair opposite the rose pink chaise longue. The room looked different from here. Maybe it wasn't a bad idea, occasionally, to change your habits, you saw things from a different angle, got a different perspective. New perspectives were what was needed on this damned investigation. Lateral thinking. He reached for the scratch pad and the ballpoint beside the telephone and after a moment, he wrote, 'Davis?' Then sat staring into the simulated coal fire, not thinking, as he usually did, of the money going up the chimney in wasted gas, but of the case for Dex having actually planted the bomb.

Alex twisted her head round and saw what he'd written. 'Not satisfied that our Dex is the right one in the frame?' she asked. 'He's a nasty customer, from what I saw of him, and so's his dad.'

'He worries me – too obvious a suspect. Far too pat, too smooth.'

All right, the obvious suspect was very often the correct one, but Dex Davis seemed just too convenient. And so did the name of this man, this John Clarke Dex said he'd got the bomb materials for, a name Mayo was bloody certain Dex had pulled off the top of his head. 'But he's suddenly acquired money from somewhere, or someone – to buy the Orion, for one thing. Nicked it may have been in the first place, but he didn't get it for nothing, even though it was through his dad. And there's still the question of the explosives.'

The possibility of subversive organizations being responsible for the actual placing of the bomb was fast receding in the absence of any claim being put forward, but they were the ones you'd go to if you wanted the know-how, the ones to give advice on what steps to take to obtain the necessary ingredients. 'Dex must have Irish connections, through his mother,' he mused aloud.

'Not everyone who's Irish sympathizes with terrorists.'

'True, but some do – though I have to admit Carmody hasn't succeeded in turning up any in Lavenstock.'

He wrote rapidly on his pad for several moments, then handed it to Alex. 'What do you make of this? It's a letter Jenny Platt turned up among Lilburne's papers, what I can remember of it, though I think it's substantially correct. Written on plain cream writing paper with a ballpoint pen. The handwriting was distinctive, spiky, a bit Gothic, feminine looking. Coinciding with the tone of the letter, which suggested to Jenny that it was from a woman.'

My dear Jack, it had begun, followed briefly by the usual congratulations, and ended: *I have never ceased to regard you with affection, for what you did for me, and I have not forgotten our agreement, but the time has come when we should meet again to discuss what concerns us both. I will telephone you to arrange a time.*

'Any comments?'

'Stilted, isn't it?' Alex said. 'But I think Jenny's right, it is from a woman. And a bit peremptory, don't you think? Though I don't read any particular threat in it.'

Was there any connection with the scrap of paper found in Lilburne's breast pocket – which had also suggested a meeting? Mayo didn't think so, he didn't think it was even written by the same person.

'No address, either, and it's unsigned, which suggests that Lilburne might have had some sort of relationship with her that neither would want made public.'

'Ye-es . . . But it's not really a lover-like letter, is it? Not the sort of love letter I'd want to get, at any rate, please note,' she added with a grin. 'But if they did have some sort of relationship going, the inference in the text is that it was some time in the past.'

'Abigail's looked into it, and she says that if the writer did ring to arrange a meeting, Lilburne must have taken the call personally, because neither his secretary, his wife nor his daughter remember him being telephoned by anyone they can't identify. I'm not sure how relevant this letter is, yet, if at all. It may well turn out to be crucial to the bombing, but . . .'

'How about revenge for an affair gone wrong? Hell hath no fury . . .'

'Unless we're talking terrorists, bombs aren't usually a woman's weapon.'

'Two people, then?'

'Well, it's possible . . .'

At the moment, he felt that anything was possible. He scarcely remembered ever having been quite so much at sea with a case.

12

After that first visit, in January, to the home Marie-Laure shared with Avril Kitchin, there began a strange period in Marc's life. Now that he'd found his mother, he was so overwhelmed he didn't quite know what to do with her, so to speak.

He couldn't – he wouldn't – bring her to his own grotty bedsitter, but time spent with her and Avril in their poky flat was something of an endurance test, the three of them squashed together for a whole evening, and not even a television set. He wanted to take her out, to see her have fun, to make her smile a bit, and was disappointed when she refused. There was the age gap, of course, which meant she wouldn't want to hang around the pubs and clubs he and his acquaintances frequented, but she wasn't the sort, anyway, he could see that. She spent all her spare time reading, the newspaper, or books from the library – dull, heavy stuff: religious subjects, and books she said had been short-listed for the Booker Prize. Whereas Marc never read anything, apart from motor magazines and the textbooks he'd had to read to get through his exams. The truth was, though it was a bitter thing for him to have to admit, they didn't seem to have much in common.

'You don't have to feel responsible for me,' she said gently. 'I'm quite happy as I am.'

He found this hard to believe. Her life was no big deal. She and Avril occupied their weekends with shopping, going to the library, walks in the park. Their evenings were spent cleaning the flat, cooking their supper, reading. Marie-Laure went to church a good deal, and Avril knitted.

She never sat down without a piece of knitting in her hands. She was an expert, able to keep an intricate pattern in her head and to work rapidly and evenly without looking at what she was doing, without dropping a stitch, her round stare fixed on Marc and his mother as they talked. Marie-Laure explained that Avril knitted samples for a woollen manufacturer: they would send her wool from the factory, and a pattern, and she would test it out for accuracy, sending back a perfect, unflawed garment. The rapidity with which she worked meant that she was able to knit for herself and Marie-Laure as well; plain sweaters and cardigans in neutral colours for his mother, the lacy things which she evidently preferred for herself, like the pink top she'd worn on his first visit to the flat. She was very fond of pink.

Despite the awkwardness, and the cramped conditions, Marc came to Coltmore Road as often as he could in his off-duty hours, since Marie-Laure wouldn't go out with him, except for an occasional walk. But the evenings were still dark and with the coming of February, they'd embarked on a period of miserable, rain-sodden weather when it was wiser to stay indoors. Marc considered it was worth it, if he could persuade Marie-Laure to talk, in her almost faultless English, about her childhood in Strasbourg, where she'd grown up, the daughter of a museum curator and his wife, about her work as a teacher in Besançon, where she'd worked until she had met Charles Daventry, a wine importer . . .

Reminiscences stopped when they got to Charles Daventry.

And the questions which Marc burned to ask but couldn't, because he feared the answers, remained unasked: why had she ever taken that last, inevitable step? Why had she given him away, allowed him to be adopted? What had really happened?

He was beginning to feel bad again, the way he'd felt before he met his mother. Angry, and as though something terrible was happening that he should do something about at all costs.

'And you, Marc, tell me about your par – about June and Frank.'

'They were all right. I don't want to talk about them.'

He was sensitive about how different his education was from what it might have been if he'd been brought up by her. The things she knew about – art, books and music – hadn't featured much in his childhood. Frank, a machine operator in a component factory, noting Marc's handiness, had shown him how to use tools, to make things; bought him his first chemistry set, taken him to football matches and taught him to swim. And

June – well, June hadn't been educated like Marie-Laure, she'd thought mothering started and ended with a kiss and a hug, seeing him clean, tidy and well fed . . .

'They were good people. You shouldn't think so badly about them,' Marie-Laure admonished quietly.

'Especially when she wasn't your born-to mother,' Avril put in, her needles click-click-clicking.

He really hated that sort of jargon, especially when it came from Avril, uttered in such pious tones. He was beginning to see he'd never like Avril very much, either, and was sure she felt the same about him. She was very critical of everything he did, or didn't do. 'Don't you have a girlfriend?' she asked, more than once.

'No,' Marc said shortly.

It was none of her business. If he wanted a girl he could get one. He objected to the way she fixed that unblinking stare of hers on him and his mother as they talked, taking in avidly every word that passed between them. He thought she bossed Marie-Laure about too much. Her everlasting knitting got on his nerves.

He tried even harder to persuade Marie-Laure to go out with him to a film, a show, a slap-up meal, but the only time he was able to get her to agree to go out for dinner, she had insisted that Avril came too, and the evening was a disaster. He had chosen the best of Lavenstock's two French restaurants, thinking to please Marie-Laure with this, but both women, appalled at the prices, chose the cheapest, and therefore the most uninteresting, food on the menu, and refused wine. Marc drank more than he should have done. Conversation languished. They'd have done better to have stayed in the flat.

Abigail provided Mayo with as many details of Jack Lilburne's background as her team had been able to gather together, from a variety of sources, ranging through his entry in *Who's Who* to a brother and sister in the north and all sorts of people who were reputed to have known him well. He familiarized himself with it by reading it through twice, then put it aside and thought about it.

Born and brought up in a sea-coast mining village in Northumberland, Jack Lilburne came of a family who had been miners for generations. His father had been a tub-thumping trade unionist of the old school who had lived through pre-war poverty and remembered the Jarrow marches: Jennie Lee and Nye Bevan were his idols. He had determined his son was going to have a better life than he'd had, knowing that Jack was clever enough to get to university if he worked hard enough – and his father had made sure that he did. He'd graduated from Durham with a respectable law degree, decided to read for the Bar but unexpectedly joined the Prison Service after a couple of years. His father's reaction to this was not recorded. He rose rapidly, came to Conyhall in 1972 and had stayed there ever since. Well known for his progressive views on treating young offenders, he had been a frequent speaker at Prison Service conferences. Leftish politics, but not aggressively so. His professional life, culminating in the award of his O B E, was crowned with success. His personal one?

Twenty-one years ago, he had married Dorothea Carrington, daughter of one of the old county families. There were those who'd said it couldn't last. People who knew him before his marriage said it would never last – not so much because he and Dorothea came from opposite ends of the social scale, but because Jack had always been known as something of a womanizer, and leopards don't change their spots.

'So, he *did* like to play the field a bit.' That was what Alex had said. He'd have to take more notice of woman's intuition in future.

'Even after his marriage, according to Claudia Reynolds,' Abigail reminded him.

'So. So, is it to be *cherchez la femme*? In particular, the *femme* who wrote that letter Jenny found?'

'Kite might have something to add to that. He's come up with something he thinks you should hear.'

Mayo rang for the sergeant and found him, for once, at his desk.

Kite was the sort who worked on intuition. Twenty years in the police hadn't yet taught him that such often led to tears before bedtime. All Mayo's caution couldn't rob him of his optimistic confidence in his own snap judgements which, to Mayo's chagrin, often turned out to be well founded. He had a way of latching on to the smallest scraps of information which turned out to be significant. Interviewing a Mrs Doreen Hancock, a civilian clerk who'd worked at Conyhall so long she was almost an institution herself, he'd recognized her as an inveterate busybody and caught a whiff of something which could fall into the 'significant' category.

Mayo prepared to hear what he had to say, knowing Kite's unerring sense for what was relevant and what was not wouldn't let him waste time in getting to the nitty-gritty. 'I know you've told all this once to Inspector Moon, but I'd like to hear it first hand, Martin.'

Kite, impatient, but knowing from past experience that Mayo would demand all the details, resigned himself to beginning at the point where Mrs Hancock had mentioned to him something which had happened years ago. She was a gossipy woman, given to clichés. She didn't like to speak ill of the dead, but she'd never forgotten the incident, somehow. A day in the Cotswolds, that was something she and her husband had always enjoyed, driving round the pretty villages or maybe visiting Hidcote Manor Gardens, having tea at Chipping Campden or an early supper on the way home. Real treat it was, or used to be, it was all getting too touristy now. Anyway, on this particular day they'd called in at this hotel on the way home for a meal, and who should they run into there but Jack Lilburne and a woman. Oh, the couple had tried to make it appear they weren't together, but Mrs Hancock wasn't born yesterday, and knew when she was having the wool pulled over her eyes, and had later happened to get into conversation with the receptionist – well, the proprietress, really – who'd witnessed the encounter and assumed they were friends. It turned out that 'Mr Norman' and his wife regularly spent weekends at the hotel.

'Disgusting, it was. At least he didn't call himself Smith,' Mrs Hancock sniffed. 'But barefaced – I ask you, not twenty miles from home! Practically under his poor wife's nose – well, it wasn't right, was it? I'm not narrow minded, but really, I can't stand that sort of thing.'

Kite had made a spur of the moment decision to run out there and check for himself.

The receptionist, who was indeed the wife of the owner, remembered the incident clearly, since it had been a cause of much embarrassment to her. 'It was years ago, but I haven't forgotten – I really put my foot in it, there! I'd seen them chatting to him in reception and assumed they were friends. "We're always pleased to see Mr and Mrs Norman," I said to that woman when she brought it up in conversation – though she was just being nosy. It was the way she looked when I said "Mr and Mrs Norman". I knew straight away, from her expression, that it wasn't his real name, and I was quite shocked, I'd thought him such a nice man. I was really naive in those days! Well, I was a lot younger, not so experienced in what goes on in hotels. The morals of our guests are nothing to do with us, but of course . . .' She let her shrug speak for itself. 'We never saw the Normans again.'

'What do you remember about the woman – the woman who called herself Mrs Norman?'

'I don't know that I'd recognize her again. It was her clothes I noticed mostly. She was beautifully dressed, always immaculate, and she'd some stunning jewellery. But she kept herself very much in the background . . . he was the extrovert, did all the talking, a really nice man. I can't believe what you're telling me. A bomb, you say? Dear God!'

'Well, Martin,' Mayo commented when Kite had finished, 'that's interesting, I'll grant you, and confirms what we're beginning to know of Lilburne's character. The question is, was this the same woman that Claudia Reynolds assumed he was meeting clandestinely, or someone else entirely? We've no evidence that she was – or whether she was the one who wrote that unsigned letter, or typed the other. Or whether any of it has anything at all to do with him being killed.'

Abigail said, 'I'll find out from Claudia exactly when it was he and this woman were meeting.'

'If it happens to be nineteen-seventy-nine, the chances are it's the same woman he stayed with at the Gravely Arms. I've already checked that was when he and the woman stayed there as Mr and Mrs Norman,' Kite said.

Marc's depression was deepened by the fact that he hadn't heard from Flora about the flowers, not even whether she'd received them or not. Then he reasoned that she wouldn't have wanted to ring him at the hospital to thank him, she would know it was more than likely he'd be on theatre duty. At the same time, it came to him that she couldn't write to him, either, since he'd never told her his full name. When she'd asked him what he was called, he'd simply said 'Marc'. From that she wouldn't know that it was spelt in the French way, with a 'c', and she probably hadn't noticed the way he pronounced it, with a short 'a'. For all she knew, there might be fifty Marks working at the hospital, which is what the woman at the flower shop would have written down when he telephoned the order. He was furious with himself for not thinking it through properly, though he wasn't sorry he'd sent them, she was the sort of girl, he knew, who'd love flowers . . . though it did seem that he didn't have much luck where women and flowers were concerned.

But no way could he give up in his attempts to contact her again. There were other ways, as Frank used to say, of skinning a cat.

At the beginning of March, Marie-Laure had told him about the new flat she would be moving into.

It was one Avril had found for her, through Search and Sell, and he'd been not only bitterly disappointed that she didn't offer to share it with him, but also obscurely affronted because, although it was small and not in the best of neighbourhoods, it was better than any he could have afforded to buy – one that would have been large enough, at any rate, for them to share. Prices seemed to have risen overnight and each time he looked at his capital, he saw it buying less and less. But it was still a mean flat, and this had never been part of his plan. She deserved better – she would have had better, if she hadn't been so self-sacrificing. He bottled up the anger he felt at this needless waste of her life, but she sensed it, all the same.

'I thought you would be pleased,' she'd said gravely. 'I can't go on sponging on Avril for ever, that's only a one-person flat she has, though she has been wonderful about letting me stay there.'

'You're not going to share the new flat with her, then?'

'What made you think that? The arrangement was only temporary. I need – how do you say it? – my own space.' She almost achieved a smile.

He felt very slightly better. Women's friendship – the deep, caring sort of relationship Avril and his mother appeared to have – was something he'd only ever heard talked about in a lubricious sort of way, and he hadn't cared to dwell on it, pushing the implications to the back of his mind. But he saw, now, that it hadn't been like that – not on Marie-Laure's part, anyway. Perhaps he was projecting his own feelings on to his

107

mother, but they were two such different personalities that he wondered, sometimes, if it wasn't merely gratitude that made her want to keep Avril as a friend.

'It's very convenient,' she'd said of her new accommodation. 'The shops are nearby. I can easily walk to Catesby's to work . . .'

'Well, I hope you won't be doing that much longer.'

'Perhaps.'

She'd agreed, after a good deal of persuasion, to try and get herself a more worthwhile job, in teaching, what she was trained for, and had applied for several positions, though so far without success.

'And the church is just round the corner,' she added.

The Roman Catholic church.

It was another part of her life that he found difficult to accept, having had to admit how deeply her religion still fitted into her life. He knew, bitterly, that her faith meant more to her than he ever could. Her inner life he was incapable of understanding, and the outward trappings of her religion irked and sometimes embarrassed him, especially when he thought of these last self-imposed years of martyrdom. How could she worship a God who'd allowed her to suffer as she had done? Yet he knew she slipped into the church every day to pray, and went regularly to mass and confession. The few books of her own that she possessed were almost all books of devotion. She wore the crucifix round her neck always, there was another above her bed.

He just couldn't understand how Marie-Laure could find peace and solace in kneeling before an altar, lighting candles in that gloomy, soot-stained building behind the market square.

'What do you see in it? What's it ever done for you?' He was totally unable to envisage a life of that sort. Frank and June hadn't been practising Christians. Churchgoing of any kind was quite outside his ken. Believing in some pie-in-the-sky religion was for cranks and parsons and Jesus freaks.

'It has helped me to go on living,' she answered, but refused to be drawn further. 'We'll talk more about it some day, when you're ready for it, but not now.'

She was very keen to move into the flat as soon as she could, and, after a great deal of argument, allowed Marc to buy for her the few modest pieces of mostly second-hand furniture which she insisted was all she needed. When he'd finished painting the sitting room for her, and they'd moved in the furniture, she was gravely delighted with the result.

But really, that was when it all started to go wrong.

He thought perhaps it was because Avril didn't seem to visit her in her new home. Maybe she'd taken the huff, or they'd quarrelled. Or maybe it was just that Avril waited until he wasn't there to call on her, which wouldn't be surprising, considering their last meeting. And if she'd told Marie-Laure of this last furious exchange, it wouldn't be surprising that there was this constraint between them that hadn't been there before, this growing coolness. Why she seemed to shrink from any attempt by him to get closer.

When he'd dropped in at Coltmore Road to pick up his mother's suitcase, Avril had accused him of putting the idea of moving out into Marie-Laure's head, insisting that he was involving her in expenses she could ill afford, when she could have stayed with her, Avril, and shared their living costs. Almost before Marc knew what was happening, they had been in the middle of a blazing row.

She'd hefted the suitcase to the middle of the floor and plonked herself down on the bed-settee so that the springs groaned under her weight, and picked up her knitting. He'd wanted to yank it out of her hands.

'Can't you see she doesn't want you?' she said. 'She got rid of you, once – why did you have to come back into her life? I've told her, Marc Daventry, that you spell trouble, and she doesn't need any more of that! And I'm warning you – you get out of her hair or I'll make trouble for *you*.'

Jealousy, fury and frustration boiled up inside him. He'd grabbed the suitcase in order to occupy his hands. If he hadn't they might have been round her throat. But a warning voice sounded in his ear. What did she mean, trouble for him?

He could easily have dealt with her, he told himself as he left the flat. But she wasn't worth bothering about. He went off to the DIY place to buy timber and put up the shelves in Marie-Laure's sitting room and told himself that the best thing she'd done was to separate herself from Avril Kitchin.

For his part, he could only feel thankful that those long, tedious evenings in her company, with her suspiciously watching his every move, those sly questions of hers, her interminable needles clicking away, were over.

13

'We've had a break, Sarge – '

D C Deeley, dependable and solid as the Rock of Gibraltar, but never the world's best communicator, broke off, staring across the flickering computer screens to the far side of the room.

'Well,' Kite said, after several moments of waiting for him to continue. 'Take your time about it, Pete, don't break your neck, but when you've thought about it, perhaps you'd be good enough to inform me what it was you were about to say.'

Deeley came to with a start. 'Sorry, Sarge. Sorry, I was just – ' Kite didn't need to follow his fascinated glance to know what it was that Deeley was 'just – ': he was just looking at Farrar, resplendent in a new suit of so light a grey it was almost silver. He wore grey leather moccasins to match, and white socks, and sported a gold chain around his wrist. Cool as a cucumber in the sweltering heat of the winter-graded central heating, he stood out like a snowdrop in a cabbage patch. Kite had had all morning to get used to the sight; moreover, he knew that Farrar was got up like a dog's dinner because he'd asked for a couple of hours off to meet his wife, Sandra, for an important appointment of a delicate nature with her gynaecologist. Kite had kept that to himself. Farrar put his back up, like he did the rest of CID, but he'd already run the gamut of basic humour over his suit, the poor sod had had his share of embarrassment for the day.

'Well, Pete?'

Deeley swallowed and smartened his attention. 'We've had a sighting on somebody hanging around the governor's house that morning, Sarge.'

'The morning of the bombing?'

'The milkman who'd just delivered to the governor's house.'

'We've questioned the milkman. And the postman – *and* the paperboy . . .'

'No, Sarge, not the regular one, we couldn't, he's been away on holiday. Winter break in Tenerife. Only just come back and heard about the bombing.'

'Tenerife? We're in the wrong job, Pete.'

'Yes, Sarge. He took the kids to Disneyland – the Orlando one – last year.'

'Strewth. Well, let's have the good news.'

'He was on his way back down the lane that leads to the house, after delivering the milk. It was still dark, around half-seven, and his headlights picked up the top of some sort of vehicle in the field over the hedge. There was somebody moving about, he thought, but he assumed it was the farmer who owns the field. Nobody else likely to have been about at that time.'

'Thought? He didn't actually see anybody?'

'He probably wouldn't have seen the vehicle, either, if he'd been going faster, but you know how slow these electric milk floats go.'

'What else does he remember? Did he see the driver? Can he make a guess what sort of vehicle it was? Colour? Not,' Kite said with sudden hope, thinking of Dex Davis's Orion, 'red?'

Deeley shook his head. 'Might've been light coloured, he said, but he can't say for sure. The hedge's four foot high, and he only saw the roof, so it was probably a car. He didn't see the driver at all.'

'Tracks,' Kite said, reaching for the phone. 'The weather's on our side, for once. Wet enough before the bomb, and cold enough since to have preserved them.'

'Unless the geezer went back and obliterated them.'

'You've been watching too much *Inspector Morse*. Nice one, though, Pete.'

It would be even nicer if Forensics managed to match up the tyre tracks with those on Dex Davis's Orion, but he wasn't optimistic, rightly so, as it proved. Tyre casts established it wasn't a farm or an off-road vehicle, maybe a front-wheel-drive car since the tread on the two front tyres was noticeably smoother than on the back ones.

'Not a lot of use to us if we haven't got a car to match them up with,' Kite said, 'but somebody up there loves us – there were footprints as well. Trainers, size eight, with a small circular mark on the heel, which SOCOs think might be a drawing pin somebody stood on.'

*   *   *

111

'Size eight? That lets Dex out,' Mayo remarked when this was later pointed out to him. 'You could do yourself an injury, falling over his size twelves.'

'Somebody smaller than Dex,' Kite agreed. 'Big for a woman – though I can think of several females not a hundred miles from here, for instance, with feet that size.'

'What is interesting,' Mayo said, 'is why that time in the morning?'

Just when the world was waking up, when the killer had had all the hours of darkness at his disposal? But it was probably why the dogs hadn't barked – they'd be used to people hanging around the house then, delivering milk, papers, mail.

'. . . and I'm truly sorry, Lois, but look, I can't give you an answer yet. Not until I've talked it over with Gil.'

'Well, I'm sorry, too, but if you don't do it,' said Lois French, 'I think you'll live to regret it. And you realize I can't keep the offer open indefinitely in case you should change your mind? I really do need a partner, I can't keep shutting up shop when I have to be out – and it's not just someone to mind the shop, I need someone with flair.'

'Then you don't need me. You're the one with the flair.'

But Alex had good taste, she knew that. And good judgement for the antiques side of the business, not to mention good sense over money. Yet she was still a little afraid that the offer was a quixotic gesture Lois might very soon repent. Brilliant Lois, flashing and skimming like a kingfisher along the surface of life, she'd always been the impulsive sister, while Alex had been the determined one, knowing where she was going and not letting anything deflect her.

'I wish you would, Alicky. Before it's too late. Next time you might not have such a lucky escape.'

'Well, whether I stay on in the police or not,' Alex said, touched by the childhood nickname Lois hadn't used in years, 'I don't know that it's a good reason for stepping from the frying pan into the fire.'

'Well, thanks! If that's how you feel about my business, darling, I agree!' Lois's laugh tinkled.

'What I meant was – well, you know what I mean.'

Lois was making light of it, but Alex sensed her sister's disappointment could be deeper than she'd given her credit for.

Recently, when having the shopfront painted, she'd had her own name removed, so that it now read simply, 'Interiors', rather than 'French Interiors', which Alex had in any case always thought misleading. This time she was leaving room for manoeuvres, hoping that Alex could be manipulated into making it into a partnership.

She stood up and began stacking their coffee cups on the tray. 'It doesn't look as if Gil's going to make it, after all. I said we'd set off if he wasn't here before half-past. Still want to come with me?'

'Seems a pity to waste the seat, though I'm not all that keen on such heavy stuff, as you know,' said Lois, who liked her music predictably easy. Radio Two, Barry Manilow. All the same, she stood up and began to inspect her immaculate make-up in the mirror over the mantel. Alex watched as she applied more lipstick, smoothed into place the shining black hair with the Cleopatra fringe and the ends curving towards her cheeks. Not a wrinkle in sight. Slim and upright as a reed (skinny, said Mayo) and too brittle (neurotic, came from the same source). Several inches shorter than Alex. Superficially rather alike facially, they differed in almost everything else, especially the number of men in their lives. Three marriages in Lois's case, all of them short-lived and, as she was fond of saying, she hadn't been neglected in between.

At that moment, Mayo's latchkey was heard in the lock. 'Saved by the bell!' Lois cried, with obvious relief.

'Are you sure you don't mind? It seems so – '

'Mind? It's a positive deliverance, not having to sit through two hours of purgatory! I'll go home and wash my underwear. Stravinsky's not my scene.'

'It's not Stravinsky, I think it's mainly Beethoven.'

'What's the difference?'

Alex laughed and felt less guilty at having messed up Lois's evening.

Mayo had remembered the concert half an hour after he'd planned to leave for home. He'd told Alex to leave if he wasn't home on time, and to take Lois, whom he knew she was seeing about now – if she could be persuaded to go – but looking at his watch, he thought he'd still make it, even though he'd walked down to the station that morning and had no car. He could have got someone to run him home, but it was a lovely evening for a walk, a positive chance to dissipate some of the tense, nervous energy that had been building up inside him.

His long strides took him past the closed, window-lit shops in the town centre, quiet for a spell until the youth of the town emerged for their evening's rowdy activity. The bellringers were practising at St Nicholas's church and the chimes rang jubilantly across the town. The clear, cold night with its brilliant, starry sky and promise of frost yet again, cleared his head of the fug of the murder room, but he couldn't rid himself of the on-edge feeling, the sense of dissatisfaction with the way the Lilburne case seemed to have reached stalemate. The break this morning, the sighting of the car, had been something, but it was only a chink in the darkness. With every stride, he tried to shake off the idea that they were getting nowhere fast, dammit. But he was beginning to have a doomed feeling about the case, which was good for nobody. It had attracted a lot of attention and he could already feel the spotlight of public criticism.

Alex felt even less guilty about her sister when Mayo asked, after Lois had gone, 'Are you wildly sold on going to this concert?'

'Not particularly,' she answered, reading the signs of his restlessness, knowing that his mind would be elsewhere and that he'd be too keyed up to concentrate on the music . . . which would frustrate him all the more, since he regarded anything less than total application as an insult to the orchestra. That the supper they'd planned at the Italian restaurant might as well be bread and cheese for all the interest he'd take in it. 'You have a hot shower, and I'll pour us a drink.'

'Make it a big one.'

An hour later, Cleo Laine on the turntable, the lamps low, a drink in his hand, she asked, 'Like me to slip out for a takeaway?'

He stretched out a hand and pulled her to him. 'I've a much better idea than that.'

The lamplight laid a radiance on her body, lay like a salve on the scars that she'd been shy of letting him see, at first. God! he'd thought, when he realized how near the heart the main scar was. The bastard had almost killed her. He lay on his back now, one arm behind his head; he let his other hand lie, heavy and lax on her thigh, unwilling to move and waken her, not wanting to remember what it had been like when he thought he might have lost her . . . knowing what he wanted for her now, and that he mustn't influence her in any way, any decisions must be hers alone.

Alex wasn't asleep, merely in a state of total contentment. 'Are you awake, Gil?'

'I am now.' He leaned over her, propped on his elbow, ran his finger along the edge of her jaw, looking down at her face in the golden light of the lamp, seeing her hair spread like dark silk against the pillow.

'I've something to tell you.'

She began hesitantly, taking her time about it, and it was what he'd expected to hear for a long time, but – 'Are you sure? Sure about your reasons? You have a future, you know, if you want it.'

'No, I'm not all that sure, it's a step in the dark, but I have to take it. And I *am* sure I don't want a future in the police – and not just because of what happened.' It was coming out in a rush, now. 'I'd always thought of myself as career-minded, but I don't like the way things are any longer – God, that's an understatement, sometimes I hate the police! I could carry on, taking things superficially, but at a deeper level I know it would be wrong for me . . . I don't believe in what I'm doing any more, I don't feel comfortable with it . . .' Her voice ran down. 'I'm not making much sense, am I?'

He'd had some inkling that this was how she felt – two people as close as they were couldn't hide feelings like this completely – but he'd thought it was a temporary disillusionment, he'd had no idea it was as bad as this. Been too wrapped up in himself, he thought guiltily. 'Go on – you're not doing so bad. I'm trying to understand.'

'It's what we have to deal with now that I can't cope with. It's a rotten, filthy world we live in, and I know somebody has to deal with the consequences, but I don't want it to be me. Carry on, and you end up brutalized – or go under.'

'That doesn't always follow, you know.'

'Oh God, don't take it personally! It's the way people like you cope that makes me feel so inadequate – '

'Inadequate? You? Never!' She was tough, a police sergeant, for God's sake. She hadn't got that commendation for nothing.

'Yes,' she insisted. 'When I see the way the children are growing up – old and experienced and cynical before they're out of primary school, into drugs and crime . . . knowing there's nothing we can do about it, it's out of control, we're losing the battle . . . I'm not opting out, I simply need time to sort myself out . . . I can't expect you to understand, you don't feel like that.'

'No.' He wasn't one of life's optimists, but if he'd felt that sort of despair he wouldn't be in the police, either. Soldiering on was what worked for him, taking things as they came, doing what was best at the time. It was people like Alex, with this need to see the world and everything in it as perfect as she wanted it to be, the need to be able to make it so, who suffered when things didn't come up to expectations.

He thought she was saying, in a different way, something of the same sort of thing Jack Lilburne had been reported as saying in his speech, the night before he was killed. But there was Jack's 'however'. Alex hadn't got as far as that. She was still floundering in the dark.

He cupped her troubled face in his hand and kissed her gently. 'You need time to get things in perspective. Don't rush it, it'll happen.'

With his arms around her, he let her talk on and felt her gradually relax, relieved for her sake that things were out in the open at last. And for other reasons, too, that maybe didn't bear examining too closely. Standards had been relaxed, a blind eye was turned these days to cohabiting officers, but a kindlier one was turned on those who conformed: the Chief Constable was a chapel-going non-conformist, a Baptist lay preacher, with old-fashioned standards.

Mayo couldn't help being aware that Alex's decision wouldn't exactly do any harm to his own standing.

14

Marc looked at his watch as he came off night duty: a digital watch, which also gave the date, and realized with astonishment that it was barely ten days since he'd met Flora. She was already so much a part of his life that he found it incredible to believe he'd known her such a short time – only since the day of the bomb which had finished off her father, Mr Jack Lilburne, OBE, the Governor of the Young Offenders' Institution, in fact. That same day Marie-Laure had moved into her new flat and that he'd hoped would mark a new beginning for her, only it hadn't.

He wondered what she'd say if he told her about Flora, but he couldn't imagine himself doing so. She'd shrunk more and more into herself, the loving relationship he'd envisaged hadn't materialized. Anyway, she'd think he was crazy, to imagine anything could ever come of his longing for Flora. He sometimes thought so himself. He'd often seen people do stupid things when they thought themselves in love; he was less contemptuous of them now. If they'd been as helpless as he was, in the grip of this infatuation . . . no, *love*, it was *love* he felt for Flora, nothing else could describe his feelings – if they'd felt like this, he could understand.

He'd tried to phone her several times but it was always her mother, or someone he guessed was the cleaning woman, who answered. Once it had been a man. They couldn't have told her he'd rung, or she'd have been in touch. A familiar, violent compulsion to do something about it came to him. He made a right turn at the next lights, and within minutes, found himself driving towards the older part of the town where she had her shop, in one of the busy, narrow streets that sloped down to the river. It was risky, but if you never took risks you might as well be dead, anyway.

*   *   *

117

It was Flora's second day back at the shop. Anthony was driving her there and she was asking his opinion on the matter of buying herself a new car.

'It's not a write-off, your Polo, you know.'

Flora shuddered. 'It is as far as I'm concerned. I don't want to see it ever again, never mind drive it. But I can't let you go on chauffeuring me around. It's sweet of you, but you don't have the time. And I do need to get into a driving seat again soon, and pretty soon, or I never will.'

'That's my girl. Though you know I don't mind what I do for you.' Anthony took his hand from the steering wheel and laid it on Flora's knee. She didn't remove it, but she didn't show any outward signs of enthusiasm. Ah well, early days yet! He had to be patient. She was already surprising him with the speed of her comeback, showing that she was Dorothea's daughter as well as Jack's, that there was a steely backbone stiffening those soft, yielding contours. She was bravely determined to pick up the threads, even to showing an interest again in what she wore.

She said suddenly, apropos of nothing, 'I'm worried about my mother.'

Anthony didn't show at his best, driving a car. He gave the impression of being in charge of a wild mustang, his arms stretched tensely to the steering wheel as if reining it in, snatching at the gears as if they might bite him, peering myopically through the screen. Sometimes, Flora wondered if he should be driving at all. The car bucked now, as he turned his head to gaze at her. 'Your mother?' he repeated.

Thankfully, they were nearly there. They'd turned down into Butter Lane, past the fashionable Interiors on the corner and Saville's antiquarian bookshop, and were now in Fetter Hill, in front of the little, half-timbered shop that was squeezed in between the art shop and an old-fashioned chemist that still had the big glass jars of coloured liquids displayed in the window. Anthony pulled into the kerb. 'What *about* your mother?'

'Something's worrying her. I mean, apart from the obvious. She isn't eating properly, and I don't think she's sleeping, either. She doesn't seem to be able to concentrate. It's so unlike her.'

'Flora, that's par for the course, in the circumstances. It'll take time – '

'I'm not talking about that. It's something else. I tried to get her to talk last night, but she wouldn't.' Flora stared absently through the windscreen for a while, then bent to pick up her bag from the floor. 'Oh, well, it'll work itself out, I suppose. Have a cup of coffee before you go back?'

'I'd better not.' Anthony had missed his breakfast in order to drive her to the shop before the morning rush, and without doubt the coffee here would be better than any he might get back at Conyhall, but he didn't want to cope with Charlie. Charlie, who was horsey and county, and made Anthony feel like a wally. And he suddenly remembered the meeting scheduled to start in half an hour – it was today, surely? Or was it tomorrow? He was usually conscientious about this sort of thing, but suddenly, it didn't matter. Something unexpected jolted inside him, some impulse making him push his luck. Everything he knew or had learned professionally told him he was playing it wrong – it was too soon, she wouldn't be ready. Despite these warnings, he found himself putting his hand on her knee again and saying just a minute, Flora, didn't she think it was time they – she and Anthony . . . began to think about . . . wouldn't it be an idea . . . well, what he wanted, more than anything else in the world, actually, was for them to get married.

Oh God. He'd blown it. Damn it to hell. Blurting it out like a callow schoolboy. Any way to do something wrong, he'd surely find it.

Flora said calmly, 'I know. It's what Da wanted, too. He told me so, just before he died.' A glow was spreading under her skin, her eyes were luminous. 'It's rather what I want, as well, Anthony, darling.'

He was momentarily stunned, then he felt the blood rush to his head, he wanted to shout and sing. It just showed, you never knew. All these months. Old Jack! Flora! He twisted round to grab hold of her but the steering wheel was in the way. And then a distinctly sobering thought occurred to him. 'What will your mother say?'

'Oh, she'll be all right. She'll be very pleased, in fact. She told me yesterday she thinks you're a very reliable young man.'

'I'll have that coffee, after all,' Anthony said, winded.

Marc drove slowly, looking for the shop. For an instant, thinking what it would be like to see Flora again, it came to him with horrifying and explicit clarity what might easily have happened to her, precisely how it must have affected her since, but the thought distressed him so much that he put it out of his mind and concentrated on finding Mark Two. Amongst the old, timbered buildings, its frontage was so narrow, barely wide enough for the name, he nearly passed it by. He was disappointed; he'd expected something much more classy.

He wasted fifteen minutes looking for somewhere to park his car. Although it was so early, the narrow street was already congested and he had an argument with a baker's delivery van driver who pulled a fast one and beat him to the only space left. His already jumpy mood hadn't improved by the time he'd parked several streets away and walked back, pushed the shop door open and entered.

She didn't look as he'd remembered her at all. He was staggered by the difference. She was dressed in a very short tubular dress that showed a lot of her legs, she wore make-up and her lips were a shiny red. Her hair had been done up in some sort of fashionable frizz. She'd looked so much more beautiful in the hospital, without all that goo on her face and with her hair falling naturally to her shoulders. He supposed she had to dress the part, but he was aware of a flicker of doubt. His sweet, virginal Flora looked – well, almost indecent, though she was more desirable than ever, in fact. He put it down to not having seen her for so long, except in his imagination.

There was some man with her in the shop, she was talking animatedly to him and smiling, but when she saw Marc, her face changed. At first he thought her expression was one of annoyance, then he realized it could be surprise at seeing him there, and perhaps embarrassment. Perhaps she wasn't supposed to have personal visitors while she was working in the shop. But that couldn't be so, he remembered she was her own boss, she'd told him she owned a half share in the business.

'Hello, Marc.' She smiled gently and said to the man, 'Anthony, this is the man I told you about, who was so kind to me in hospital.'

Beaming all over his face, the other man shook Marc by the hand and said Flora had told him how he'd kept his eye on her, and thanked him, as if he'd done *him* a favour as well. Then he said he must be going and took both Flora's hands in his and looked right into her eyes. Marc didn't like the proprietary way he did this, as if he owned a share in her, much less the way Flora didn't seem to mind. The lingering way she smiled at him, in fact.

'Have you known him long?' he asked jealously when the Anthony person had left.

'Oh, ages,' Flora said casually, and Marc recalled that the man had been years older than Flora. Probably an old family friend. He was almost certain he was the one who'd answered the phone when he'd rung.

'Did you get my flowers?' he asked.

'Oh, so it *was* you? How sweet of you.'

She explained why she hadn't thanked him, and it was just as he'd thought – she hadn't wanted to ring him at the hospital, she didn't know his last name – 'Daventry,' he said, 'Marc Daventry, Marc with a "c".' Repeating it twice so that she'd remember. 'You're looking better,' he added – meaning that she looked less ill than she had.

'Oh well, you have to make the effort. As you said to me, life must go on.'

She smiled, but it was a smile that wobbled at the edges, and while registering pleasure that she'd remembered what he'd said, he saw she was, underneath, still the lost little girl he remembered in the hospital, and that had an immediate, cheering effect on him.

The shop didn't appear to be busy. There were no customers, although there were a lot of fancy clothes on the rails and displayed on models. Marc found the atmosphere very claustrophobic. The shop was extremely small and had a low-beamed ceiling, thick grey carpets and big mirrors that showed disconcerting reflections of himself, and the air was heavy with the residue of expensive perfumes. Flora began folding a raspberry-coloured silk suit that was laid out on the large glass-topped table that served as a counter and said, 'We-ll?' Looking at him expectantly.

'Will you have dinner with me one night?' he blurted out, coming to the point much more quickly than he'd meant to, suddenly feeling his nerve giving out, afraid that he might leave the shop without ever having asked her, if he didn't do it immediately.

She gave him a quick upward glance from under her lashes, then lowered them and went on smoothing down the suit skirt.

'I don't think that would be a good idea, Marc,' she said quietly, at last.

'Why not?'

'I – I don't have much spare time, for one thing, and for another – '

'I'm not your social class – is that it?' he interrupted, quick on the defensive, unable to keep the bitterness out of his voice.

'No, of course not, not at all! It's just that – '

A woman came in from the back of the shop. 'Flora? Anything wrong?' she asked in a cut-glass accent.

'No, Charlie, Marc's just going, aren't you, Marc?'

Charlie – what sort of stupid name was that for a woman to call herself? Marc judged her to be a few years older than Flora, heavily made up, with shiny, streaky hair tied back with a black velvet bow, wearing a very short-skirted navy blue suit that showed legs with knobbly knees, and enough gold chains clanking round her neck to anchor the *QE2*. She gave Marc a look that froze.

After Flora's unwillingness and that look, he wasn't going to hang around to be humiliated further. 'I'll ring you,' he said to Flora. 'You must have *some* free time – this week, next week – '

'Don't, Marc, it won't be any good.'

He wasn't all that experienced in asking girls out, but this was supposed to be how some of them reacted, wasn't it? Played hard to get? He didn't believe that was Flora's style, yet she couldn't really mean what she said.

'Why not? Why won't it be any good?'

The Charlie woman began, 'Look here – ' But Flora interrupted her.

'Because for one thing, I'm engaged to be married.'

'I – I don't believe you.'

'Yes, I am. To Anthony. Anthony Spurrier, the man you just met.'

He was stunned. 'You can't be. You're lying!'

'You'd better go,' the other woman said coldly, though he could have sworn all this was news to her, too.

'Yes, Marc, I think you had,' said Flora. Her eyes were huge, and her face had gone very pale.

They stood there, looking at him, and he had absolutely no idea what to say. He couldn't have spoken anyway at first for the tumult boiling up inside him, churning his stomach. At last, he managed it. 'All right, but I'm not going to leave it there. You let me think . . . You *kissed* me when you left the hospital!'

'Oh, Marc, that meant nothing – except that you'd been so nice to me! Everybody kisses, it doesn't mean any more than shaking hands.'

It was true, people kissed all the time, when they met, when they said goodbye, even people who didn't know each other very well. But not Marc. Kissing was special, for when you wanted to show affection, or love, for someone. Using kisses in that casual way debased their currency.

He was bitterly disappointed in Flora. Disappointed, and so angry he felt that he couldn't breathe. She'd made him look a fool in front of that other woman he'd taken an instant dislike to. But if she thought it was over with, she was wrong. He wouldn't be put off so easily, he hadn't finished yet, far from it.

Without another word, he turned and left the scented, feminine atmosphere of the shop and stepped out into the workaday bustle of Fetter Hill. The sense of isolation which he so often felt had never seemed greater.

15

The Mayor's new rose garden outside the Town Hall, of which he'd spoken so enthusiastically to Dorothea on the night of the dinner, was still a collection of bare, lifeless twigs set in square cushions of earth. Bordered with massed purple and white crocuses, a thing of pride and joy to the municipal mind, the beds were cheerful, if not aesthetically pleasing, on a miserable morning. Or what Abigail could see of them as she perched on a desk in the incident room, the telephone to her ear.

'Yes, that's it, that's the name,' she answered Anthony Spurrier. 'Clarke. John Clarke.'

'Well, I've been through the records, way back, and we've never had a John Clarke, with or without the "e". Sean Clarke, yes. Michael, Justin, Andrew. Even a Tristram, poor devil. But no John, ever, not even as a middle name. Funny, when you think how common it is.'

'Maybe that's why it was chosen. If the owner of it ever existed, outside Dex Davis's mind.'

'Giving you a hard time, is he?'

'No more than we'd expect.' No more than insisting he was telling the truth about this John Clarke. But he would, anyway. He was up to the neck in it. Tip and Farrar had done a good job in tracking down the source of the explosives, which had indeed come from the quarry, via a light-fingered truck driver doing regular pick-ups of stone for the new Hurstfield bypass. He'd admitted leaving the explosives in a car boot, picking up the money left there, just as Dex had said. 'Well, thanks anyway for your help, Mr Spurrier.'

'Er – before you ring off. There's – er – something you might be able to help me with. I've got a problem, well, sort of. At least, not me, personally, not exactly – '

'Whose is it, then?' Abigail asked, looking at her watch,

mindful of how long it took Spurrier to get to the point.

'It concerns Flora – Flora Lilburne. My fiancée, you know.' There was a pause which seemed to call for some comment.

'Oh, I didn't know you were engaged.'

'Only just,' he answered with a proud bashfulness that managed to convey itself over the phone.

'Congratulations.'

'Thanks.' Another pause.

Abigail sighed inwardly, made a drinking motion towards Pete Deeley, indicating that a coffee would be welcome. He stuck his thumb up and as he went to get her one from the machine, she said, 'What's the problem, Mr Spurrier?'

She listened patiently while he told her that Flora Lilburne was being pestered by someone named Marc Daventry. Telephone calls, flowers – even hanging around her shop – and now it was letters . . .

'He's threatening her, you mean?'

'No, not exactly. Rather the opposite, I suppose. He seems to have taken a shine to her, and won't take no for an answer.' Her own crispness was sharpening him up, and he managed to give her a fairly succinct account in less than the five minutes it took to drink her coffee, of how the situation had arisen. It seemed to Abigail a fairly familiar one – a pretty girl giving a young man too much encouragement, and then regretting it. She didn't see what Spurrier expected of her, since there had so far been no threats to Flora's person, but she told him to leave it with her and she'd see what she could do. Which, with all the goodwill in the world, she didn't think would be much. Considering all the department had on just now, it wasn't a priority.

'You – won't mention this call to Flora? She feels sorry for this bloke, thinks it'll all blow over.'

Abigail promised, but she thought it prudent to make a few inquiries, and when she'd collected the results, to report what she discovered when the team met for the morning briefing.

'What do you say his name is? Daventry?'

Mayo knew most of what went on in Lavenstock, it was his patch and he made it his business to know, but this name was a new one to him.

'Yes. I've had him checked, there's nothing against him, personally. But he was connected, as a child, with a big murder case that happened around here some time since.'

Several people, those who'd been in the district long enough, remembered the Daventry case.

'Must've been twenty years ago,' Kite said. 'I was just thinking of joining the police. A Frenchwoman who murdered her husband with a carving knife, wasn't it? Created a regular furore round here.'

'Eighteen years ago, to be precise,' Abigail said.

A typical domestic murder, it had been, following the usual pattern of a happy enough marriage, a couple apparently devoted to each other and to their small boy, until the dark river of discontent and unhappiness running beneath the surface had erupted in blood and death. The truth emerged only at the trial.

An attractive woman whom Charles Daventry had met when on business in France, his wife had turned out to be not the thrifty French schoolteacher he'd expected, but hopelessly extravagant – at least, in his eyes. He'd evidently tried to keep her on short commons all their married life, subjecting her to interrogations on how she'd spent his money. Although a man with a substantial business as a wine importer, he had possessed a streak of miserliness which the defence might have claimed had made life a misery for his wife, had there been any defence.

'But she wouldn't plead mitigating circumstances, as I remember it,' Atkins said. And he *would* remember it, he never forgot anything. Elephants had nothing on George.

'Go on.' Mayo stopped twiddling with his newly acquired reading glasses (which he didn't really need all that much, of course), a sure sign that he was interested.

'It's all in the records, but she admitted it from the beginning, said it was all her fault. She'd been spending extravagant sums of money on clothes and such, and he blew his top.' She'd ended six years of humiliation by driving a kitchen carving knife between his ribs.

'Her prints were all over the knife, there was blood on her clothes commensurate with her having done it. Made no attempt to deny it.'

'A classic case of "I don't know what came over me"?'

'Not quite in the heat of the moment. Waited until he was in bed before she attacked him.' The prosecution had made much of a discrepancy between when Daventry died and when his death had been reported. She had stated that was because she'd been too distraught to think clearly, belated fear of what would become of her child. Whether this had any effect on the jury or not, she had received a life sentence.

Leaving behind her child. The child who had been called Marc, and who was now making a nuisance of himself over Flora Lilburne.

'What did you say this Marc does for a living, Abigail?'

'He's an operating-theatre technician. The people he works with speak highly of him. He's been there about two years, came to them from one of the Birmingham hospitals.'

Mayo asked for all the documentation that was available on the case and, after reading it through, sat thinking about Marc Daventry and Flora Lilburne. Two victims of tragedy, both of them with a murdered father. Was there anything between them other than the simple coincidence of having met in the hospital? The trouble was, he didn't like coincidences, simple or not. But however he looked at it, there was nothing on present showing to suggest there was the slightest link between Charles Daventry's stabbing, and Lilburne being blown to death.

The call came in just after half past nine the following day, when George Atkins was just finishing his early elevenses, a small snack comprising a pint mug of coffee and two sticky buns, and was looking forward to a concluding smoke. He was making the most of his pipe-smoking days, sensing they were numbered. It didn't take much imagination to realize that a new non-smoking super would lose no time in making the office a no-go area as far as tobacco went. As far as George's noxious pipe went, nobody would be sorry to see this — except George himself, who hoped he'd be too far gone into retirement before that happened to worry about it.

He immediately set the routine procedures in motion, then put himself through to Mayo to relay the information, though not before he'd gulped down the rest of his coffee and plugged his pipe into his mouth, not unlike a baby with a comforter, one or two unkind souls had been heard to remark.

'Sir. Looks like we have a suspicious death.'

Mayo, surrounded by papers, was tetchy. 'Looks like? Well, have we or haven't we?'

'No details yet, sir, except that the victim's female. Flat in Coltmore Road, Branxmore. I've alerted Inspector Moon. Organized SOCOs — and Doc Ison's on his way.'

'Good man, George.' Mollified, Mayo surveyed the day's tasks lying before him, did a rapid mental review on what was lined up for him in his diary. He had a full day, including a working lunch with the ACC (Crime) which he couldn't put off. Nothing else of world-shaking importance. And every suspicious death on his patch was his business, his presence was necessary, he reminded himself, squaring his conscience at the eagerness with which he welcomed this diversion. 'I'll be down there myself, George, soon as I can.'

Coltmore Road led off the busy Coventry Road, but went nowhere except to a parade of dingy shops and other similarly drab streets, distinguished from them only because it was one degree more respectable and had municipal acers, rowans and Kanzan cherries planted at intervals along its length, some of which had survived the attentions of vandals.

By the time Mayo arrived, the phalanx of police vehicles was creating havoc in an area where congested on-street parking left little room to pass. The pathologist's gleaming vintage Rover was nowhere in evidence, but he could see Henry Ison's blue Ford Scorpio parked halfway down the street, and the scenes-of-crime van, double parked with a patrol car in front of a house remarkable for its fresh paint and a tub, crammed with vivid primulas, at the foot of the front steps. The house had been cordoned off, a uniformed constable stood guarding the entry, trying not to look frozen stiff, his nose red and his breath clouding the frosty air. Mayo shouldered his way past the usual knot of gaping sightseers who were intent on disregarding the attempts of another constable to keep them back, and spoke briefly to the West Indian couple who were huddled in the doorway of the downstairs flat. Running up the narrow stairs, he found Abigail at the top, looking sick. She was standing outside a door opening into a very small room where Sergeant Dexter and his white-overalled scenes-of-crime team were already in action, sidestepping and generally falling over each other in the cramped space, while Napier endeavoured to do his stuff with his cameras.

'Morning, Henry.'

Ison, the police surgeon, was kneeling on the floor beside the body of a woman, half dressed beneath an open dressing-gown. A sticky red stain spread across the front of her pink slip. She lay on the carpet, across the front of a bed-settee. A gas fire fixed to the wall had evidently been left on. Though now switched off, it had left the small room unbearably overheated. The smell of death was nauseating, the feeling of violence palpable.

Ison flapped a hand in greeting. 'Be with you in a minute, Gil. Thought you were T-L. Taking his time, isn't he?'

'He'll be along shortly. Finishing off a PM, I'm told.'

Abigail and Mayo stood bunched awkwardly at the door, careful not to touch anything, looking in at the room, every detail of which was visible from the doorway: the bed-settee, taking up a lot of the available space, two wooden-armed, upholstered chairs with splayed legs, one of them overturned, coffee table ditto, a small sideboard, a curtained alcove with the curtains drawn back, revealing a neatly made bed and a single wardrobe. A door at the opposite end of the room presumably led to a kitchen of sorts. The open door of a shared bathroom and lavatory was behind them on the landing.

'Who is she?'

'Avril Kitchin. Worked at the house agent's in Lorrimer Street, Search and Sell. Lived here about twelve months.' Abigail paused. 'Before that, she'd been doing time.' Mayo raised his eyebrows. 'The flat was found for her by her probation officer.'

'How was she discovered?'

'Mr Johnson downstairs, the landlord, found her. He came upstairs to start redecorating the next flat, presently empty – the attic flat's occupied by a single girl, but she's off with her boyfriend somewhere just now – and saw the door wide open, with her on the floor, as you see her.'

'Somebody broke in and attacked her, hm?' Mayo could see her handbag, lying on the floor beside her, the contents spilling out.

'Not so much *broke* in. The outside door at the bottom's never locked after the milk's been taken in at about seven-thirty, apparently. No sign of forced entry up here – so this door wasn't locked, either, or else she let in whoever did it. Or they had a key. But more likely they were after money – purse, cheque book and credit cards seem to have gone missing from her handbag.'

Ison snapped his bag shut and got to his feet, removing himself out of Dexter's way. 'OK, I've finished, Sergeant. You can have a bit more leg room now. Straightforward stabbing,' he said to Mayo as he reached the door. 'In or near the heart. Difficult thing to achieve, to hit exactly the right place without catching a rib. So the killer was either lucky, or knew what he was doing.'

'The weapon?'

'Steel knitting needle, left on the floor.'

'Here, sir,' Dexter said, holding up a tagged plastic bag with the grey enamelled needle inside it, and indicating a bundle of fluffy yellow knitting, resembling a dead chicken, lying on the carpet in front of the bed-settee.

'Size twelve needle, fairly thin, which is why there isn't as much blood as you might expect,' added Ison. 'Though there was probably a good deal of internal bleeding.'

'Has she been raped?' The victim appeared to have been dressing when she was interrupted. A coral-coloured blouse and a light brown skirt were draped over a chair. What clothing she was wearing appeared to be undisturbed, apart from her pink, fleecy dressing-gown being unfastened. But it was a question that had to be asked, nowadays, whether the victim was eight or eighty.

'Not interfered with at all, as far as I can tell. She was spared that.'

'How long – ?' began Mayo.

'A matter of an hour or thereabouts, probably not much more. She's still warm. Say around eight o'clock. Difficult to say exactly with the gas fire on. As for anything else, I'm only here to certify life's extinct, you'll have to wait until Timpson-Ludgate opens her up for the drama – though I doubt there'll be any surprises. Right, I'll leave you to it and see what I can do for Mrs Johnson downstairs. She's understandably a mite upset. Give me a buzz if there's anything else I can do.'

Brisk, bespectacled, like a small beaver, he inched past them and clattered down the stairs.

16

'I just don't know,' Mrs Johnson sighed, in the spotless sur-roundings of her downstairs sitting room, after Ison had left. She was calmer now, dispensing home-made ginger cakes and pouring tea – not, Mayo noticed to his satisfaction, into mugs (what the hell did you do with the spoon?), but into violet-sprigged china cups with matching saucers. 'I don't know, you think you're doing right, trying to help, and then this happens. I won't do it no more, I tell you that.'

'Now then, Pearl!' Her husband put an arm around her plump shoulders and squeezed. 'She's upset,' he explained apologet-ically. 'We offered to take Mrs Kitchin in when we was asked, we try to do the best we can, you know. Pearl, these people need help, you know that.'

The Johnsons were a Jamaican-born couple of late middle-age who had struggled for twenty years to keep up the mortgage on their house. When their four children had left home, they'd converted the bedroom and attic floors into three flats in order to pay off what they owed to the building society. Through their local church, they'd been approached to take in occasional released prisoners as tenants. 'And up to now, we've had no trouble of this sort, no trouble at all,' Mrs Johnson said.

'Be fair, *she* was no trouble, neither, Pearl,' Leroy Johnson gently reminded her. 'Kept herself to herself and no bother.'

'Well, that's right,' his wife conceded. 'I have to say that. The bathroom always left nice and clean, and no wasting the hot water, even when that other one was here.'

'What other one was this, Mrs Johnson?' Abigail asked.

'The friend who stayed with her.'

'Never did think we should've allowed that, you know,' put in her husband, 'that flat's not big enough. Not to say they was getting two for the price of one! But we reckoned, if she was another one down on her luck, we'd turn a blind eye for the moment, especially as Mrs Kitchin – Avril – seemed so happy to have her here. Never saw her smile until her friend came. Well . . . anyway, she left a few weeks ago.'

'What was her name?'

The couple looked at each other. The husband frowned. 'Not sure. We hardly saw her, never mind spoke to her.'

'Mary Lou,' said Pearl Johnson suddenly, 'That's what Mrs Kitchin used to call her – Mary Lou, or some such. She wasn't English.'

'American?'

'No, oh, no, not American. More like French or something, I'd say.'

Mayo put his cup and saucer down on the small lace mat that had been provided. Abigail said, 'Could it have been Marie-Laure, Mrs Johnson?'

'Why, that's right! That's just what it was.'

Abigail glanced at Mayo. He was perfectly still, but gave the impression that whereas before he'd been coasting along in neutral, he was now, suddenly, in top gear, as though the engine was running light and swift.

'What sort of woman was Avril Kitchin?' Abigail was asking.

Mrs Johnson shrugged. 'All right, you know. All right. I didn't know her well. We hardly spoke, all the time she was here.' As if realizing how she was damning the woman with faint praise, she added, 'She was no trouble, and I can't say more than that.'

'What about visitors?'

'We never saw any. Except maybe a young chap, a couple of times that I know of, but that was only when her friend was here. She had her own doorbell.'

'Could you describe this young man?'

But it had been dark the time Mrs Johnson had passed him on her way out, and the next time she'd only seen the back of him through the window. She'd only had a vague impression and wouldn't commit herself to describing anything about him.

Mayo stood up. 'Thank you for your help, Mr and Mrs Johnson. You've been very cooperative. Sorry for all the disruption, we'll try and let you get back to normal as soon as possible. If you need anything, any help, just ask one of my men.'

The body would not be moved to the mortuary until the pathologist, Timpson-Ludgate, had seen it. He still hadn't arrived, and now that fewer people were around, Mayo went back upstairs for a closer look, taking the stairs two at a time.

He paused at the top, scanning the room, again from the vantage point of the doorway. A typical bedsitter, minimally furnished. Almost aggressively clean, the net curtains starched and white, the floorboards polished around the square of cheap carpet. Nothing personal to prettify the place, no photographs, no books. The cream-painted walls were bare, not even a Suzie Wong department-store picture. The yellow knitting hadn't been removed and still lay on the floor, a complicated piece of work which appeared to be the almost-finished sleeve of a jumper, pulled free of the needle which had been plunged into the woman's chest. Its companion was still stuck into the ball of fluffy wool. The killer hadn't come armed with a weapon, then. Yet an opportunist thief, surprised in the act of filching the missing contents of the handbag, seemed an unlikely scenario, given the time of day, before people had left for work: miscreants didn't normally enter premises when there was the likelihood of encountering anyone.

Something in the thought set up an echo of a previous conjecture, but when Mayo tried to grasp it that was all it was, an echo, gone like lost footsteps.

A quarrel, had it been, then? Better, though the Johnsons had heard no struggle, no sounds of anyone coming or going, they'd seen nothing. But he could sense violence in the room. There was something not only murderous, but vengeful, about that knitting needle.

If the victim had been the knitter, she'd been clever enough with her hands to fashion an intricate piece of work, though they were stubby fingered, thick and clumsy looking. He studied her more closely. Alive, she couldn't have been physically attractive. A sturdily built woman with heavy shoulders and muscly legs. A broad face with coarse features. Death had wiped away all traces of anything which might have moderated this impression. He was left with a strong, if unjustified, feeling that she'd been unlovely and unloved, a desolate epitaph for anyone. As always with murder, he felt an immense sadness at the waste of a life, a life in this case that had led a woman to a prison sentence and was unlikely to have been a happy one. He wondered what she'd been inside for, which prison it was where she had met Marie-Laure Daventry.

He walked to the window and stood looking out over a narrow strip of back garden, bisected by a concrete path – flower borders and grass on one side, neat rows of vegetables on the other. Terminated by a six-foot wooden fence separating it from the back garden of the house in the next street. Hands in pockets, he watched a lean tabby cat strut between the rows of Mr Johnson's cabbages and Brussels sprouts.

Marie-Laure. She seemed to have an unfortunate habit of being around when murder happened. It occurred to him also that the name Daventry was cropping up with rather too much regularity to be coincidental. First in connection with Flora Lilburne, now this. He suddenly recalled the letter to Lilburne, its precise phrasing. Non-English? The spiky-looking handwriting – Continental? From Marie-Laure, in fact? The same woman, perhaps, with whom he'd stayed at the Gravely Arms, the one he'd met behind Claudia Reynolds's cottage? Mayo checked this unsupported theory before it ran away with him and turned back to Dexter.

'Tell me what you've found so far, Dave.'

'No prints, apart from the victim's – not even on the needle, but we'd have been lucky if there were. Gloves, I suppose, but then, you don't normally grab a knitting needle with your fingertips, and if you use it for what this was used for, you'd hold it in your fist.' He demonstrated with a graphic, downward thrust of his balled fist.

'I see what you mean.'

'Blood, possibly. And some contact fibres on her slip. Dark-coloured, but I wouldn't care to say what type until we've had them analysed. And the knitting wool's angora, which sheds hairs all over the place. The killer could hardly have avoided getting some on his clothing when he picked the knitting up. Maybe some of her hairs, too – she didn't appear to have finished doing her hair – only one side's fastened with a slide.'

Mayo grunted. 'First find your suspect – then hope he hasn't got rid of what he was wearing.' Macabre, though – that last, intimate exchange, the close contact of bodies, that obscene conjunction which left something of the killer at the locus of the crime, and transferred to him some unsuspected trace of his victim. 'Did she struggle?'

'No apparent signs of it. Doc Ison says there were no bruises.' Mayo thought it likely she'd been taken by surprise, looking at the position of the body where it lay, suggesting that the chair and table had been overturned as she fell.

'Well, keep at it, Dave, keep me informed.'

'That's not all, sir.' Dexter, who had a quirky sense of timing, had been keeping the best until last. 'Looks like we've found the typewriter. An Olympia 66, anyway. Haven't tried it out yet, of course, but at first glance, I'd say it fits the bill.' Mayo peered through the film of polythene now enclosing it and discerned a shabby, leatherette-covered zipped case. He recalled his feeling that the two communiciations hadn't been from the same person. But if Marie-Laure hadn't sent the typed one, then presumably Avril Kitchin had.

Where the devil did she fit into all this?

Abigail was at the foot of the stairs, talking to one of the uniformed sergeants. A house-to-house call on the neighbours was being organized. It was routine, it would have to be done, but it probably wouldn't yield much. In this street of houses turned into flats, bedsitters and student pads, strangers came and went, nobody noticed, or minded anyone else's business. One day you had one neighbour, the next a new one, or several. Scarcely anyone knew who lived next door to them, or cared.

'We need to trace Marie-Laure Daventry as a priority,' he told her heavily. 'You know where to start.'

Hearing the tone of his voice, she threw a quick glance at his grim face and had no trouble in following where his thoughts were leading. She'd recalled the reports of the Daventry case as well, and she didn't like the idea that they might have a repeat performance killer here any more than he did, but it couldn't be ignored. Charles Daventry had been killed by his wife, named Marie-Laure. A Marie-Laure had been a friend of the dead woman, there was a similar M O in both cases.

Within a couple of hours, they had the information they needed on Avril Kitchin. She had once been a nurse in an old people's home – before she was sent to prison for using violence against the patients in her charge.

'And she wasn't exactly a model prisoner, either,' said Gillian Short, her probation officer, who'd offered, when Abigail telephoned, to make a few inquiries and then pop into the station for a chat. 'They had to keep a watchful eye on her because of her anti-social tendencies – against the other prisoners and sometimes the screws, I gather.' She was a fair-haired woman with a fresh complexion and perfect teeth, who looked like a tennis-playing head prefect, but Abigail had come across her before and knew her to be a woman of understanding and sympathy, who knew precisely how to deal with her probationers. 'But she was in for a long time and I suppose eventually it occurred to her that she was forgoing most of the privileges accorded for good behaviour, and losing remission. At any rate, she calmed down. Eventually she was transferred to the low-security prison at Gormleigh.'

'And that's where she met Marie-Laure Daventry?'

'Who was serving the last years of her sentence there, yes. Strangely, they seemed to get on well – though they weren't particularly close. Over-close friendships aren't encouraged, for all sorts of reasons, as you know. The psychologist in charge of her case was certain there were no lesbian tendencies on Marie-Laure Daventry's part, though as far as Avril Kitchin went, I gather nobody would have been surprised at anything.'

When Avril was released, Mrs Short had found her the Coltmore Road flat and an interview for a job at the house agency, Search and Sell, whose owner was enlightened enough to take a chance on her. 'She didn't disappoint him, I'm happy to say. She was always conscientious, though she kept herself to herself and didn't associate with any of the other employees out of working hours.'

'What about her husband?'

'She wasn't married, presumably she thought the "Mrs" added respectability. People like her have a very low self-esteem, you know.'

'And Marie-Laure Daventry?'

Marie-Laure, it seemed, had been released under licence five years before Avril, also having served a reduced sentence, with remissions for good conduct. After her probationary period, when a close eye was kept on her, she was more or less free to do as she wished.

'Do you know where she's living now?'

'She's out under life licence and therefore required to keep her probation officer informed of any change of address, and she's well out of order if she doesn't, so yes, I can find out where she is for you.'

But she rang later to say there was no recorded address after that of Avril Kitchin's flat in Coltmore Road. 'So where was she before that?' asked Abigail.

'A *nunnery*?'

'A convent.'

Semantics. What difference did a name make? If Abigail had said Marie-Laure Daventry had been living in outer space, Mayo couldn't have been more taken aback. He knew no more than the next person about nuns, those anonymous black-clad figures, subjects of ribald bar-room jokes about their unnatural life, a life against nature. And like most people, he couldn't begin to comprehend religious convictions so strong that human beings were led to shut themselves away from the world. Call it ignorance, but the very idea was to him slightly suspect.

And an ex-con, a murderess, living in a nunnery?

'But it's not an enclosed order, it's actually a convent boarding school,' Abigail corrected. 'And she wasn't exactly a nun. I suppose she worked there in a lay capacity,' she added vaguely. She didn't know a lot more than he did about the religious life.

A lay capacity? And what was that supposed to mean, Mayo wanted to know. If she hadn't taken vows – wasn't that what they called it? – then why had she chosen to be there at all? As a form of penance? To hide? Had she become so institutionalized that she'd seen this as the only viable alternative to life outside? It was something quite outside his ken, but anyway, it was for the moment irrelevant. The question which was paramount was, where was she now?

17

'Well, whether she should have reported her new address or not, the fact remains she hasn't done so.' Mayo swung his spectacles irritably by their arm. 'Which is a fat lot of help to us.'

'I've not yet seen Marc Daventry,' Abigail said, mentally docking another week or two off the life of the specs. 'He should know where his mother is, surely? We can but try.'

Mayo put his specs down and rasped his hand across his chin. He'd had his usual shave and shower first thing that morning, but he felt an urgent need to repeat the performance, as though it were a necessary ritual cleansing to purge himself free of the contamination of murder. And then to consume a large hot meal and a dram of the malt. All of which were unlikely to be fulfilled for some time.

'You say he works at the hospital? Let me know how you get on with him – no, have him brought in. I'm interested to see this young man.'

He sent out for a sandwich, and it was Carmody and Jenny Platt who were detailed to seek out Marc Daventry at the County Hospital.

They were directed – after a careful scrutiny of their warrant cards, a routine established after one or two scares about un-authorized people getting on to the wards – to the Pargeter wing, a newly built extension dedicated to a local industrialist, the better part of whose fortune had enabled it to be built. They followed signs through the crowded waiting room, with its tea and sandwich bar, along corridors to satellite waiting areas designed to accommodate smaller numbers of people, and were finally filtered to a three-seat area, not in use that day, outside a consultant obstetrician's door.

Waiting for Marc to arrive, there was nothing to do but sit staring at the decor, which was dispiriting, considering how new it was. Porridge-coloured walls. Grey carpet tiles. Old magazines. An exhausted Swiss cheese plant drooping in the corner, as though waiting for urgent resuscitation techniques. Cardboard boxes of brightly coloured plastic toys for children.

'Jeez, how long do they expect patients to wait?' Carmody said, casting his eyes up at a bookcase full of paperback novels.

Mercifully, their own wait wasn't long enough for him to get through more than the first three pages of *The Reluctant Heart* before Marc arrived.

He'd been in the theatre setting up preparations for the next operation when he was summoned. He hadn't been told it was the police who wanted to see him, but he guessed that was who they were, even before they introduced themselves with a polite request that he should accompany them to the station so that Superintendent Mayo might clear up one or two matters.

'What sort of matters?'

'Couldn't say, sir.' The spokesman, a detective sergeant, was a pessimistic-looking character with a Scouse accent you could cut with a knife, a big bloke you'd be stupid to argue with. His sidekick was a smiling young WDC with a mop of curly hair and a china-doll complexion, but Marc wasn't fooled by her, either; she could probably have your arm locked behind your back and break it in two seconds flat.

'I can't come at the moment,' he objected, indicating his theatre garb, his green top and trousers, white shoes, his paper cap and the mask dangling below his chin. 'Mr McNulty's list isn't finished.'

'They tell me somebody can take over your duties, sir.' The Liverpudlian was unmoving, stolidly communicating to Marc that there was no point in prevaricating, or letting himself be angry.

'Give me a few minutes to change, then.'

They made no objection to that, and within ten minutes he was sitting in the police car, the sergeant driving, the girl sitting next to Marc on the back seat. There was a bald patch on the back of the sergeant's head, the steering wheel looked like a toy in his big hands. The girl was wearing a short navy jacket and a pleated plaid skirt, and her ankles underneath it looked neat in low-heeled pumps and navy tights. She wore a light perfume smelling of spring flowers. No one spoke as the car covered the short distance to Milford Road.

He was taken into a small room where the sergeant stayed with him until presently the superintendent joined them. Marc was confronted by a big, unsmiling man with a quiet, no-nonsense air about him, a penetrating gaze and a direct form of speech in which Northern vowels were apparent, as he told Marc his name and asked the sergeant to remain, sitting himself down opposite Marc.

Mayo, in his turn, saw a slim young man of middle height, well-dressed, presentable, a handsome lad, but taut and guarded, obviously ill at ease, though that conveyed nothing. Most people were uncomfortable, however innocent they were, when being questioned by the police. Mayo poured a little of the tea he'd requested – stipulating a pot, if you please, with cups and saucers – inspected it and, evidently finding it satisfactorily strong, filled two of the three cups and pushed one across the desk before shunting the tray across to Carmody to help himself. 'Sugar, Marc?'

'Two, please,' Marc said, and shovelled four in. Nervous. Had to swallow twice before he could get out the question as to why he'd been brought here.

'Yes, of course you want to know, Marc. We've asked you here because it's possible you might be able to help us on a case we're working on at the moment. There's been a fatality, a sudden death – '

'Whose?' The cup clattered slightly as it was put back on to the saucer. Marc Daventry was pale, but he'd been pale when he came in, possibly it was a natural pallor.

'You're acquainted with a Miss Avril Kitchin, of Coltmore Road?'

'Yes. What's happened?'

'I have to tell you she's been murdered.'

Shock registered on his face – astonishment, shock, horror. None of which cut a lot of ice with Mayo, since it might or might not be genuine. They were all accustomed, at Milford Road, to dealing with suspects, guilty as hell, acting out the role of innocent or injured party. Some of them were good enough to apply for an Equity card.

'When?' Marc asked. 'When did it happen?'

'This morning. We think about eight o'clock.'

'I was at the hospital – I'm on standby and working a split shift this week.'

140

Mayo raised his eyebrows. 'Well now, Marc, I don't think we're as far down the road as all that. You're not under suspicion, as yet. We can leave the question of your movements until later, if indeed, we need to ask it.' He finished his tea, sat back and made himself comfortable. He was in no hurry. 'Do you always work shifts?'

'I enjoy it. Gives me free time during the day.'

Mayo nodded. 'Tell me how you came to know Miss Kitchin.'

After a moment's consideration, Marc said, 'She's – she was – a friend of my mother's.'

'What did you think of her?'

Again, he took his time, but his reply, when it came, was frank. 'I didn't like her much, but I didn't have to. I just kept out of her way as much as possible.'

'When was the last time you saw her?'

'Can't honestly remember – weeks ago, must be. My mother shared her flat for a while, but she's moved now. I haven't seen Avril since.'

'I see.' Mayo paused to replenish his cup and offer the pot to the others, which they declined, and to regard the young man thoughtfully. Deep, this one. Thought before he spoke. Weighed up the consequences. You'd never know when you had him, as they used to say, up where he was a lad. 'Well, you've been frank with me and I'll be frank with you – we know how and where your mother and Miss Kitchin met. We also know where your mother's spent the last years. What we don't know is what brought her back to Lavenstock – and that's where you come in.'

Marc stiffened and was immediately on the defensive. 'That really is sick! She has a record, therefore you assume she must be the one who killed Avril Kitchin! She couldn't kill anyone.'

That was an astonishing thing to say, with the thought of Charles Daventry hanging in the air between them. Perhaps he should have said, 'She couldn't kill anyone *now*.'

'Take it easy, lad. We're not in the business of assuming anything, but we're not just playing marbles, either. This happens to be a murder hunt, don't forget. We shall have to question everyone Miss Kitchin knew – and that, I'm afraid, includes your mother. Where does she live, Marc? How can we get hold of her?'

He seemed to be debating whether there was any point in refusing. Finally, reluctantly, he gave her address.

'Does she have a job?'

'At Catesby's. She's a waitress in the restaurant,' he added after another pause, as if the words stuck in his gullet. He saw Carmody writing this down. 'But it won't be any use you going to see her there.'

'Don't worry,' Carmody said, 'we'll be discreet.'

'It's not that, she won't be there. She's taken the day off – to attend to some private business.'

Mayo studied him for a moment. 'Are you telling us the truth?'

'Why should I lie?'

'Where's she gone?'

Marc shrugged. Mayo stared hard at him and eventually he muttered, 'If you must know, she's gone down to that convent where she used to live. She's worried about something – I don't know what – and she seemed to think they could help her.'

'What time did she leave?'

'She caught the early bus. She doesn't drive. I offered to take her, but she wanted to go alone.'

Mayo thought for a minute or two. 'All right, Marc, I think that wraps up that bit.'

'I can go?' His eyes flickered, he seemed momentarily disorientated. Maybe he hadn't expected to be let off so lightly, but he soon recovered and began to lever himself up, ready to go.

'Not yet.' Mayo waved him to stay where he was. 'There's something else I want to talk to you about.' And as Marc subsided, he said, 'You haven't asked how Miss Kitchin was murdered. Aren't you interested?'

'Not particularly, but I should imagine that someone bashed her over the head, or strangled her.'

After a long, considering look, Mayo spoke deliberately. 'No. She wasn't strangled, or hit on the head. She was stabbed, Marc. Stabbed with one of her own knitting needles.'

He made a choking sound, quickly turned into a cough. 'I'm sorry, but that's – well, if you'd known what she was like with that knitting! She never had it out of her hands, drove you round the bend, watching her.' The final irony of the murder weapon evidently afforded him some grim amusement.

It was not shared by Mayo. He let a few moments pass, then said abruptly, 'What's your interest in Flora Lilburne?'

Any amusement, if that was what it had been, faded from Marc's face. The atmosphere was suddenly charged. His facial muscles stiffened, and he appeared to find difficulty in answering.

'Fancy her, do you?'

He swallowed hard. 'If you must put it like that. I like her. I've asked her to go out with me.'

'I know you have, Marc, and she's refused. But you still go on pestering her.' Marc said nothing, still white round the mouth. 'Did you know her father – the Governor of Conyhall Young Offenders' Institution? The one who got blown up, you remember?'

'Of course I remember. That's how I got to meet Flora – she was injured in the same accident – '

'Accident? That's one way of looking at it. But what I asked you was, did you know the governor?'

'No, I didn't, I never clapped eyes on him. Why should I? And I don't see what all this has to do with Avril Kitchin's murder.'

'Neither do I, Marc. Not yet. But take my advice, lad. Keep away from Miss Lilburne, or you'll find yourself in trouble. She's said no and she means no. And so do we.'

A mixed-up lad, if ever there was one. Dangerously on the edge of obsession, and not only over his determined pursual of Flora Lilburne. Overprotective of his mother, perhaps with more reason than her unhappy past indicated. Why? Pondering on the situation, Mayo was becoming more and more certain that not only was Marie-Laure their prime suspect for the murder of Avril Kitchin, but that she was the key on which the Lilburne case turned. Questions abounded. Why had she come back to Lavenstock, the last place one would have thought she'd wish to return to? Why had she now fled back to what had for the last years been, as Mayo saw it, her self-imposed prison? Was it the need of confession, to absolve herself of guilt? To hide? he wondered, vaguely remembered history lessons of medieval fugitives in sanctuary crossing his mind. Or had she simply been pulling the wool over Marc's eyes, pretending she needed to seek advice from the Mother Superior at the convent, when really it was an attempt to cover up that she was running away, and had never had any intentions of going there?

No satisfactory answers had yet occurred to him when he and

Abigail drove down to the convent, to what he persisted in thinking of as the 'nunnery' – a large, secluded building on the outskirts of an affluent suburb near Stratford upon Avon, set back from the road, behind the reputedly expensive girls' school that was run by the nuns.

'Funny how-d'you-do, her living here all that time after she came out of prison,' he commented as they swept up the weed-less gravel drive, adding a few terse remarks as to what the parents of these privileged girls would have said had they known a convicted murderess had been teaching their daughters.

'Oh, I don't know. Wouldn't like to guess at the backgrounds of some of the teachers at my comprehensive!'

Mayo tut-tutted. 'So young, and yet so cynical! They couldn't have been so bad. They got you to university, didn't they?' It was against his principles to believe that what you were didn't matter, that it was possible to separate your public and private persona.

'I'd like to think I'd something to do with it, as well.'

'Ouch!' He grinned, and they left the car and walked towards the heavy front door. He wasn't precisely sure what he was hoping to gain from this visit – except that Marie-Laure was a woman at the centre of two murders, perhaps three, and that even if he wasn't able to see her in person, here in the convent was at least one woman who might provide answers to some of his questions, if she so chose.

She faced them, the Reverend Mother Emmanuel, across a highly polished table in a prim, chilly parlour, a pink chrysanthemum in an ugly majolica-type cache-pot dead centre of the table. He'd half expected to see a woman in a great starched headdress and a long black habit, but she wore a sober, calf-length dress in dark blue, a simple veil and wimple, and a rosary at her breast. She had steady blue eyes in an austere face that might have been carved from wax. Her speech was clearly modulated, classless but pedantic. She looked about sixty, but her life might equally have added to, or taken years from, her real age.

It was barely three months since Marie-Laure had left the convent, she told them, after listening attentively to Abigail's brief explanation of why they were here. Then Abigail sat back, her role from now on merely to observe, but the Mother Superior was reluctant to discuss either Marie-Laure's reasons for leaving the convent or choosing to live within it in the first place, except to say that she had known of their community through retreats she'd regularly attended before the tragedy which had befallen her, that it had been a refuge to which she'd turned when leaving prison. 'Suffice it to say that when she returned here she helped to teach French – and science, her own subject – to the younger girls, until she found courage to face the world again.'

'Did she tell you why she'd decided to go back to Lavenstock?'

'She did.'

Mayo waited, and so did she. He was no novice at this sort of game, but he spoke again before the silence became too long, fully aware that in a contest to see who would first break it, he stood no chance.

'Were they reasons of which you could approve?'

She's got me at it now, talking like a flipping English grammar! he thought, avoiding Abigail's eye.

The Mother Superior's level glance rested momentarily somewhere above his eyebrows, and then she sighed. 'I see no reason why you shouldn't know, since her motives for returning were entirely laudable. She heard that the people who had adopted her son had died tragically, and she thought he might be in need of her . . . she began to feel she had been wrong to have severed all connections with him.'

Mayo studied the serene face. 'And now? I was told she'd come down here to see you today. If she's still here, may I see her?'

The silence of the house was profound. Thirty women lived here, occupied in the tasks of maintaining themselves and keeping the house immaculate, teaching in the school which accommodated a hundred girls, but not a whisper, not a footfall, not the slightest sound of a closing door could be heard. After a while, the nun opposite, sitting rigidly erect, without touching the chairback, raised her eyes from her clasped hands. 'I'm afraid I could not allow that.'

But she *was* here. He said gently, 'You could be putting yourself in an awkward position. Wasting police time, failure to cooperate might be the least of it.'

Her eyes were lowered over her clasped hands. After a moment she raised them once more to the level of his forehead. 'She came here because she was in need of spiritual guidance. She is free to stay, or to go whenever she feels so inclined, but I will not force her, nor be a party to anyone else doing so, nor will I allow you to question her.'

It seemed they'd reached deadlock. Was there really nothing he could do? he asked himself, never having had to face such a dilemma before. No, nothing short of obtaining a warrant to search the convent, dragging out the suspect, questioning the Reverend Mother's integrity . . . he quailed before the very thought of any such action, not knowing which alternative would be worse. What he wanted to ask was whether she thought Marie-Laure capable of committing a second murder, but the question froze on his lips. He would in any case receive no direct answer, he knew. So he phrased it rather differently, asking carefully, feeling as though he were walking on eggshells that he mustn't break. 'Would you act otherwise if I told you we've reason to believe she's deeply involved in this second murder?' There he went again.

She'd provided the weakest coffee he'd ever tasted, and fig-roll biscuits. He manfully drained his cup but abandoned the biscuit, which was sticking to his teeth, mentally awarded Abigail several brownie points when he saw she'd finished hers, wondering whether the nuns were forced to eat them as penance.

'If that question were a matter of academic debate, I would enjoy taking you up on it,' the Mother Superior said at last, and Mayo had no difficulty in believing that she would, noticing the spark of animation which flashed across her face as she spoke, making him wonder what she had been 'in the world'. 'But as I presume it is not . . .'

He sighed. 'As it isn't, you won't.'

'As things stand, I need to consider it. And to pray, Superintendent,' she said simply.

'And there's no answer to that,' Mayo remarked gloomily to Abigail, as they drove back.

18

Flora Lilburne was painting her face, always a serious undertaking. And thinking deeply while she did it, which was not as painful for her as some would have liked to make out.

Contrary to the impression given by the way she dressed, her light-hearted approach to life and the sexy figure with which Nature had endowed her, Flora wasn't the shallow, air-headed bimbo she seemed to be. She was quite aware that was what people thought and it gave her a flick of amusement . . . She was never going to qualify for *Brain of Britain*, right, but she had more sense than she was given credit for. And more discrimination – Anthony, for instance, was the only man she'd ever slept with, and that only after she was as sure as she could be that they were right for each other.

She blotted her Red Forever lips, added a touch of gloss, picked up a thick, soft brush and lightly stroked amethyst shadows above her right brow. Catching sight of the silver-framed photo of her father on her dressing table, for a moment her lips quivered. But she breathed deeply and the dangerous moment passed.

Her dearest da had wanted nothing more for her than to be happy – how often had he told her this? So, happy she'd be. Never mind the hurt that she had to push away, bury deep, deep down, the tears that sometimes, alone or with Anthony, soaked her pillow. As for the bad dreams – well, they couldn't last for ever. And after the initial, debilitating shock of the tragedy, she'd found a new energy in herself, as if the trauma of losing Da, not to mention her own near approach to extinction, had made her see how precious life was, made her feel there wasn't a moment to waste.

And that was just what she was doing, she told herself – wasting too much of it lately on thinking what to do about

Marc Daventry. The thought was sobering.

She brushed the left brow to match the right and, satisfied with the result, stood up, smoothed her frock down over her hips and stood by the window, looking out over the garden. She knew she ought to do something about the Marc situation – and do it herself. She couldn't expect her mother to cope with it and it was no use hoping that Anthony would dash along on a white charger, ready to slay dragons. He'd be perfectly willing to have a go at slaying dragons or anything else for her – darling Anthony – but he'd probably steer his horse in the wrong direction and forget his sword.

She'd have done something already if only she knew what. If she'd had any sense, she wouldn't have encouraged Marc in the first place, though she'd only thought she was being nice to him when he kept popping into her room at the hospital to see how she was. At first, she'd shrugged it off, thinking he'd soon get over it. But he was refusing to take no for an answer . . . flowers, chocolates, telephone calls . . . trying to make out she wouldn't go out with him because he wasn't good enough for her, not in the right social class and all that load of rubbish. As if she cared about that! Of course, you couldn't convince someone properly over the telephone that you wanted nothing to do with them, especially someone who doesn't want to be convinced. That was probably what had made him come to the house last night, to try and talk to her in person, only she hadn't been there. Her mother had, and it had really upset her for some reason, far more than Flora would have imagined. Little things do assume big proportions, though, when you're distracted and unhappy . . . and Dorothea had looked awful for some time. Flora worried a good deal about her mother. There was a lot of love between them, if not always expressed.

She'd never before been in this sort of situation. She was beginning to feel a bit – well, uneasy. Nothing more than that, she told herself. It was just an unpleasantness she'd have no trouble in dealing with, once she decided how. But, looking out across the flowering shrubs and the wide green lawns, she shivered.

It was just that he seemed, in some odd way, to be always there, on the edges of her mind. Sometimes, she even dreamed about him, and the way he looked, with those deep, dark eyes that seemed to be trying to compel her to do something she didn't want to do. And it was silly, really, but occasionally, she'd look round and almost imagine him there. Once, she'd been certain she'd seen him in the distance, but she decided it was only the reflection of someone looking in a shop window.

It had seemed a waste of time, after their interview with the Reverend Mother, even to call at the address Marc Daventry had given as his mother's, but Mayo sent someone round to check, all the same, with the expected result. No one answered the door, there were no lights in the upstairs flat. The tenants in the rooms below, a young couple with a baby, had heard no sound from above.

'And believe me, we would have if she'd been there,' the young woman said. 'She's very quiet, specially after the last lot who had the flat – he was a drummer with Serpent's Tongue – but you could hear a mouse sneeze in this place.'

The telephone call Abigail made the next morning brought a better response. A few questions to Catesby's personnel department had elicited the fact that one of their employees, a waitress in the restaurant, was French. Her name was given as Mrs Nicoud, but it seemed certain to Abigail she must be Marie-Laure Daventry.

'I'm on my way,' she informed Mayo, popping her head round his door, 'before she has the opportunity to change her mind and disappear again. She must have arrived home at the flat last night after we called. Unless she spent the night at the convent and went straight to Catesby's from there. At any rate, she's gone in to work this morning.'

'Has she, by Jove? I'd like to think that shows she's nothing to hide, but I'm more inclined to believe it's the influence of the Mother Superior. Extraordinary.'

Abigail smiled to herself, noting how much the Reverend Mother Emmanuel had impressed Mayo, despite the grumbles which had accompanied them all the way home at the way he considered she'd outsmarted him.

The personnel officer at Catesby's was a Mrs Patterson, who had no option but to agree, in the face of Abigail's warrant card, to fetch 'Mrs Nicoud' from her duties, though it was with some reluctance and suspicion that she did so.

'What's going on? She was very late this morning, as it is, and this is our busiest time, you know.'

'I know, and I'm sorry, but it's either that, or we take her down to the police station.' Abigail was adamant, knowing it was certain to be both.

Curiosity unsatisfied, a little piqued, Mrs Patterson disappeared, leaving Abigail and Jenny Platt in her office, a blandly pleasant, neutral sort of room with a group of chairs set around a small table in front of a big window. Green-carpeted. Chairs covered in grey, royal blue and kelly green. Catesby's colours. The room was at the end of a corridor, removed from the bustle of the main offices, and was very quiet. Presently, the personnel officer returned, accompanied by a slight woman with dark hair and brown eyes, a sallow complexion. It was easy to see Marc Daventry's resemblance to his mother.

'Please sit down, Mrs Nicoud. Thank you, Mrs Patterson.'

'I'll leave you to it, then.' Dismissed, the personnel officer shut the door with a precision just short of a bang.

'Mrs Nicoud – '

She came forward hesitantly and took the seat which Jenny pulled out, offering a wary smile.

Breaking bad news was something Abigail was used to but hadn't yet learned to do dispassionately, especially when it was news of a death; even more so when that death had been a violent one, and the recipient of the news was someone close to the victim. It was all too easy to empathize with the distress of the other person, difficult to find the right words of condolence, while at the same time keeping a sharp eye out for the sort of reaction the news produced. In this case, a sudden, draining pallor, a loss of focus in the dark eyes.

'Put your head down between your knees,' she ordered, rushing to the chair where the other woman sat and pushing her head down in case she might be going to faint, while Jenny, who had noticed a drinks dispensing machine in the corridor outside, nipped out of the door. But almost immediately Marie-Laure sat up. Her lips moved, she crossed herself, and for several moments her eyes stayed lowered, her hand on the ivory crucifix which hung on a chain at the neckline of her overall. She was either a very good actress, or genuinely shocked. Or could the reaction simply be panic on hearing that the body had now been found?

By then, Jenny was back with a paper cup of scalding liquid. 'Drink this and you'll feel better. Sorry it's not water, tea was all I could find.'

Marie-Laure obediently took the steaming tea, so hot she was able to sip only a tiny amount. 'Avril?' she murmured.

'I'm afraid so, Mrs Nicoud,' Abigail said. 'I'm sorry, I know she was a friend of yours – I understand you lived together for some time.' On the face of it, two very ill-assorted women, but Abigail had seen odder associations.

'I stayed with her until I found a place of my own. Hers was very small – only big enough for one ... I don't understand, there was nothing to steal ... she had little enough, God knows.' She spoke with barely a trace of an accent. She was fine-boned and good-looking, with slender legs and neatly groomed hair. Out of the depersonalizing candy-striped green uniform she was probably a very elegant woman. The degradations of prison had left no obvious, coarsening mark. 'Why?' she repeated.

'Her purse is missing, possibly credit cards and cheque book.'

'She did not have credit cards. Did someone break in, then?'

'It would appear not. She may have *let* someone in, someone she knew.'

There was a silence.

'Did you know any of her acquaintants? Or anyone who might want to harm her? Someone she'd got across with at some time? Someone she knew before she went into prison?'

Slowly, the other woman met Abigail's gaze. 'If you know that,' she stated flatly, 'then you must know about me, too.'

'Yes. We know she was in Gormleigh, and that was where you met and became friends.' Abigail watched her carefully. 'You changed your name when you came out of prison, Mrs Nicoud, so obviously you want to make a new life. Didn't it occur to you that in keeping up with her, once outside, you might be in very suspect company?'

That, at least, provoked a reaction. 'Avril was going straight! She had cut herself free from all that. She was very good to me. She gave me somewhere to stay when I needed it.'

'Why did you need it?' The Reverend Mother had said she had returned here to find her son but that wasn't necessarily the whole truth. 'Tell me why you came back to Lavenstock? It can't have many happy memories for you.'

151

'That is my business. You have no control over me now, or what I do.'

'You're wrong there. We're investigating a murder, which is very much our business. If you've any sense you'll help us to eliminate you from the inquiry.'

'But I had nothing to do with it,' she said stonily. 'And I have nothing more to say.'

Abigail sighed. 'All right. I think it's better we continue this interview down at the station.'

19

'Lavenstock Divisional Police.'

'My name is Lilburne – Dorothea Lilburne. I should like to speak to the officer in charge of the bombing at Conyhall – Mr Mayo, I believe.'

'I'm sorry, Superintendent Mayo's not available at the moment, ma'am. Can I put you through to someone else?'

'No. I've something very important to say to him personally about my husband's murder. I don't have a car at the moment so if he'd be so good as to come here . . . but tell him, not before ten, please.'

Dorothea Lilburne couldn't have known when she rang the police station that her request to see Mayo had pre-empted an earlier decision of his to see her again on that same day. He'd already made up his mind that she'd been left simmering on the back burner for long enough, and he congratulated himself on the strategy that had prompted him to leave her there in the first place. She had, as he'd known she would, finally seen the sense in telling what she knew. He felt momentarily annoyed at her peremptory summons, the assumption that he could leave everything at the drop of a hat, but standing on his dignity wasn't going to get him anywhere. It was a token grumble anyway. It was *his* problem, trying to squeeze a gallon into a pint pot, if that was how fitting his new duties and responsibilities in with the urgent priorities of an important case could be described. That was how it felt, for sure, though it was a challenge that had the merits of keeping the adrenaline flowing.

In any case, though Dorothea's summons might have sounded like a royal command, he sensed an urgency in it that he couldn't ignore.

Abigail he needed with him, he decided, remembering the

affinity between the two women the last time they had talked. Marie-Laure Daventry, who had just been brought in, would have to be left in Jenny Platt's hands until his return.

Abigail drove to Conyhall in the silence she knew Mayo preferred, smoothly and expertly, leaving him to his own thoughts. Mid-morning now, and the countryside, in the grip of this unexpectedly hard overnight frost, was only just beginning to warm up. The road, where the traffic had melted the rime, was a black ribbon between the stiff white grass verges. A pale sun shone and the trees and hedgerows glittered. The beauty of the day brought a catch to your throat. A day to be working outdoors in the garden, with the sun warming your face, exercise sending the blood coursing through your body. Not to be thinking about Jack Lilburne and Avril Kitchin, dead and cold and never to feel the sun again. Despite herself, Abigail shivered a little.

Mayo gave her a sharp glance, then sat up and began to take notice as she made the right turn, a few hundred yards along the main road past the entrance to the Young Offenders' Unit, down the lane which led to the governor's house.

A pretty lane, with fields and high skeletal hedges either side, where cow parsley blossomed in summer, its dead umbels frosted now like Christmas-tree decorations. A gate, halfway along, where the car had stood that morning when the bomb went off. Mayo rubbed at the frown between his eyes. What the blazes was it that was niggling him, every time he thought about the milkman seeing that car parked there? That seemed to connect it with the Coltmore Road murder? And then he had it. The answer to why the two murders had been committed at roughly the same time of day. Because they could *only* be committed then. But the question of why they'd been committed at all was something else. During the next hundred yards it took to reach the house, he'd taken several further imaginative strides, all of them, unfortunately, seeming to take him in every direction but the one which must be right. He abandoned supposition as they swept into the gravelled drive of the house. There weren't enough facts as yet to support fancy theories, and guessing games weren't exactly his line of country.

It was a pleasant entrance, a hint of money and prosperity – an impression immediately banished when they rounded a curve and came upon the house itself, and saw the scaffolding still netting the front, the polythene sheeting hanging pallidly from it, half obscuring the ruined, collapsed barn. A constructivist stage set, almost a metaphor for the wanton destruction of life.

Mrs Lilburne opened the door immediately, as quickly as if she'd been waiting behind it. 'Thank you for coming, for waiting until now. Flora left about ten minutes ago. I didn't want her to see you here.'

Mayo exchanged a mystified glance with Abigail, but neither of them commented or showed surprise. He wondered if she was as shocked at the change in Dorothea Lilburne as he was. Anyone else, and he would have said she was falling apart. Something had surely happened to upset her, but why did Flora have to be kept out of it? He wouldn't jump the gun by asking. Best to let things take their course, see what would happen — find out what *had* happened . . .

She opened the door into the same room as before, where they were greeted with noisy enthusiasm by the two spaniels, destined for ever, it seemed, poor beasts, to be turfed out. When they had shambled out, Abigail, invited to sit down and observing dog hairs on the chair near the warm fire, chose another, less obviously comfortable one, but one which had compensations, a better view of the garden, affording a glimpse of the little lake and the old summerhouse perched on the raised bank above it. Bowered in frost-limned shrubs and trees, some hardy shrubs in flower, the bulbs adding their own grace notes, the sun sparkling over all, it was a charming sight – the curtain risen on another stage set, for a play by Barrie rather than Brecht.

Mayo sat himself in the same comfortable chair which he'd occupied before, looking searchingly at the woman opposite while being careful not to show that he was aware of her ravaged face. However little he knew about the opposite sex, he'd learned enough to be sure that no woman likes to see in other faces what her mirror has already told her is not good. The set expression of dogged determination, the early telephone call told its own tale: she'd spent sleepless nights, wrestling with her conscience, and had come to an unpalatable decision. Though he was impatient to know what it was she had to tell them, he forced himself to let her take her time.

All the same, for the sake of his schedule, he was glad it took her no more than a few minutes to pull herself together. Coffee was ready, she said, if they should want it. Abigail offered to pour, and Mrs Lilburne was beginning, before the cups were half filled, on what was evidently a prepared speech:

'Something's happened which I feel you should know about. It may – it may well have some bearing on who killed my husband.'

She accepted a cup of coffee from Abigail and stopped to put it down on the small table at her side. A log fell with a shower of sparks into the rosy ash beneath it. A vehicle was heard to draw up outside, and someone walked over the gravel, the dogs as usual making their presence felt as the post slithered through the letter box into the hall. The mail van drew away, leaving a silence behind. The thread of Mrs Lilburne's narrative had been interrupted. He willed her for God's sake to get it grafted together again quickly, but in the event she scarcely paused, obviously wanting to get it over and done with.

'A young man came to the house yesterday looking for Flora,' she began again, looking at the carpet as she spoke, and so missed the quick glance which passed between Abigail and Mayo. 'She wasn't in, so I spoke to him myself. It seems that he works at the County Hospital, where Flora was looked after. He met her there – and apparently he'd been pestering her ever since to go out with him, despite the fact that she'd told him she doesn't want to see him again, that she's engaged to be married. I wasn't aware that this was happening . . . I'd never met the young man before . . . but, I immediately recognized him. Even before he gave his name . . .'

'You recognized him?'

Her large, pale hands, bare but for her wedding band, were clasped so tightly together that the knuckles were white. Her feet, similarly long and elegant, were pressed closely together. 'He's the image of his mother – his mother as she used to be, as I remember her.'

'Who was this, Mrs Lilburne?'

She stirred her coffee but made no move to drink it. 'Her name was Daventry – Marie-Laure Daventry. He was her son, Marc.'

She looked directly at Mayo, evidently expecting to read recognition in his face, but he gave no sign that the name meant anything to him.

'Don't you recall the Daventry case, sixteen years ago?' she asked. 'The Frenchwoman who killed her husband with a carving knife?'

'I know which one you're talking about.'

He'd been sure, from the beginning, with that copper's instinct for spotting evasions, that Dorothea Lilburne had known, or suspected, more about her husband's murder than she'd been prepared to say, but there'd been no way of forcing her to tell what she knew; it had taken the shock of finding Marc Daventry on her doorstep to make her admit at last what he devoutly hoped would now be the truth. It was taking an unconscionable time to get at it.

'Mrs Lilburne, let's get this straight. You say you believe this old tragedy has something to do with your husband's death. You must have your reasons for saying that. Tell me what your connections with Charles Daventry and his wife were?'

'They were simply acquaintances, nothing more, as far as I was concerned. I scarcely knew them. It was Jack who had the connections. With her, at least – with Mrs Daventry.' Her eyes, as she spoke, were on Abigail, not him. He nodded, willing enough to let Abigail take it, if Dorothea felt happier responding to her. 'You understand what I'm saying?'

'They were having an affair?' Abigail's voice was gentle.

Dorothea gave a dry little cough that was probably meant to mean yes, reached out and sipped the now cold coffee, grimaced and put it down with distaste. Waved away Abigail's offer to pour fresh and sat rigidly upright. It was hard for her to admit betrayal, but she was going to do it courageously, with as little loss of face as possible.

Mrs Lilburne's secret wasn't the astonishing revelation to them, by now, that she must have thought it would be, after having stayed undisclosed all these years. But how had Lilburne, Mayo wondered, not always as circumspect about his affairs as he might have been, managed to keep his liaison with Daventry's wife from emerging at her trial? By virtue of the others, possibly – in that it had been thought just another affair when they'd been seen together, with nobody curious enough to wonder who she was. Yet Dorothea had known . . .

'It wasn't something that came out during the inquiry, Mrs Lilburne,' he remarked.

'No, I'll give her that. She had the sense to keep quiet about it – but there was no reason why she *should* implicate him, was there? After all, she was the one who'd killed her husband. Jack had nothing to do with it.'

157

Abigail said bluntly, 'This young man you say has been pestering your daughter – this Marc Daventry – do you have any reason to believe he's your husband's child?'

'*What*? Oh, heavens, no, there's no question of that! The child was two or three years old when they came to live in the district – before she and Jack ever knew one another.'

'Then what makes you think he could have anything to do with your husband's murder? If he's implicated in any way, wouldn't he be likely to keep away from your daughter?'

'I'd have thought so, yes, that's what I can't understand, but he struck me as being a very strange young man – oh, he was polite enough, but there was something – well, not quite right about him. One never knows what that sort will do.'

'Even to planting a bomb? Thinking your husband morally, if not actually, responsible for his father's murder? Is that what you're saying?'

Dorothea looked thoughtful. 'You could be right. No, I hadn't thought of that.'

Not true, Mayo thought. She'd worked that one out, all right, but she hadn't wanted the suggestion to come from her.

'I could be overreacting,' she admitted, 'though I'm not easily alarmed, and there was something about him that made me nervous.'

'Mrs Lilburne, where was your husband the night Charles Daventry was killed?' Mayo asked suddenly.

She stiffened. 'He was here, with me, all night.'

'All night? No emergency at the Young Offenders' Institution, or anything like that?'

'Nothing like that,' she said, looking him straight in the eye.

He sighed gently.

'Are you suggesting, Mr Mayo, that *he* murdered Charles Daventry? That's preposterous! Jack, sticking a knife into someone? Never! He was *for* life, not against it – no one more so.'

She surprised him, then. After taking a deep breath, she said in a rush, 'If anyone was to blame, I was.'

No one spoke. She looked frightened. A plane droned across the sky. He wondered if she'd meant to say that, and then realized this was why she'd sent for him, why she'd wanted Flora out of the way. But –

'Well, there you are,' she said in a tired voice.

'That's not all, though, is it?'

After a moment, she shook her head. 'No. She killed her husband, of course. But not simply because of a quarrel over money. Whatever her reasons were for saying that, I've no idea, but it wasn't true. She killed Charles Daventry because he found out about her affair with Jack.'

'How can you know that?' Abigail asked.

'For the best reason I can think of. I told him myself.'

Her back stiff, she looked at nobody as she added, 'I cannot imagine now what made me do something so – so vulgar. Jack had had affairs before, but none that lasted. I'd valued my marriage enough to ignore them. But this was different . . . it had gone on too long, it had to be stopped before it got too serious.'

'How did you find out?'

'What? Oh, one knows. We'd met them socially, and when I saw them together . . . a woman knows these things . . .' Doubtless that was partly true, Mayo thought, if her suspicions had been alerted in the first place, but it was too simplistic to be wholly convincing. In the circumstances, he decided to let it pass, until the next time he questioned her. It wasn't the only thing she'd been lying about.

So this was Marie-Laure, the woman who had killed her husband, sitting on the other side of the interview room. There could hardly have been a greater contrast with Dorothea Lilburne, the woman he'd just left.

Dark, slender; brown eyes in a pale face, a wide Gallic mouth. Not the face or demeanour of a murderess, but if criminals wore their guilt or their malevolence on their features, he and a lot more people would pretty soon be out of a job. She had, apparently, been very upset when told the news of Avril Kitchin's death – though she'd reportedly shed no tears – but she'd seemingly recovered and now appeared self-controlled and determined to say as little as possible.

Prison had taught her when to be silent, when words might incriminate. Living in the convent, where unnecessary speech would no doubt be discouraged, had possibly, though in a different way, reinforced this lesson. But while silence in a nun might be admirable, the refusal of the woman in front of him to communicate in anything more than a few words was irritating.

'Mrs Nicoud – do you prefer to be known as that, or Mrs Daventry?'

159

'Daventry is still my legal name.'

'Mrs Daventry, then. When did you last see Miss Kitchin?'

'When I moved out, and into my own flat, about three weeks ago.'

'Three weeks? That's a long time, to say you'd previously been living together.' She shrugged. 'Did you by any chance have a disagreement – was that why you left? Failing, incidentally, to report your new address? You're in trouble there, you know that?'

'It didn't occur to me. Perhaps I forgot. I was very preoccupied. It was always understood I would leave, as soon as I found somewhere of my own. Her place was too small for two people to live comfortably.'

'Didn't she help you to move in?' Abigail asked. 'Or even come to see your new flat, to see how you were settled?'

'She would have done, in time.'

He let her take a drink of water. 'What brought her to live in Lavenstock after she was released? She wasn't from these parts.'

'She knew I would return here, eventually. We were friends. She didn't have many.'

'You didn't appear to have much in common, if I may say so.'

'She was a strong woman – she helped me to survive in prison – she gave me confidence.'

He was wondering what made her think she lacked confidence, for he certainly didn't think so, unless they had different perceptions of the meaning of the word, when Abigail asked, suddenly, 'Do you still have the set of keys to her flat she gave you when you lived with her?'

'Keys?' She looked blank. 'Oh, yes, as a matter of fact, I have.'

Abigail held her hand out and after a moment when it looked as though she might be about to refuse, Marie-Laure produced from her handbag two Yale-type keys on a ring with an enamel tag. 'I had forgotten about them.' She surrendered them reluctantly, watching warily as they were slipped into a plastic bag and tagged.

'Why did you go to the convent yesterday?' Mayo asked abruptly.

She studied the lion and the unicorn stamped on the copy of PACE which hung on the wall, as if every detail had to be committed to memory. 'I had something personal I wished to discuss with the Reverend Mother.'

160

'As personal as confessing to her that you'd killed Avril Kitchin?'

'I have told you, I had nothing to do with Avril's death.' Her words were low and dispassionate, there was still nothing in her manner to show that she was upset, or grieved for her friend. Which didn't mean that she didn't feel anything, of course, only that she held her emotions on a very tight rein indeed.

He asked her the same question he'd asked her son, interested to see whether her reaction would be the same as his. 'You haven't asked how she was killed.'

'If you want me to know, no doubt you will tell me.'

'Perhaps you already know that she was stabbed with a knitting needle. Pierced through the heart with it.'

The announcement provoked no other reaction than a slight flicker in her eyes, a tightening of her mouth. 'I did not know.'

'All right.' Mayo leaned back in his chair. 'Never mind that, for the moment. Let's talk about something else. You must have heard about the bomb at the Conyhall Young Offenders' Institution, and Mr Jack Lilburne, who was killed?'

'I read about it in the newspaper, yes.'

'Did you have any hand in that killing?'

She stared at him. 'I did not.'

'Do you know who did?'

He hadn't expected an affirmative, though it was a valid question. Both women had been inside for a long time – they could have made contacts, they knew the score. And he'd sensed fear, smelled it, when Lilburne's name was mentioned . . .

This time, he'd at least provoked a reaction. 'You insult me,' she said. 'I committed a grave sin once. Am I to be under suspicion for the rest of my life, for every murder that is committed in this town?'

'But you were acquainted with Mr Lilburne, weren't you, before you went into prison?'

The tape machine whirred. She was so long answering he thought she was again taking refuge in silence.

'Come on, now, we know you were. That he was meeting you on a regular basis, that he stayed with someone on several occasions at the Gravely Arms near Chipping Campden, and we have witnesses who can prove it was you. We also believe you recently wrote him a letter, suggesting a meeting. Can you confirm this?'

She still didn't reply.

'Mrs Daventry,' he reminded her, 'we can if necessary compare the handwriting on that letter with yours. Did you write to him because you wished to resume your relationship with him?'

'No. Not at all. You're quite wrong!' She stared down at her hands, clasped together on her lap, then raised her eyes to his face, eyes that were clear and luminous. 'Very well. I did write to him, but not for those reasons. When I went to prison, he made arrangements for my son to be adopted, and during this time – and afterwards – he kept me informed of Marc's progress . . .'

'Why? Why did he agree to do all this?' When she merely shrugged, he went on, 'I suggest it was in return for keeping his name out of it. For not revealing at the trial the real reason you and your husband quarrelled?'

He thought she was going to deny it, then she sighed. 'Charles had found out about us, I don't know how – he was threatening divorce, to take the child from me, to make a scandal for Jack . . . in the end, it was too much . . . I was telling nothing but the truth at my trial when I said my life with my husband had been a misery. I killed him, I have never denied it. But nothing would have been gained if I had made my affair with Jack public.'

Naming him at the original inquiry wouldn't have saved her, that was true. Might have put her in a worse light, and would have ruined more lives, Dorothea's and Flora's, not to mention blighting Lilburne's career. On the other hand, she might have received more sympathy from the jury than simply knifing her husband in cold blood had earned her. He watched her hand tighten round the little ivory crucifix. Could they believe her? She was a clever woman, she could be a very convincing liar. He could, very easily indeed, imagine her wielding a knife – or a knitting needle – and killing someone. Yet . . .

Dorothea Lilburne, he was sure, had lied about her husband being at home on the night of the murder.

He was familiar with all the vagaries of human nature but he'd never yet met anyone willingly prepared to serve a life sentence for something they hadn't done. So what kind of a woman would admit to a murder she hadn't committed? What kind of man would *let* her do that for him?

And what kind of son would not want revenge if he saw Lilburne getting off scot-free, while his mother spent the best years of her life incarcerated for something she was, putting the very best construction on it, only partly to blame for?

'Please go on, Mrs Daventry.'

'When he wrote and told me that the couple who had taken Marc had been killed in an accident, I thought – I *knew* – it was my duty to contact my son and see if I could help. I wrote to Jack, suggesting we should meet to discuss it, but he did not think it wise that my son and I should be reunited, and he refused to help me.'

'What reason did he give for this?'

'He would not explain. But his help was not necessary. In the end, it was Marc who found me.'

'How did he manage to do that?'

'By chance.' She told him how they had met, through Marc's encounter with Avril Kitchin at the place where she had worked.

He looked steadily at her when she had finished, knowing that this was the core of it, where it all began. They were a close pair, she and her son, and they both knew the truth of this whole business, even if they weren't telling it. He sensed some sort of complicity, though in a way which bothered him, and for some reason he couldn't define.

She said, 'I wish to go now. You have no reason for keeping me here.'

She was right. He'd no cause to hold her at the moment. He said, 'You can go presently, as long as you don't disappear again, Mrs Daventry. We shall need to see you again. But first, I want you to tell me more about your son – how much he knew of the circumstances in which your husband was killed.'

'He knew nothing until after his adoptive parents were killed, when he found the papers relating to the trial.'

'Nothing more than that?'

'There was no more to know,' she answered, looking at him steadily.

'These adoptive parents. What was their name?' he asked. He thought, Don't tell me, let me guess.

*   *   *

163

They showed Dex Davis a photograph, an identity photo taken by the hospital as part of their new safety measure campaign. 'That's him,' Davis, now back in Conyhall on remand, said triumphantly. 'That's John Clarke. Now will you believe me?'

20

The church of Our Lady of the Assumption was an unappealing Victorian edifice of soot-blackened bricks, with a tall steeple, its steps opening straight off the street. Marc waited across the road, loitering in a shop doorway until the priest had left the presbytery, watching him until he'd crossed to the church and entered by a side door. He waited another ten minutes before following him into the unfamiliar church.

He slipped in silently and stood in the flickering dimness near the stand of votive candles at the back, blinking slightly as he searched for her in the shadowed nave where she knelt alone, a solitary figure at the end of a pew, her head bent, kneeling upright, unsupported. A posture she could keep up without any seeming effort. You'd have thought she'd have had enough religion by now. But he'd known she'd come straight here after being questioned by the police: the woman at Catesby's, when he'd rung to speak to her, had told him disapprovingly where she was. He was impatient, but controlled it – if she'd already made her confession, it couldn't be long before she was ready to leave.

It wasn't a prepossessing church. Apart from a Burne-Jones stained-glass window, it had little of either architectural or ecclesiastical merit. Nor did it seem to be particularly well-cared for: there was a mingled odour of dust, damp, incense and burning wax tapers that was not wholly pleasant, but the riot of pre-Raphaelite yellows and browns from the window bathed the altar in a dappled glow which even now, when the light was beginning to fade, and the body of the church was dark, gave a spurious illusion of sunlight flooding into the interior.

Not yet ready for what he knew he must do, reluctant to approach the kneeling figure, Marc let his gaze rest on the source of the golden light, and a recollection, sharp and clear in

165

its totality, came to him, of a bright morning long ago. A warm, early summer's morning and himself a child, running down the narrow, high-walled passageway that was a short cut from the High Street to the playground where the swings were. He'd run ahead of the other two, rejoicing in the freedom of wearing shorts for the first time that year, feeling the sun on his face and the air against his legs, wanting to skip, jump, climb trees, run . . .

She'd appeared before him like some great black bat, her arms outstretched to catch him, blocking his way, cackling, her face contorted with crazy laughter: the madwoman who walked about the town, strangely dressed in voluminous garments, talking to herself, waving her umbrella. The old woman they called Mad Motty, the one all his class at school jeered and laughed at – though from the safety of the other side of the street. He'd screamed in terror, and run. But the stony alleyway was slippery, his rubber soles had skidded on the loose, flinty pebbles and he'd fallen, bloodied his knee and cracked his forehead painfully. For a moment he lay, winded, on the upward slope of the path, then he began to roar, never mind that he was seven and big men didn't cry. And in a moment his mother's arms were round him, his head was pillowed against her soft bosom, shutting out the horrible sight, he was safe, nothing could hurt him any more.

'It's all right, lovey, it's all right, she doesn't mean any harm.'

To the deranged old woman, uncomprehending of why the child had been so afraid of her, when all she'd wanted was to scoop him up and cuddle him, and who was now trying to pat him and wanting to kiss him better, his mother said kindly, 'Leave him, Miss Mott, leave him to me, he'll be all right. You be on your way, now.'

The madwoman finally went, and June mopped him up and tied a handkerchief round his knee, and his father hoisted the wounded soldier on to his shoulders, the bright morning came back and terror receded, to be forgotten altogether until now.

June. His mother. His *mother*.

The pain he'd never felt when she'd died, when Frank had died, pain obscured by anger, now ripped through him like a knife, so that he swayed and had to hold on to the back of the pew in front of him. The dizzying revelation of what he'd tried not to acknowledge over the last few weeks came to him in full

166

– that the dark figure kneeling in the pew in front was as unreal as the figure of the Madonna in the niche by the altar. She'd given him birth, she'd passed on physical characteristics – but nothing more, except that one thing, so monstrous that his mind blotted it out.

His mother, in everything that mattered, had been June. His father had been, not the unknown Charles Daventry, but Frank.

Simple, uncomplicated, kindly people. Unimaginative, but well meaning. Too late, he felt regret – for not appreciating the love and happiness of their home, the kindness, the careful nurturing, everything that he'd taken for granted as a child – for things he'd sometimes despised them for, as a self-centred teenager. Their only failure had been, not a deliberate attempt to keep him ignorant of the true facts of his birth, but an inability to know how to tell him what a fearful heritage was his, a lack of the necessary insight. It was true, he knew, that he'd been a difficult child to communicate with. He wasn't like them. A cuckoo in the nest. Perhaps they'd been a little afraid of him.

And he'd been seduced by an idea, a mistaken concept of what his true mother was, by a romantic myth of suffering and martyrdom. He saw now how wrong he'd been, how bitterly he'd been let down. She'd never really wanted him, not after she'd given him away. The years between had made her into someone who had no need of, or no wish for, personal relationships. Duty had made her acknowledge him, but they could never have anything truly meaningful to say to each other. After all he'd done for her, she was too occupied with the dark, inimitable forces within her.

It was that part of his genetic inheritance which he didn't want to think about, not now, not ever again.

He'd come to the church before leaving, intending to ask her to walk in the park near the river with him, thinking he might find it easier there, in the dark, with the distant sound of traffic and the rush of the weir nearby, to say so many of the things he had to say, all of which he now saw as pointless.

He left her kneeling there and went out as silently as he'd entered.

A squad car sped off to Branxmore, to the address Marc Daventry had given. Farrar drove. Kite had a warrant in his pocket. Deeley and Tip were there as back-up. While it was on its way,

Mayo conferred with Abigail, looking at the profile they'd already drawn up of the putative bomber.

A man of middle height, who wore size-8 trainers – Reeboks, well worn, the pattern on the sole worn smooth at the inner edges, with a probable drawing pin embedded in one heel.

A man who drove a car whose tyre tracks should match up with the ones found in the field.

Someone who committed his crimes in the early morning . . . because he had been working during the night previous to both crimes. Someone, like Marc Daventry, who worked shifts, irregular hours.

Someone who had negotiated to buy explosives and had made them into a bomb – and whom Dex Davis was prepared to identify. Not exactly the best of witnesses to produce in court, but the best they had.

'But where did he get the money?' Abigail asked. 'And why Lilburne? Did he really believe he killed his father? And why, for God's sake, Avril Kitchin?'

'That's what he's going to tell us when we bring him in,' Mayo said grimly.

But he wasn't happy that all the links they had so far were with the Lilburne murder. What about Avril Kitchin's? Apart from the fact, on his own admission, that he hadn't liked her, there was nothing to say Daventry had murdered her, too, or why. Her killing, whether Marie-Laure was implicated or not, seemed entirely pointless.

The keys Marie-Laure had handed over had been dusted for prints but the surface, according to Dexter, was too rough to provide anything useful. The enamel tag on the key ring, however, was a different matter, with two distinct prints, one of them matching up with Marie-Laure's, taken while she was at the station. The other print wasn't Avril Kitchin's. It might, with luck, prove to belong to Marc Daventry, but as evidence of murder, it was inconclusive.

The squad car turned into Evesham Street.

Although it was only a short distance away from Coltmore Road, the respectability was several degrees lower down the scale, the flat itself being no better. It was on the ground floor of a small terraced house, whose minuscule front garden was a repository for everything representative of a throwaway, takeaway society. They rang the bell marked 'Garden Flat' and, receiving no answer, didn't bother with a second ring but went round the back. Another tiny garden, rank with weeds, a tumbledown shed leaning drunkenly against the back railings. No answer to their knock.

'Give it a push, Pete,' Kite said. But the rickety-looking wooden door was remarkably resistant to Deeley's buffalo-charging fifteen stones. 'Try the window.'

The scullery window splintered glass into the sink below, already full of dirty washing-up water and crockery. With Farrar's usual luck, he was the one delegated to climb through, the most finicky of the four but also the slimmest. Avoiding the sink as best he could, he presently opened the door, an expression of extreme disgust on his face, as though there were a bad smell under his nose. The place was clean enough, however, if in a bad state of disrepair, with the half-done washing up appearing to be there simply as a result of the occupant having been in a hurry when he left.

Almost all his personal possessions had gone with him, with only some dirty linen remaining, stuffed into the bottom drawer of the big, old wardrobe. A couple of shirts, underclothes, and an Arran sweater which Deeley held up inquiringly. Kite shook his head. 'Probably not. It's something dark – maroon – we're looking for.'

Everything else appeared to have been cleared out.

'Done a runner, hasn't he?' observed Deeley after a few minutes' more unrewarding search, which blinding statement of the obvious was rewarded with a terse instruction from Kite to check the other occupants of the house.

He came back with the news that none of them appeared to be at home, but in the back shed, amongst garden implements which hadn't been touched for years, hidden under a pile of old sacks, he'd found a biscuit tin, full of electrical equipment, mercury tilt switches. Kite's reaction wasn't the jubilant one he'd expected.

'Take a look at this, Sarge,' Farrar had said, a minute or two before.

Kite was now staring at what had been revealed when the DC had unhooked a long mirror, hanging somewhat lopsidedly inside the back of the wardrobe, with something protruding from behind. The mirror had been hung over a pinboard, easily visible from the bed if the door were left open. Drawing-pinned to it were dozens of photographs. All blown-up snaps of the same girl, taken outdoors and seemingly when she was unaware of the camera, a tawny blonde with an amazing figure and short skirts revealing long legs.

'Very tasty,' Deeley remarked.

Farrar said, 'Could Daventry be our happy little photographer? If so, maybe the gardener will identify him.'

'These are Flora Lilburne,' Kite said sharply.

His eyes travelled over the snaps and fell on one different from the rest. It was a shocking invasion of her privacy, more so than the others, taken when she was asleep in what was obviously a hospital bed. One arm was flung outside the bedclothes, a large dressing was on her forehead. 'What the devil – ?' And then, looking at the last of the pictures, Kite added softly, 'My God.'

The snap showed Flora again, this time walking in the street, hand in hand with a man. She was laughing as she turned her face to him. It was still possible to tell that she was laughing, and to recognize the man as Anthony Spurrier, even though both faces had been slashed viciously across, twice, with a sharp blade.

'Move!' Kite said. 'And you know where to.'

21

He had no plans, other than to drive to Coventry railway station or Birmingham International – it didn't matter which – abandoning the car in the long-stay car park, where it would probably remain undiscovered for days, and then to take the first train to London. But without knowing why, he found he'd turned off the main road, aimlessly taking side roads with unfamiliar signposts, driving deeper and deeper into the country until finally he drew his car into the side of a narrow lane, doused the lights and sat staring through the windscreen as the light faded.

Two rabbits hopped across the road and disappeared into the hedge. A lean cat on the prowl, probably from the farm halfway up the hill, suddenly materialized and stalked towards the hump-backed bridge about fifty yards further along, where it leaped up in one neat movement and sat on the parapet, gazing down at what must be a railway line, or a canal. Marc left the car and walked to the bridge to join the cat, where he stood leaning his arms along the low parapet, staring down at the water below. Automatically, he stretched out his hand to stroke the animal's tabby fur. Offended, or sensing his dark mood, it leaped down.

In London, he could disappear. He'd cleared out his bank account, all that was left of the sale of the Rumbold Avenue house, so that money, at least, wasn't a problem for the immediate future. He could take an anonymous room until he could find some way of getting abroad without a passport. It didn't matter where he went, just generally 'abroad'. He had a vague idea things would be easier there – that he could, if it later became necessary, find a job, anything, in a hotel kitchen maybe, one of those places where no questions were asked. But that was all in the future. For the moment his aim was simply to get away from Lavenstock. Yet he knew now that his original plan, to reach London that night, was impossible. He was overcome by exhaustion, a lassitude so enormous that the idea of driving to Coventry, or Birmingham, or anywhere at all for that matter, was out of the question. He'd had nothing but a cup of coffee since the previous day and his stomach felt hollow through lack of food, his mind blank with exhaustion. The persistent nagging headache he'd had all day was growing worse. He desperately needed a hot meal, and a bed. He ought to look for a pub and buy some food, but he was afraid he'd have to spend an uncomfortable night in his car.

Dismayed by the thought of a long search along these dark, empty anonymous lanes for somewhere which might provide meals, unnerved by the thought of the stares of strangers, he stared down the length of the canal. The night had all the smoky nostalgia of a Whistler nocturne – a fitful sky, vapour rising between the banks, a string of barges moored a hundred yards or so away, laid up for the winter, covered by tarpaulins. From one of them curled a plume of smoke, its lighted reflection quivering in the olive waters of the canal.

He thought, where there's a navigable canal, there are pubs, offering food. The fact of the boats being moored there suggested it, though he could see no sign of anything resembling a hostelry from where he stood. But all he had to do was walk along the towpath and he'd soon come across it. He went back to the car, drove it back to where he'd noticed a derelict, tin-roofed shack next to a rusted gateway. The gate wasn't locked, held only on the latch, and he drove the car into the field, leaving it behind the shed, where it would be shielded from the road. Good enough for the time being.

He went back to the bridge and scrambled down the side of it on to the path beside the canal. It was cold down by the water and he began to shiver, already half regretting his decision. Wouldn't it have been wiser to keep himself out of sight? How long in any case might he have to stumble along in the dark on this muddy, unlit towpath, treacherously undercut in places, before he came to a pub? Who was to say that he'd taken the right direction when he left the bridge?

He approached the line of barges and came alongside the lighted one, saw it was called the *Lucy with Diamonds*. Patched with rust, it had seen better days. Its roof was stacked with logs, the smoke curling from the chimney was sweet with wood-smoke. Light glowed dimly from the windows, promising warmth and comfort as he passed. The back half of the boat was in darkness.

Without any conscious decision of what he was doing, without pause to question the wisdom of his actions, Marc stepped, cat-footed, silently into the cockpit. For all his care, the boat rocked gently, the water slapping against the metal sides. He waited several minutes after it had steadied, and then tried the handle of the cabin door, the top half of which was curtained glass but showed no chink of light. He was surprised to find it unlocked, and he gradually eased the door open and slid into the unlit interior. He stood for a while until his eyes grew accustomed to the darkness, became aware of unmade-up bunks set either side, against the sloping sides, a further door in front of him. Slipping his Swiss army knife from his pocket, more to give himself courage than anything else, he moved forward then, abandoning caution, pushed open the door.

Heat hit him, an atmosphere thick and fetid as in an animal's lair, a smell compounded of sweetish smoke, something savoury cooking in a pot and something other, something rank, animal.

The space, lit by a single dim lamp, was dominated by a dark green stove, its doors open to reveal a fiercely glowing interior, and next to it was an armchair in which a man was sitting, a huge man with long hair and a beard, wearing a seaman's navy-blue guernsey and corduroy pants. He was holding a roll-up between his fingers and a gun across his knees and looked expectant.

Something moved in the shadows.

At first Marc thought it was a dog, a terrier of some kind, and then he saw the bright, fervid eyes, pointed muzzle and big ears, the mask of a fox. The animal moved forward, awkwardly, it seemed to Marc, and the man laid a restraining hand on its head, to which it immediately responded by sitting on its haunches, head cocked, its unblinking, feral stare on Marc. He saw then that the reason for its awkward movement was that it only had three legs.

'Welcome aboard,' said the man. 'And you can put that bloody knife away. You can have whatever it is you want, without that.'

*   *   *

173

Rick, he said his name was, just Rick, no names, no pack drill, right? It took Marc no more than a minute or two to realize he was more than halfway stoned. Not much longer to believe him when he said the gun was unloaded.

When Marc said that all he wanted was some food and somewhere to sleep for the night, that he was willing to pay, the man simply grinned and told him to help himself. 'All friends here, mate,' he said. 'Fellow travellers.'

Later, when Marc was replete with a bowlful of hot, good-tasting stew that was unidentifiable in content and probably better to remain so, and with rough, wholemeal bread that Rick told him he made himself, all washed down with a can of lager, Rick began to talk. Rambling and incoherent, and presently maudlin, maybe from the bottom of the several bottles strewn on the floor round his chair. Marc thought vaguely he was being entertained by the story of Rick's colourful, itinerant and quite possibly lawless life, but since he couldn't make head nor tail of more than half of it, he made no struggle with the attempt to keep his eyes open and never heard how it was that Rick had ended up living on a canal barge in the back of beyond.

He woke in the early hours of the morning in a terrible panic, thrashing around, his heart thumping inside his ribcage, lathered in sweat, constricted by the narrow confines of where he lay, wondering where the hell he was. He tried to turn over and banged his elbow against something hard and metallic, then everything came back to him.

Last night, Rick must have heaved him on to one of the bunks and thrown a blanket over him, which was rough and smelt horrible, as though it might have been used as bedding for the fox. Underneath it, he was fully dressed, even to his shoes.

His first thought was disbelief at the unlikely scenario he'd stumbled into, at his own preposterous actions, and then he remembered why he'd acted as he had done last night. He squirmed with embarrassment, but it didn't matter, nothing could make things worse than they already were.

He listened to a faint, irregular scratching on the roof over his head, lifting the hairs on his skin. At first he thought it was rats and then recognized the noise was simply birds who were pattering on the roof of the barge, that it was growing lighter, it was almost dawn.

He was grateful, now, for the immense weariness that had

caused him to act as he had done last night. Had he felt able to make the journey to London, he'd have been regretting it by now.

At least he'd had some food and sleep. If he'd spent the night in his car, doubtless hungry and cold, he'd be fit for nothing today, and he couldn't afford that: he'd been in such a panic to leave Lavenstock that he'd failed to make sure all the loose ends were tied up, that he'd left nothing incriminating behind. He was *almost* certain he hadn't, but something at the back of his mind was nagging, bothering him like a sore tooth.

The trouble was, his mind felt no clearer than it had last night. He felt as though he'd entered a state where little, if anything, made sense. Like that time before, he was apparently functioning on a normal level, while having no control over his actions, as if he were two people, his thoughts jumbled and incoherent, with only his subconscious dictating his actions.

The one thought clear in his mind was that he couldn't leave Lavenstock when he had unfinished business with Flora to complete.

It took him a long time to find his way back to the main road. He'd driven further out of the town than he'd thought.

When he left the barge, Rick had still been snoring, dead to the world in the armchair, where, after hefting Marc on to the bunk, he'd presumably spent the night sleeping off the effects of the booze and whatever had been in the roll-ups. Marc had simply poured himself a tumblerful of water, and left money, though not sure that it would be welcomed, underneath the empty glass. But he'd had unbelievable luck, chancing upon somebody like Rick and his *Lucy with Diamonds*, and he needed to show somehow that he was grateful. The three-legged fox, watching his every movement alertly from the corner where it lay curled up, had made no sound.

22

'I reckon Mayo must be off his trolley. It's too rarefied up there where he is now, his brain's getting short of oxygen . . .'

Deeley opened his eyes, shifted his weight and tested the seat adjustment lever once again to try and ease his legs into a more comfortable position, but the front seat was already as far back as it would go. He yawned and looked at his watch, closed his eyes again. Another half-hour and they'd be relieved and off down to the station canteen and tucking into a good breakfast of sausage, egg and bacon, with a double portion of fried potatoes, lashings of toast and gallons of hot, sweet tea. He was a big lad and needed to keep his strength up . . .

'Off his trolley,' the young P C in the passenger seat repeated monotonously. He wasn't used to this malarkey, he was only here to make up the shortfall, and didn't think much of it. If this was C I D, he'd stick to uniforms. 'Keeping us here all night. Bet you a fiver the laddo won't come back.'

'Ours not to reason why, if Mayo thinks there's a chance,' Deeley mumbled, resettling himself. 'Thank your lucky stars you're off in half an hour and stop moaning.'

A minute or two later, his eyes flew open again as he was nudged sharply in the ribs.

'Think this might be him, Pete.'

The new car Flora had ordered hadn't arrived yet, and Anthony was still taking her to work each morning. The only flaw with the arrangement that Anthony could see was her rather ambivalent attitude towards time. It was all right for Flora, whose customers weren't the sort to arrive much before ten, and it didn't bother him too much, generally, but this morning he couldn't afford to be late.

Jenny, the young policewoman who'd been staying the night

with Flora and her mother, waved to him as she drove off. Anthony left the car, where he'd been sitting ready for the off, halfway down the drive, pointing in the right direction, and went into the house to try and chivvy Flora along.

Marc drove slowly, looking for somewhere near his flat to leave his car, but Evesham Street was still jammed with overnight parking, and although lights were coming on in windows all down the street, nobody had yet left for work and vacated a space. He might never have noticed the two men slumped down in the front seats of the dark green Rover, if he'd been driving at normal speed.

Two men, sitting there, that time in the morning?

His heart thumping, he drove past them, on towards that end of the street which joined the Coventry Road, hardly able to believe his luck when the big white furniture pantechnicon which had turned into the street just behind him drew up at a house with a For Sale sign in the garden, just beyond the parked car. Ready for an early start, no doubt. The driver jumped out, leaving the van in the middle of the road, effectively blocking the Rover's route. Even if they'd recognized him, by the time they were all sorted out, he'd be long away.

He slipped into the traffic stream on the main road and kept an eye on his mirror for some time, but they hadn't followed.

He found his hands were slippery on the wheel, his legs trembling. Yesterday's headache was again threatening, a tightening band across his skull. He looked at the clock on the dash. Much too early. She didn't leave home to go to the shop until half past eight. With that slob Spurrier, he thought, grinding his teeth at the thought of him touching Flora. Well, there were ways of preventing that. If Marc couldn't have her, then Spurrier wouldn't, either.

It seemed a long time since he'd eaten the stew: he was ravenously hungry again, and desperately needing hot coffee and aspirin, not to mention a shave and a shower; worst of all, his clothes reeked of the blanket that had covered him last night. Normally so fastidious, he hated that.

He drove along, looking for a café that might be open, but this was Lavenstock, where people had their breakfasts at home and didn't demand coffee at ungodly hours. The supermarket which offered all-day breakfasts in its coffee shop didn't open until

177

eight – an hour to go yet – and it was too far to drive to the nearest motorway services.

He turned into the park and pulled up on the hard standing near the lake. It was a mild, heavy morning, with the rain coming down soft and insistent, the sky like pewter, the sort of day that would be dark until evening. He leaned back in his seat and closed his eyes. If he could snatch some sleep, maybe his head would clear . . . but he soon realized that no way was he going to be able to do that for the noise the damned ducks were making, and the barking of unruly dogs, being taken for their early-morning runs.

Images of Flora swam before his closed lids, Flora or his mother, he couldn't properly tell, the focus seemed to be wrong, and somehow they were blurred together. The photographs, that was what he'd left behind, those damning photos . . . how was it possible he'd forgotten *them*? Well, it was too late now. If it *had* been the police, waiting for him to come home, they'd surely been into his flat and would have seen them.

There must be something wrong with him, the way he forgot essential things at crucial moments . . . like forgetting the typewriter at Avril's flat, after going there that morning specifically to pick it up. The *only* reason he'd gone back there, after swearing he'd never step through the door again . . .

He willed the memory of her to recede, her hectoring voice to cease, but she wouldn't go away.

'What do *you* want?' she'd demanded as she opened the door, pink from her bath, wearing a fluffy, baby-pink dressing-gown hastily tied, partly revealing a pink slip. 'This is my flat, you're not welcome here.'

'I've come for my typewriter. My mother left it here and now she needs it; she wants to make another job application.'

'Take it and go.'

If she'd left it at that, that's where it would have ended. But she had to go on. 'So she hasn't come to her senses, yet? Still thinks the sun shines out of your bum, does she?' she began aggressively, and, just as the previous time they'd met, in no time at all she was hurling further abuse at him . . .

'Shut up!' he'd ground out, when he could get a word in, disgusted at her coarseness. 'Shut up, shut up!'

But she didn't. She went on and on . . . I should never have let you meet her . . . all you've done is make her miserable . . . quite content before you came . . .

At last, pushed to his limits, he'd grabbed the nearest thing handy, snatching up her knitting from the settee. He pulled the needle out from the row of stitches and lunged, only to find his wrist caught in a vice-like grip, Avril's contorted face inches from his own.

'Look what you've bloody done!' she hissed between her teeth, more concerned with the knitting than with his attack on her. And well she might be – with reflex actions like that, and a strength he hadn't guessed she possessed, she'd no need to fear.

She dropped his arm. The belt of her dressing-gown had come loose, and it flapped open, revealing more of her unappetizing flesh than he wanted to see, but she didn't seem to notice. 'You've gone too far. I warned you once before I could make trouble for you. I've only kept my mouth shut because of Marie-Laure, but there's a limit. You've always looked on me as dirt, you patronized your mother – oh, yes, you did, think about it! – and all the time you were worse than either of us – and thinking we didn't know you'd done that bomb.'

He was suddenly aware of the cheap, tinny alarm clock on the sideboard with its loud, insistent tick, that seemed to underline his every heartbeat.

'How did you know that, Avril?' he asked, feeling all at once cold and clear, dangerously calm. 'How could you have known?'

'There's knowing and knowing. I'd nothing to prove it but once I'd thought about it, it was obvious from everything you said. The police'll work it out the same way, once they've got your name and know who you are.'

He remembered the avid way she'd hung on their words, the questions she'd asked, the clever way she'd turned conversations in the direction she'd wanted them to go. He shouldn't have underestimated her.

She was regarding him with scorn. 'You're a fool, you know that? You'll never get away with it and take it from me, doing life is no picnic!'

'I don't care about that. He killed my father. He let my mother go to prison for it.'

She stared at him as though he were some different sort of species, arrived from another planet. 'Is that what you really believe? Do you honestly think she'd have done a life sentence for something she didn't do? Oh, for God's sake, get real!'

'I *know*. I *saw* him there, that night.'

He'd wakened with the need to go to the toilet and, pattering along the landing, he'd seen, through her open bedroom door, his mother and a strange man, bending over the bed where his father lay. She was crying, and he'd been terrified, though he hadn't known why. His mother had seen him and taken him back to bed, and cuddled him until he went off to sleep again, telling him he'd had a nightmare and that everything would be all right when he wakened up in the morning. But it hadn't been. Nothing had ever been the same after that.

After Frank's death, when he had found the letters clipped to the newspaper cuttings, the letters which Lilburne had written to Frank over the years, he'd contacted Lilburne to ask for help in tracing his mother and, after some reluctance, Lilburne had agreed to meet him. Immediately he saw him, Marc had known that this was the man he'd seen that night, when he was four years old, the man whose face he'd never completely forgotten . . . seen in dreams and half flashes of memory ever since, though never entirely recaptured. Lilburne had refused to help him in his search for his mother. He'd talked to Marc for nearly an hour, trying to persuade him, without success, that it would be better for everyone to leave things as they were.

When Marc, without his help, had eventually found Marie-Laure, he became immediately convinced that Lilburne's reluctance to help him to trace her had sprung from a desire to save his own skin . . . for Marc had refused to believe that Marie-Laure was anything but innocent of the terrible crime of murdering his father. And if she had not taken Charles Daventry's life, then who else but Lilburne could have been responsible – and been despicable enough to let Marie-Laure take the rap? Why she'd allowed herself to be sacrificed in this way, what her reasons were, Marc could only speculate, but he knew enough of her by now to know that she was capable of a certain degree of martyrdom.

There had never been any question in his mind, after meeting his mother, that Lilburne should be made to pay, not only for killing his father, but for robbing his mother of the best years of her life. Marc felt no compunction for what he had done, but oh, it was a cruel irony that he had met, and now surely lost, Flora through that very same action!

Avril broke into these dark thoughts, saying scornfully, 'What sort of proof is that? The word of a four-year-old?'

'I saw him there, I tell you. I know my mother didn't do it. I know she couldn't have killed anybody.'

She'd laughed. 'It's obvious you *don't* know her, Markie boy. Take it from me, she killed him.'

Whether it was the laugh, or the 'Markie boy', or the fact that somewhere deep down he sensed there might be a grain of truth, but it was then that he'd lost control.

'What was that you said about the bomb?' he asked softly. 'Marie-Laure *knew*?'

'She did when I faced her with the facts. Oh, she said she didn't believe it but she's not a fool, she – '

He still held the knitting needle in his hand. He felt it in his fist, the knob under the ball of his thumb, the prick of its sharp point where he'd been tapping it against the palm of his other hand. It was surprising how easily it went through her flesh, how quickly she died.

He left the house, and it wasn't until he was back at home that he remembered he hadn't picked up the typewriter.

Flora was ready at last, after Anthony had spent another ten minutes champing at the bit. He was somewhat short with her, telling her to hurry up for God's sake and she gave him the sort of look that said, oh, you're changing your tune now you've got your ring on my finger! Instantly appalled – surely this couldn't be their first quarrel, and at a time like this? – he said he was sorry, kissed her gently and told her how lovely she looked in her yellow suit, but they were both still a little taut when they opened the front door and came face to face with Marc Daventry, standing right there on the top step.

'What the hell – ?' Anthony began, as they both backed away, Flora turning white as a sheet with shock.

'Don't be frightened, Flora, I don't want to hurt you,' Marc said. His voice was slurred, he was unshaven and his eyes were very bright, there was a rank, unpleasant smell on him. 'I'm going away. I just wanted to tell you how sorry I am that you've been hurt . . .

A volley of barking sounded from the back of the house.

Marc's head came up, his eyes swivelled to the door leading to the kitchen but the dogs grew quiet, evidently silenced by Dorothea. His gaze went back to Flora. 'I'd no choice, you know. Your father was bad, he wouldn't help me trace my mother. You know why? He was afraid of me because I knew he'd killed my father.'

He took a step towards her and she recoiled.

She shouldn't have done that, stepped away from him, as if he were some unpleasant species of humanity.

Anthony saw the knife in his hand and before he was aware of what he was doing, charged forward. Too late, he saw blood spreading all over the front of Flora's yellow suit. It was a moment or two, a lifetime, before he realized it was his own blood, that the knife had ripped through the sleeve of his jacket, he was bleeding like a stuck pig and that he'd performed the one and only heroic action of his life.

And that Marc still had Flora in his grip, the knife in his hand . . .

She kicked backwards, catching him painfully on the shin with her heel, and for a moment he was caught off balance. Anthony prepared to charge again, only, suddenly, the hall was full of men, erupting through the front and back. He saw the knife clatter to the floor. Two policemen had Marc's arms behind his back and another was saying, 'Marc Daventry, I'm arresting you on suspicion of . . .'

And then he had to go and spoil it all by passing out cold.

Mayo took them out for lunch the next day, Abigail and Kite. The completion of a case was traditionally a time for celebrating, but he didn't feel anything more than a pie and a pint in the Saracen's Head was called for at this juncture. The echoes were still too close, especially the echoes of that last interview he'd had with Marie-Laure, which he didn't seem able to get out of his mind.

But inevitably their talk over lunch turned to Marc Daventry and the evidence against him. Apart from Dex Davis's testimony — for what it was worth — forensic evidence indicated that the bomb had been made in the kitchen at Evesham Street: traces of weedkiller and sugar had been discovered between the cracks of the ancient lino on the floor. Together with the rest of the stuff in the shed, not to mention the typewriter and the car tracks and all the rest of it, it added up fairly conclusively.

'He thought he was being clever, using a bomb, I suppose,' Kite commented as the pies were brought to the table and they began to eat. 'Unless he was an expert, he couldn't have been sure of killing Lilburne with a gun, and anything else would've involved personal contact with the governor, which wouldn't have been easy.'

Abigail reached for the mayonnaise, having declined the pie and opted for salad. 'With all that against him, you wouldn't think he'd be having such difficulty in coming to terms with the truth. I've never heard such a pack of lies and evasions. What do you think'll happen to him?'

Mayo shrugged, and took a long swig of his bitter. 'Hard to tell. He won't be in circulation for a long time, at any rate.'

'Never'd be too soon for me,' Kite said, spearing a pickled onion with a fierce jab of his fork. He hadn't forgotten the slashed photos.

Abigail gave him a quizzical glance. 'You're not usually so vindictive, Martin.'

'We don't usually have double murderers to deal with – nearly triple, if you count old Spurrier – do we? Look at the way he did for Avril Kitchin, and what for? I mean, I can understand Lilburne, in a way, but why her?'

'He's just clamming up about it. But my bet is he was jealous of her relationship with his mother,' Abigail hazarded.

Mayo wondered what the prosecution would make of that. He thought of his first meeting with Marie-Laure, and what she'd said about Avril helping her to survive in prison. But most human beings have only so much capacity for gratitude. And the two women had separated – allegedly without acrimony but possibly with a certain coolness . . . About what? Not having known Avril Kitchin, he could only speculate, but he had a shrewd suspicion that it might have concerned Marc. And that Marie-Laure knew that, too. But she'd retreated into one of her silences on the subject.

She was less of an enigma now, Marie-Laure, after the long session they'd had with her, after her son had been arrested, but he still didn't feel that he, or perhaps anyone, would ever know her. But during that interview, at least, she'd been willing to talk . . .

'I will tell you all I know, Superintendent, everything that happened the night my husband died,' she had told him, looking drained and exhausted, consumed with guilt. 'I must. If I had not taken Jack Lilburne as a lover, none of this would have happened. Three people would still be alive. And Marc – and Marc – '

He had interrupted her without too much ceremony. 'If Charles Daventry hadn't married you, if he hadn't been the man he was . . . No, Mrs Daventry, I don't go along with all this "if" business – otherwise we'd soon be back to Eve and the apple. Carry on with the night your husband died.'

But she hadn't been ready to start on that. Not until she'd offloaded more guilt, about Marc. 'All the years when I was in prison, and afterwards,' she said, in a low voice, 'I would not allow myself to think of him too much. I shut him out of my mind, except for when I had the letters from Jack, telling me he was well . . . And then, in the convent, when I heard that the people who had adopted him had died, a small corner of my heart opened . . . I thought, I hoped, he might need me.'

'Only then, you see, when we met, I found I had nothing to give him. He was no longer a child, he was a grown man, his character already formed and, and – ' Her voice sank, so low he could hardly hear her. 'I could not love what he had become. I could feel for him, I could pity him. But I could not love him.'

A noisy, cheerful argument broke out at the bar over Lavenstock United's chances in the coming week. Rude comments were shouted and returned full measure. The decibel level rose above what was usual in the Saracen's and the landlord made signs to the participants to quieten down. Two of them drank up and left, leaving the rest to continue the argument more decorously . . .

As if nothing could be worse, having confessed her feelings towards her son, Marie-Laure had taken a grip of herself and begun to tell him about the night Daventry died. He had begun the quarrel, accusing her of having an affair with Jack Lilburne, and then storming off to bed. Someone had told him, some busybody, no doubt . . .

'I wonder she didn't suspect it was Dorothea Lilburne,' Abigail remarked now, over a forkful of salad. 'Or perhaps she did.'

'It wouldn't surprise me if she worked it out, in retrospect. She said she'd no idea who it was, didn't she, but who knows with Marie-Laure?'

. . . 'I sat in the kitchen, thinking of the impasse I was in,' she'd continued. 'I was in a state of madness when I picked the knife up, I simply wanted to end it all. But it was only after I'd killed him that I came to my senses and began to think of what it was all going to mean – especially to my child. I didn't know where to turn and the only person I could think of was Jack. I telephoned him and he came straight over. We must have disturbed Marc with our talking because he came out of his bedroom and saw us. I don't think he actually saw that his father was dead. It's only in retrospect that he has remembered what he thought he saw. I took him back to bed and afterwards Jack and I talked, and talked. We knew there was no way of avoiding the consequences. He promised to look after the child, and I promised not to mention his name. He went home, and I telephoned the police. There was nothing else he could have done.'

He could have stayed by her, Mayo thought. He could have testified at her trial. Would it have helped? Probably not.

'Frank Clarke kept Jack's letters, and when Marc found them after he died, he wrote to Jack repeatedly, asking for his help in tracing me. I think they did meet, once. I, too, met and talked with Jack when I came back to Lavenstock, but he refused to put us in touch with one another. He said he wasn't sure of Marc's real motives. He thought him unstable and that I might be in danger, that it was possible Marc couldn't forgive me for his father's death.'

'When actually, it was Lilburne he blamed – without any real justification. Except that he just couldn't accept the idea of his mother as a murderess. Will he ever?'

'He'll have plenty of time to think about it,' Kite said, polishing off what was left on his plate. 'Another pork pie, anybody?'

'That's what I like about you, Martin. You always get your priorities right.'

23

Claudia Reynolds walked across to the governor's house from the Young Offenders' establishment by way of the garden, knowing, without having to make too much effort about it, that she would find Dorothea there. She found her triumphantly contemplating the helpful work of a thrush: empty snail shells scattered like broken, translucent porcelain along the path, where small, delicate irises thrust themselves through the cracks at the edges. In the distance, lordly crown imperials glowed like balls of fire in the April sun.

'I came to tell you that I'm leaving, Dorothea.'

'Well, well. I take it that congratulations are in order?' said Dorothea, adding with a smile, 'It *is* promotion?'

'Yes.'

Claudia returned the smile and the two women stood regarding a *Rosa rubrifolia* just beginning to show its new, as yet glaucous leaves, full of promise for the great, arching fountain of blossom it would later become. Only Dorothea knew it was a *Rosa rubrifolia*, and what it would look like when it was in full bloom, its tiny pink flowers starry against the plum-coloured foliage and ruby-red stems – a rose hardly like a rose at all, yet what a treasure! But Claudia had learned to feign interest.

They talked for a while, Claudia outlining her plans, telling Dorothea of the establishment for female prisoners in the north where she hoped to start within the month.

'You'll be happier there,' Dorothea said, pausing to pull out a dandelion which had seeded itself into a crack. 'Damn, why do I always believe they'll come out whole, and not snap off at the root?'

'What Dr Johnson called the triumph of hope over experience.'

'How right he was – only he was talking about second

186

marriages, not dandelions, wasn't he? Well, Claudia, I know you'll make a success of your new job – you're so good with women and girls. I mean good, in that you understand them.'

'Thank you,' Claudia replied, smiling faintly. 'That's not how some people would interpret it.'

'Then they'd be wrong, wouldn't they?'

'Yes.'

'You always knew how to deal with Flora. I've never been able to thank you properly, for the way you helped her – and me – that time,' Dorothea said, referring to several stormy, early-adolescent years when she herself hadn't the vaguest notion how to cope with a rebellious daughter.

'It was the least I could do, in the circumstances, to try to make amends.'

Claudia was one of the few people Dorothea could talk to with ease. They understood each other without much need for explanations. They always had, even all those years ago, when Claudia had first worked at Conyhall, younger and unsure of herself. They had neither of them ever before referred to the occasion when Claudia, touchy at being reprimanded over some slight thing by the governor, wanting to get her own back, had hinted to Dorothea about Jack's extra-marital affair. A hint was all Dorothea had needed to make her act, quite out of character, by employing an inquiry agent and then informing Charles Daventry of what she'd found out . . . Neither woman had dreamed what the terrible domino effect of that action would be.

'Don't feel guilty, my dear. Someone else would have told me if you hadn't. It was my decision to do what I did, and if I have to learn to live with it, that's my problem,' Dorothea said. Then, in her new refusal to let the past cloud the present, she added, 'And that's enough of that. I have news for you, too. I'm leaving, as well.'

If the Queen had announced she was leaving Buckingham Palace, Claudia could not have been more astonished. Dorothea smiled at her incredulous face. She was quite surprised herself, hearing it put into words for the first time, though the words had slipped out so easily that she knew the idea had been in her mind for some considerable while, waiting for the right moment to emerge.

'Are you sure?'

Dorothea was. Though not so sure of her reasons. Was she making, in fact, a kind of atonement, a whacky kind of sacrifice to the gods? It didn't matter, she knew without question that she was doing the right thing. She would sell the house. She would wait until the bomb damage had been repaired and Flora was safely married to Anthony, and then she would put it on the market. It should fetch a good price. Jack had insisted on buying it when they came here, remarking ironically that he couldn't see her in Prison Service quarters. They had both loved the house from the start, and she had been enchanted with the garden, or at least the prospect of it, for it had been a wilderness then. The lovely, burgeoning thing it was now, she had created with her own hands, her own love; her knowledge had grown with it . . .

'You're prepared to leave your garden?' Claudia asked, wonderingly.

And for a moment, Dorothea's heart quailed.

'I shall start another,' she replied stoutly. 'I'll find a smaller house, but one with some land around it, and I'll make another garden. It'll be quite a challenge.'

She could already feel the quickening of interest at the idea, a growing excitement stirring her blood as she thought of the plans she could pore over during the winter evenings. There would be much to do, here and now: earmarking favourite things she might legitimately take with her, there would be seeds to sow, cuttings to strike. And, speaking of roses, there was a sumptuous fragrant Bourbon, Mme Pierre Oger, that she'd always wanted and never found the ideal place for . . .

Claudia took her leave. 'I'll see you again before I go,' she said, turning to go back the way she'd come. She wasn't sure that Dorothea had even heard her. She was already on her knees, grubbing out yet another recalcitrant root of ground elder.